BLOOD MANSION

ROBERT HOWELL

ISBN: 978-1-964619-38-5

CONTENTS

CHAPTER ONE

THE WEDDING, SPRING 1994

"So, what do you think?" asked Dick of his fiancé as they exited the car.

"Spectacular!" answered Suzie. "Do you really think they will rent us this place for our wedding at a price we can afford? I mean look at it. This is a billionaire's house. I know you have contacts, but even my parents wouldn't be able to pay for this."

They had been searching for the perfect place to have their wedding since their original choice, where they had already booked their event, burned to the ground a week ago. However, it wasn't until a partner at the law firm where Richard Stein worked mentioned that one of his clients might be interested in renting them a place that would make the most audacious wedding scene ever, that they had finally found a place they could both agree on, and that was available.

"That's the beauty of it. The owner specifically asked for Jack to find someone to have a wedding here and all we would have to pay for is cleaning and maintenance of the place during and following the wedding."

"Why would he do that? He could rent this place out for a fortune for some Hollywood star's wedding."

"He didn't want the type of publicity that would involve. "

"I can understand that, but still, why a wedding to inaugurate this place? He hasn't even moved here himself."

"Jack told me the owner is very spiritual. He thinks that having a union of love as the first event here would fill the place with Qi positive life force. He's heavily into feng shui. When Jack mentioned that someone in his office was looking for a place to have a wedding, he immediately offered this place."

"So, no other conditions? We just clean up after it's over and that's it?"

When her fiancé did not answer right away, Suzie looked him in the eye and said, "I know you, Richard Stein. When you hesitate like that there's something wrong. What is the catch?"

Suzie using his full name like that told Dick he had better come clean and do so fast.

"Nothing bad. He just wants us, and our guests, to spend our wedding night in the house. He will even have the master suite set up with champagne, rose petals, and of course clean sheets on the bed."

"Yeah, and hidden cameras too, I bet."

"Why would some billionaire, who could get all the porn he desires, want a video of us? Anyway, we can check it out and if you feel uncomfortable, we will just say no."

"Won't that put you in difficulty with your boss? After all, you may be only a year away from becoming a partner. Would you be willing to sacrifice that because I may have doubts?"

"Hey, there are other partnership opportunities with other companies. There is only one you."

The look Suzie gave him confirmed that he could not have put it any better than that. No need to tell her that his future partnership had already been confirmed and was not reliant on this house.

"So, let's go see where we will be consummating our marriage," Suzie suggested, giving his butt a good squeeze.

It was about a hundred meters to the entrance to the house from where they parked the car just outside the gate. The gate was locked, but a side entrance had been left open for them. Suzie may have used the word spectacular to describe the house, but the same word could easily have been used to describe the natural setting around the house, and even the landscaping leading up to it.

The driveway was wide enough for three cars and made with some type of beautiful stone, interlocking like uni-pave, but in a way that seemed more like a perfect jigsaw puzzle. If they stared at any one spot long enough it felt like they could almost see a picture forming, but of what, they could not figure out. As they got closer to the house, the driveway narrowed down to two lanes and became circular, with a beautiful fountain in the center, surrounded by aromatic flowers of a type they did not recognize.

Standing by the fountain was a tall, slim man, easily in his 70s. He wore a three-piece suit; with the shiniest black shoes they had ever seen. His silver hair shone like a flair as the sun hit it. The wide smile on his face put them at ease.

Reaching the man, Dick took the hand that was presented, noticing the firm grip, but also how cold it was.

"Welcome to my home. My name is Peter Vanderbilt, and I built this house. Oh, not the manual labor of course, but every piece of material I selected, and every design was done to my specifications." His voice was deep, but smooth, with hardly a trace of an accent.

"Mr. Vanderbilt, it is a pleasure," responded Dick, shaking the offered hand enthusiastically. "I wasn't expecting to meet you here. Jack Spence from my office said there would be someone here but did not prepare me to be greeted by the owner himself. I'm Richard Stein, and this is my lovely fiancé, Suzie Milton."

The aging gentleman moved with a grace that belied his age as he reached past Dick and took Suzie's hand in his own, surprising her as he leaned over and kissed it. He stood just over six feet tall and although Peter Vanderbilt was in his 70s his face had few wrinkles.

"I am sincerely pleased to meet you Ms. Milton, and you too, Mr. Stein. But please call me Peter. I have too many officious bureaucrats running around my office calling me Mr. Vanderbilt. At my home I prefer to go by my given name.

It was Suzie who responded.

"It would be an honor to call you Peter. And you must call us Suzie and Richard."

Peter Vanderbilt let out a laugh that sounded like the tinkling of broken glass tumbling onto a concrete floor.

"I am sure that Richard would prefer it if I called him Dick; am I right, Dick?"

"Well, that is what my family and friends call me, except of course when they're upset with me," he replied, giving Suzie *the look*.

Peter let out that laugh again and looked Suzie in the eyes. "I don't stand on formality, dear. Not in my home. I have always gone by Peter, so for me it is informal, but when someone has a preference about their name, I prefer to use it. For example, I must know a dozen Roberts. Some go by Bob, some Rob, some Robin, some Robbie and so on. If I insisted on calling them all Robert, none of them would know whom I am speaking to." Again, that unusual laugh.

Before either could respond, Peter turned to the fountain and started talking about his home.

"The first thing you will notice is this lovely fountain."

"That looks just like the Trafalgar Fountain in Ottawa," exclaimed Suzie. "Did you have a replica made?"

"Of course, I did," replied Peter. "How else could I have acquired the original if I had not had a duplicate made. But the duplicate is in Regina, as there were two fountains, one sent to Ottawa and the other one there." He said it in such a cavalier way, they had no idea if he was joking or not, but concluded he must be since there was no way the government would have let a national monument like this out of its possession.

"Let me tell you the history. A pair of fountains made of red granite from Peterhead Quarry, Aberdeenshire, by McDonald and Leslie Aberdeen to Sir Charles Barry's design, were erected in London's Trafalgar Square in 1845. They rested in the square until 1939 when they were removed to make way for larger fountains. These fountains were brought to the attention of the National Art Collection Fund of Britain, which acquired them for presentation to a Dominion capital. Canada accepted the gift and one of the fountains serves as a memorial to Lieutenant Colonel John By, founder of Bytown, which was later renamed Ottawa. The mate to the Ottawa Fountain was relocated to Wascana Centre on the east side of the Legislative Building in Regina. There is even a rumour it is haunted, but who believes in that nonsense," he said, again finishing with his unusual laugh.

"Haunted?" asked Suzie.

"Oh, just rumours and stories of course," replied Peter. "They say a young girl drowned in the fountain and her spirit haunts it to this day."

"That's terrible!" she exclaimed.

"I said rumor because no one was ever able to verify that anyone had died there. No name of a little girl missing at that time, even. So most likely just a story that made the fountain more fun for some to visit."

"To think, social media didn't even exist back then and still rumors and fake news were common," commented Dick.

Peter gave Dick a smile but withheld his unusual laugh.

"Please, let us go to the main entrance now. I want you to enjoy the beauty of this house, and a little of the history of its construction. Yes, I am very biased when I say this is the most unique residence in the world, as I took great pride in every aspect of its construction."

They arrived at the entrance, a double arched door of solid wood. Carved into each door was a single gargoyle, the one on the left with an open mouth featuring sharp teeth, the other with a closed mouth holding a large brass ring to be used as a door knocker.

"Even before we started construction on the house, I had these doors. They were actually taken from the Voergaard Castle in Denmark. I happened to be in Dronninglund at the time they were doing renovations. When I was told they were going to replace the doors, I knew I had to have them, so made an offer they could not refuse." Peter ended the sentence with his patented laugh.

"Of course, they did not look like this. I had a craftsman reshape and work them to my design. Notice the door knocker? One would think that using it would not call anyone in a house so large." He turned to Suzie and added, "Go ahead and try."

Wondering if there was some type of trick involved, but not wanting to insult their host, Suzie reached over and pulled on the brass ring, expecting it to be heavy. However, it was far lighter than even her large silver earrings, and on pulling it, a tone straight out of *2001: A Space Odyssey* sounded.

"Thanks to speakers, that tone plays throughout the house, so no matter where anyone is, it will be heard. It even plays in the secondary building you can see in the distance.

Peter indicated a large structure over five hundred yards away.

"That's kind of far away to park cars," commented Dick.

"That is not where we will park our cars," Peter clarified. "That is where we will repair them. It is hard to see from here, but there is a large, double bay entrance at each end of the building, and inside an oil change pit. As you can see, further in the distance, are maple trees. We plan to use the maple syrup from the trees to make maple wine. The second storey of the building consists of offices. There is also another building behind it, where we store the equipment used to maintain the property. I plan on running a maple wine business there on my retirement. Not because I need the money, but because I need a hobby, and since my first taste of maple wine a couple of years ago, I decided that's what I wanted."

"I know many people like to work long after retirement age, but I have never understood why," said Suzie. "If I had millions of dollars I would retire and spend my time travelling and having fun."

"Yet it is not millions, but billions in my case. However, I have been waiting for the right person to come along and properly run my companies. I want my reputation as a fair employer and businessman to last longer than I will. Since I have no children, finding the right person to trust has not been easy. When this much money is involved greed usually far surpasses trust. It is only recently that I have found someone I can depend on to take over the businesses and run them as I have. My assistant James Neighbors will be ready to handle it all within a year, so I will be able to take my retirement then.

"As for why most rich people don't retire young, my opinion is that they are so used to working they just can't stop. To prevent this from happening to me I plan on having a side business that will be my hobby. It will be fun instead of work, and not making money will not be a concern."

"Now that's the way to retire," commented Dick.

"Indeed," replied Peter. "Now let us continue the tour."

Peter used a large brass key with a skeleton head as its base to open the left side of the solid oak double doors. Just above and on each side were two distinctive windows that Suzie thought kind of looked like eyes watching. A part of her felt comforted by the thought that the house itself was protective of those who entered—then a cold shiver passed through her as her thought changed to: *The house is watching all who enter and deciding whom it will allow to leave again.*

Yet, once Peter opened the doors, those feelings disappeared with the beauty she found before her. It was a grand entrance hall, with large windows filtering in lots of sunshine in some places and glowing with stained-glass designs in others, as some of the windows were like panes from a church.

Realizing that Peter had been saying something, Suzie looked away from the windows and said, "Pardon? I'm sorry I was so absorbed in the beauty of the windows that I missed what you were saying."

"That is quite alright, my dear. Even I get stunned sometimes when I walk through these doors. My master crafters did a marvelous job of reproduction. Should you ever go to Montreal and visit Notre-Dame-de-Bonsecours chapel you will see where the inspiration for these windows comes from."

Suzie was now able to see that most of the sunlight was coming from the wall above the entrance doors. Since the ceiling here was about twenty-five feet high it gave a good fifteen feet above the doors for window space.

The entrance hall was some twenty feet in diameter, being

circular in shape. Directly in the center, hanging from a delightful ceiling with various mosaics both crafted and painted, there was a marvelous chandelier with multiple layers of beautiful crystal and what looked like real candles, though how that could be Suzie could not figure out since someone would need a huge ladder to light them.

"I see you admiring the chandelier. Once again, my craftsmen outdid themselves. They created a duplicate of a chandelier hanging in the Chateau de Brissac in France," he explained before ushering them deeper into the house.

The tour lasted for over an hour as Peter took them to the various spaces. On the main floor alone, there were more than a dozen rooms, many of them quite spacious. One contained an Olympic-sized pool, another, a theatre that contained thirty seats. They passed through a library, two kitchens, a dining room that would seat fifty, a smaller, more intimate dining room that would seat ten, and several bathrooms. As well there was a small chapel near the rear of the mansion. The pool room itself had an attached area with a full bathroom, jacuzzi, sauna, and his and hers shower rooms.

The second floor had access both from the central entrance, by way of a spiral staircase, and from the back of the house where two different staircases were located. This second floor consisted of twenty-five suites, some having just two beds, and some having a lounge area and a table. All the suites had their own bathrooms. Most of them also had balconies.

The real treat, though, was the third floor. There were only three doors in the hall as they reached the top of the staircase. The first door led to the master suite. The second door led to an observatory. The third door led to Peter's personal workshop for his other hobbies. He did not elaborate nor offer to show them; he simply explained that it would remain locked and out of bounds.

Instead, Peter took them into the observatory. There was equipment there that neither Suzie, nor Dick understood, but the telescope itself was something to behold. It was probably the largest such instrument, not owned by the government or a university, that they had ever seen. Above the telescope the roof was completely made of an unusual type of glass.

"I do not know a lot about telescopes, but I asked my people to acquire the best one they could that would work here. They say it makes the TAL-65 look like a child's toy. The glass above is custom made so as not to reflect and is something new called self cleaning glass. It has a special hydrophilic and photocatalytic coating that is activated using UV rays present in daylight and rain to wash away organic dust. They tell me it is twenty years ahead of its time. I do know that it is not available to the public. Thanks to my contacts with the U.S. military research division, I was able to obtain it. The rest of what you see here is some type of computer equipment. I am afraid that it won't be of much use while you are here since it has not been set up yet. Once I move in, an expert will come and finish the setup and explain it all to me. However, if you sit in that chair under the telescope, you will still be able to manually operate it."

After the observatory they entered the master suite, which had a bedroom, a small kitchen, a miniature theatre room, a lounge, a bathroom, and a balcony that wrapped around at least half the manor. Suzie was awed at the size of it. The bed was double king size. The bathroom had a double jacuzzi bath, as well as a shower large enough for two, a toilet and even a bidet, which she wondered about, having been told Peter was single. The tour of the master suite ended in the miniature theatre room, which featured only two full sized recliners. He invited Dick and Suzie to try them out, and once they were seated, he pushed a remote and the chairs started vibrating. He showed them the remote.

"This button controls the vibrations. These two change the level of the seats from fully upright to fully reclined. This last button though is special. It turns this into a full 3D setup. So, if you are watching a movie that features an earthquake, then the chair will move as if you were actually feeling it. If jet planes are blasting off, your seat will vibrate as if they are flying directly overhead."

"Wow, that is amazing," Dick said.

"This is going to be my final home, so I might as well make it as comfortable as possible."

"Your home is truly magnificent, but isn't it a bit much for one person?" asked Suzie.

"Alas my dear, my days of travelling will soon be behind me. I no longer want to go away. Instead, I will be having my friends, of which I have made many, and associates come to me. I still love lots of company, so I want to have plenty of space for my visitors.

"Now before we leave this suite, I want you to know that the bed will be fitted with the most comfortable sheets imaginable for your wedding. My assistant will be leaving a nice bottle of champagne and some special snacks for you to enjoy. As well, as many of your guests that wish to stay, may stay. All twenty-five suites on the second floor will be prepared for company. Do you know how many of your wedding party will be staying here?" Seeing the look on Suzie's face he added, "That is if you would like to have your wedding here. I surely hope so, as an event like that will just bring this place to life, and I feel that will give me years of enjoyment."

Suzie looked at Dick who nodded.

"We would love to, and we thank you so much for this," she replied. "Although the wedding party will consist of over two hundred people, I think that about twenty or so couples would probably want to stay."

"It is *I* who thank *you*. You have no idea how much this means to me. You can tell your guests they can stay here for a full week if they would like. I believe you mentioned that you were planning a June first wedding. That is just two months away and a lot of preparations to make, so if you need anything, please feel free to ask and I will have it provided."

"Oh, just about everything has been arranged already," replied Dick. "We even had arranged for the ceremony to be held at a hotel, with those guests coming from out of town staying there. But last week there was a big fire. The hotel sustained major damage, and we were told our reservations were cancelled. You don't know how much of a life saver you are offering us this place. Both our families would have been quite upset if we had to postpone, as many are flying in and would have had a hard time getting refunds on their tickets."

"Dick, I think furious would be a better term for how some of them would have reacted."

Peter laughed his broken glass laugh.

"Then the circumstances just worked out for everyone."

As he led them to the front door, Dick thought to ask, "Is there no basement in this mansion?"

"Just a wine cellar and storage, accessed through the kitchen. A key will be left for your catering company to access the wine cellar, and please feel free to sample the wines. Some are quite good."

They exited the front door and Peter shook both of their hands.

"I will not be seeing you again before your wedding as I have business overseas that will keep me away until July. I wish you happy nuptials, and if you need anything just contact my assistant, James Neighbors. Your office, Dick, has his contact info. And please do not be shy to ask for anything."

* * *

The day of the wedding could not have been more beautiful. Although the wedding planner had rented and set up a couple of event tents in case of rain, the day was bright without a cloud in the sky. Even the temperature could not have been better, a warm seventy-five degrees Fahrenheit. If anything, the tents would be used to protect people and food from the sun.

The guests had begun arriving an hour earlier, and Betty was rushing from station to station to make sure everything was running smoothly. This was the largest wedding she had been responsible for, and a good showing here could really launch her new company.

After making sure the tables in the tents were properly set up, she rushed over to the area where the ceremony itself was to take place. There was less than an hour to go, and Betty saw right away that something was wrong. Grabbing one of the workers, she pulled him over to stand where the Rabbi would be presiding. It was two o'clock and the sun was shining directly where she had expected it to, which was why the podium was badly placed.

She pushed the worker forward and told him to go stand behind it.

"So, what is wrong Miss Betty?" the crew foreman asked.

Betty moved to where the couple would be standing.

"How many fingers am I holding up?"

"I can't see Miss Betty."

"Why not?"

"The sun is in my eyes."

"Now do you see what is wrong? It is going to be even worse when the ceremony begins."

"Yes Miss Betty. I will have my workers make the changes right away."

Betty stood there while his crew of five shifted the position of the podium, and then all the chairs. They also had to adjust the flowered arch that the bride would walk through, which took a little more time since it was securely staked to the ground.

Finally satisfied with the positioning, she made a final tour of the area, and then went to see the bride to let her know that all was ready. She was intercepted by the bride's mother before she was able to see Suzie.

"When Suzie told me that you would be her wedding planner, I seriously had my doubts," said Mrs. Milton, her nasally tone and arrogant attitude grating on Betty. "I know you two have been friends for many years, but your business was too new for me to think you could pull this off. But I am impressed. The setup is perfect, and I have spoken with the caterer and all the Kosher meals we had requested arrived on time. I will recommend your services to my friends at the synagogue."

"Thank you, Mrs. Milton. It has been an honor to do this arrangement, and close to my heart, as I want everything to be perfect for Suzie. Speaking of which, I wanted to let Suzie know that all was set before I went to get ready myself."

"She's busy sorting out the dress arrangement with the tailor. He forgot to attach the bow on the back like she asked and is doing a last-minute adjustment. I'll let her know for you."

"Thank you, Mrs. Milton, and thank Suzie for me for arranging a place here where I can change."

Before Betty had even finished speaking, Suzie's mother had turned away and was heading over to speak with the Rabbi. Having known Suzie and her family for many years, Betty was used to her attitude and did not let it bother her. The fact that she had received that type of praise from her friend's mother in the first place was surprising, and she would keep that as her favorite memory of the day, aside of course from the wedding itself.

Being considered more hired help than friends and family, Betty did not warrant a suite, however she was given the entire bathroom area off the pool to herself. She took a quick shower and then changed into her dress, a simple green and yellow gown with sunflowers and daisies. She kept her long hair in a simple bun. Looking at herself in the mirror, she applied some lipstick, and a little rouge, but not being a big make-up person, she kept it simple. Satisfied with her appearance, she checked the hour and realized she still had plenty of time left.

Looking back at the mirror she spoke aloud to herself. "You know what is missing, Betty. A nice bottle of wine. Since I am not allowed to stay for the reception, not being Kosher enough, I think I will sneak out a bottle of wine. Suzie told me there was a wonderful wine cellar off the kitchen. Time to check it out." She nodded again and left the bathroom to head for the kitchen.

Since the reception was going to be held outdoors, none of the catering staff was in the there. Looking around she spotted the door that likely led to the basement. Happily, she noticed it was unlocked, and though solid and imposing, it was easy to open and made no noise. There was a light switch at the top of the steps, which, when flicked on, lighted the staircase itself, but not the basement. She hoped there would be another light that was easy to find when she got to the bottom.

About halfway down the stairs she started shivering. Although it was much cooler here than anywhere else in the house, she did not give it a second thought. After all, it was a wine cellar. Of course, it would be cooler. She reached the bottom, and as she expected, on the wall by the last step, was another switch. She turned it on—and gasped.

The size of the place was unbelievable. A corridor led straight ahead, but off to each side were various alcoves. She could see the first alcove from where she stood. It went back at least fifteen feet and was about ten feet wide. The walls on both sides were lined with racks full of wine bottles. Each rack had a plaque on it, designating the type of wine, the place of origin, and the year it was bottled. The corridor she was facing ran at least fifty feet, and evenly spaced on each side of the corridor were more alcoves of wine racks, the same size as the first one, and equally full.

"My God, there must be thousands and thousands of bottles here," she said aloud. Her voice echoed throughout the area, which caused her to jump.

"Okay Betty, keep it quiet and quick. Grab a bottle and get out of here. This place is kind of spooky." Hearing her own voice this time was more soothing as she practically whispered. No more echoing. She looked into the first alcove and saw on the plaque, white wines from Germany. A lot of the labels read Liebfraumilch. She preferred red wine, so she passed that alcove and went to the next, which read champagnes. She kept walking until she came to one that intrigued her. Red Chiantis.

"Now this is more like it."

She started reading the different plaques in this section. Then spotted a 1963 Fattoria Montagliari Chianti Classico Riserva.

"That's the one. I could never afford this on my own."

She pulled the bottle off the rack and was studying the label when she heard it. A door opening and footsteps. What was strange though was that the steps were coming from the wrong direction, instead of from the stairs, they were coming from the back of the wine cellar. Yet she had seen, as she had followed the corridor down, that it ended in a stone wall. There was no door there. Then again maybe someone else had the same idea as she did and was just in one of the furthest alcoves picking up a bottle.

"It is okay, young lady. I won't bite. It gives me pleasure that someone would enjoy a bottle from my collection." The voice was deep, but smooth.

Betty peeked around the corner and saw a man standing a little further along the corridor. She could not see much of his face but noticed the full head of silver hair. She stepped out of the alcove, knowing that she had been discovered. She hoped Suzie would not be upset with her.

The man stepped up to her, took her hand, and kissed it.

"My name is Peter Vanderbilt. This is my home, and you are very welcome to that bottle of Chianti." Betty only realized then that she still held on to the bottle.

"I'm sorry. I didn't know you were here. Suzie told me that you were travelling overseas."

"Alas, my trip ended early, and I decided to set up a little wedding surprise for the couple. You being here now must have been fate, since I could use some help to finish the preparations."

"Preparations?"

"For the wedding surprise. Would you mind? I think it is something that will blow them away if I do say so myself. It will be quite the surprise for everyone. And you would be the only one with advance knowledge, so will get to see the expressions on their faces when it comes to pass."

Thinking fireworks, or something like that, Betty was only too quick to agree. She was a little unnerved when he headed away from the staircase, but his smile and calm demeanor left her feeling at ease. When they reached the stone wall, he appeared to reach between two stones and push something, and the wall moved inwards, displaying another corridor. Thinking how wonderful it was, a hidden room, a wedding surprise, and her being part of it, she practically skipped through the arch, following Peter Vanderbilt. She did not notice the wall closing behind her.

Betty was never seen again.

* * *

"Where is she?" Suzie was upset with Betty. She knew her friend wasn't happy that she could not be one of the bridesmaids, but still her seat had been reserved, and it was glaringly empty. She needed her friend's support since her mother had taken control of so much of the wedding planning—including who her bridesmaids would be—and Betty was to be her anchor.

Her mother was born Catholic, but converted to Judaism when she met the man she would marry. Suzie had been raised in Jewish tradition, and loved her life, her synagogue, and her friends from there, but no one was more "Jewish" than her mother. Everything had to be Kosher. Thank goodness Dick's family was far more laid back then her mother was. As for the woman's arrogance, she must have gotten it from her Catholic grandmother who was quite similar.

The music was starting up, so no more time to worry about that, as her father stepped beside her to take her arm.

The rest of the day was a blur to Suzie, from the ceremony itself, to the reception after. She had not given Betty another thought. It was close to midnight when many of the guests started to leave. Soon the only ones remaining were those that would be spending the night, so the party moved indoors.

For the next couple of hours, the guests milled around the dining room, as the caterer had laid out more food. Then they started leaving in pairs for their assigned rooms. Those who were staying had been given a number corresponding to a number pinned to the outside of their guest suite, so they could easily find their accommodations. Soon only Dick and Suzie remained in the dining room, along with two hired waiters who were putting away the remaining food. They took away what was left to store in the kitchen and wished the couple a good night, saying someone would be by around ten in the morning to finish cleaning up, and another crew would come by at the same time to make breakfast for the guests. It had turned out that each of the twenty-five rooms were occupied, some with more than just one couple, as those who had been drinking a little much decided to crash for the night. In total, besides Dick and Suzie, there were another sixty-four people there for the night.

They wearily climbed to the third floor. But when they got to their suite a burst of energy spurred Dick to sweep Suzie into his arms, push the door open, and carry her across the threshold. It was the first time they had had a chance to enter their suite since Peter Vanderbilt had given them a tour of the place. All of Suzie's and Dick's clothing preparations had taken place in their respective parents' suites.

The first thing they noticed was the champagne and hors d'oeuvres spread on the table in the living area. The food was on ice, and covered in plastic, so was still fresh. Although both had changed out of their wedding clothing hours before, they decided to get more comfortable with Suzie putting on a negligee, and Dick just pajama bottoms, as the room was quite warm. They noticed that someone had brought up their wedding clothes for them and put them in a closet. Then they headed right to the table. Dick pulled out the bottle.

"Dom Perignon, 1973. Wow that is some champagne." He popped the cork and poured wine into the two glasses that sat beside the bottle, handing one to Suzie.

"To the most beautiful woman in the world."

"To my loving husband, and the wonders tonight will still hold," she replied, with a coquettish smile. Dick almost spit up his champagne. Before he could say a word, she picked up one of the enticing pieces of food on the platter and shoved it in his mouth.

His eyes opened in surprise. "I don't know what this is, but it tastes amazing," he said as he picked up another piece and put it into Suzie's mouth. Her eyes widened as well. They kept feeding each other different pieces from the platter and sipping their champagne. Soon the platter was nearing empty, and the champagne was half finished.

"I have an idea," said Dick.

Suzie looked towards the bed.

"No, not that, at least not yet," laughed Dick. "Let's go check out the theatre. Maybe there is a movie ready to go and we can try those seats." His eyebrows arching as he said it.

Suzie giggled and headed towards the theatre, pinching Dick's ass as she walked by.

"Do you know how this system works," asked Suzie, as she turned on the lights.

"Not really, but I think everything is already prepared for us." He indicated what looked like a recording device that lit up when Suzie turned on the lights.

Still holding their champagne, they sat in the seats, noticing then that there was a place holder for their glasses. In his place holder was also the remote, which Dick picked up so he could place his glass there. He noticed that the button marked 3D was flashing so he pushed it. The screen came to life, the lights in the room dimmed, and the chairs started vibrating softly. Whether it was the activities of the day, the champagne, or something else, their eyes closed, and they could not see what was on the screen, but they could hear the voice as they entered a trance-like state.

Had their eyes been open they would have seen on the screen their host, Peter Vanderbilt, dressed in a tuxedo, and looking like he had just come from a wedding himself. His voice, however, filled their heads with love, and they would do anything he asked.

"I want to congratulate you two on your marriage, and the life, or afterlife, that you have been chosen to share. It is time now to complete my plans. You will see at each of your sides a box. Inside the box is a knife, sharper than anything you can imagine. It has also been especially treated. You will each pick up your knife and head towards the guest rooms. Starting with your parents, you are to slit the throats of everyone in the house. None will awaken, I have taken care of that. Once you have finished your task you will head out to the garage and go down into the oil pit. In the pit you will find an opening in the back. You will crawl through that opening and once you have passed through the doorway, you will see a handle. You will push the handle to shut the door behind you. Then you will fall asleep, a sleep from which you will not awaken."

THE NEXT DAY

The 911 call came early that morning from the catering company that had returned to clean up. They had been given a key to enter and instructions to knock on one of the bedroom doors before they left—the bedroom closest to the top of the staircase, occupied by the parents of the bride.

They had arrived at six and by eight had finished the kitchen and dining areas and removed the leftover food. "Sofia," said the supervisor to his lead hand. "I think we're finished here. We just need to check in as instructed."

The two of them climbed the stairs and knocked on the door to the bedroom but received no response. Their instructions were clear though. The mother of the bride had to be informed when they were done, and they knew what the repercussions would be if they did not follow instructions.

After the third knock failed to produce a response, Sofia was told by her supervisor to enter the room. It being dark, she turned on a light. This was a suite, and from where she stood, she could see the living area, which had a table on which stood a half empty bottle of champagne, and through an open door, a small part of the bedroom.

"Mrs. Milton," whispered Sofia, trying not to cause too much of a disturbance. The wrath of the matriarch was well known.

Getting no response, she walked up to the bedroom door and tapped lightly, once again calling out the name. In the dim light coming from the hall, she could make out that there were two forms on the bed and not much else. Wanting to wake up only Mrs. Milton, she quietly made her way over, but as she neared the bed,

Sofia slipped and almost fell. She lifted her foot to see what she had slipped in and saw that her shoe was covered in something red. Pulling out her pocket flashlight she shined it on the bed.

Her screams rang through the house.

* * *

Dozens of police cars, ambulances, and other emergency vehicles lined the driveway leading to the Vanderbilt mansion. Already the morgue vehicles had left and returned multiple times. The local morgue only had three vehicles. It had never been set up to receive multiple bodies, let alone over sixty at one time. Due to the prominent social standing of many of the families, Detective Ron Harris knew this was going to be a shit storm. Already there were television crews trying to access the property, despite the police cordon set up. A couple of cameramen had even tried to enter the mansion through a back door via a path in the maple forest behind the house.

To make matters worse, this was an international incident. There were families from both sides of the border. The local sheriff's office would soon be losing control to state troopers and probably RCMP officers from Canada. Ron wanted to get his report over and done with and handed to them as quickly as possible so he could wash his hands of this. Some would think that this type of incident could make a policeman's career, but Ron preferred the simple life he had with his family. He had been a cop for eight quiet years and wanted the rest of his life to go the same way, peaceful and happy.

It was his job to write a wrap up report based on the observations of the first police on the scene. This report would then be turned over to the state police. He wanted it done quickly and competently so that he would not have to return to this mess.

"What have you got, JP?" JP Larock was a junior detective who had only been with the department for a little over a year. Ron noticed he looked a lot paler than normal.

"Bodies all over the place, spread through twenty-five suites, a total of sixty-four. All were found in their beds, except the bride and groom, Suzie Milton, and Dick Stein."

"Where were they found?"

"They weren't. We searched the entire house, the grounds, and the other building. No sign of them. They were supposed to be in the master suite. We checked there. The bed was not slept in. It looked like the theatre room off their suite had been used, but other than two near-empty champagne glasses we found nothing else."

"Murder-suicide or just murder—it makes no sense. How could they go through the entire house and kill everyone without a single person waking up and resisting?"

"I might be able to answer that," said the coroner coming from the suite that had been occupied by the parents of the bride. "I will have to have it analyzed to see what was used, but based on the residue I see, it looks like the champagne was laced with some type of sleeping compound. If that is the case with all the guests, then they slept through their deaths."

"Sixty-four dead and two missing. The press will have a field day with this."

"Pardon sir, but there may be three missing," said an even younger policeman standing by the front door.

"Who is the third?" asked Ron.

"Betty Cooper. She was the wedding planner. We found her car near the garage. I confirmed with her office that she never returned yesterday."

"Any connection between her and the newly married couple?"

"According to the wedding list she was an invitee, so probably more than just the planner. But not close enough to warrant a suite as we have a list showing the room arrangements and her name was not on it. We also compared the list to every dead body that was found, and the numbers match."

"So, a mass murder and three potential suspects."

Another officer approached.

"Sir."

"What now?"

"The FBI has arrived." He pointed out a tall man in a dark suit.

"Just what I need."

Seeing that he was being looked at, the FBI agent walked up to Ron and held out his hand.

"Special Agent Montgomery. Please fill me in on what you have. I'll be taking over the case."

Ron sighed with relief. This was one situation he wanted out of as quickly as possible.

There was not a lot to tell, other than bodies all over the place, a coroner's suspicions, and three missing people. It took only a few minutes.

"I want the coroner's report sent to me as soon as possible," Montgomery said, handing Ron a card. "You will be my point man with local authorities, and to set up any questioning of local people if necessary. Do you have any information on the owner of this place? Was he here as well?"

"Thank God, no. The owner is a multi-billionaire named Peter Vanderbilt."

"*The* Peter Vanderbilt?"

"There is only one multi-billionaire of that name that I know about. According to word around town, he had let the wedding party use his house after their original site burned down—the Hotel

Astoria. You may have heard about it. Anyway, the groom worked for the lawyers that represent Mr. Vanderbilt, and when he heard of their situation he offered his residence, since he would be out of the country at the time. I will give you the contact info of his representative, James Neighbors, in my report."

"Okay. Finish up your report and send it to me. Other than that, your job here is done." Montgomery once again shook Ron's hand and then turned away to speak with another agent.

Ron heard the beginning of the conversation. "I want an APB put out on Suzie Milton, Richard Stein, and Betty Cooper. Yes, I know it will create a shit storm with the press, but we have one here already. I want it done five minutes ago."

The rest of what the special agent had to say Ron did not hear, nor did he care. He finished at the scene as quickly as possible, went back to his office, and wrote his final report. With any luck, he thought, that would be the last he would ever have anything to do with the place.

* * *

Luck, however, was not on Detective Harris's side. Four more times he was called to investigate unusual deaths in that house. And the last time was the strangest of all, since it involved James Neighbors, the custodian of the estate.

Ironically, the death of James Neighbors caused everything to change. The trust fund set up to pay the expenses of the estate was folded. No one knew why. Two years later it was sold for back taxes.

Because of its reputation, buyers were few and far between, and it went for a tenth of its value to a man who believed, more than others, in the supernatural. He also had the financial means to have the place investigated to its fullest.

CHAPTER TWO

THE GHOST ELIMINATORS

"We have now spent forty-eight hours here in Winfred Manor, said to be the most haunted estate in Wisconsin. As you, our viewers, have seen and heard, we have spoken to many spirits, some fearful and basically harmless, but a couple that were evil and tried to hurt us many times.

"Using the exclusive equipment we designed, and the experience we have acquired, we confronted each and every ghost, including the infamous Blackjack Scorpion, said to have tortured and killed dozens here before his death—and even more afterwards. You have seen the wounds we have taken, from the scratch marks on Bryan's back, to the bite marks on Michelle's arms.

"Fear is not something the Ghost Eliminators will give in to. We will stand up to any and all evil forces that try to drive the rightful occupants of a home away. We will fight them to the end, and we will win. This is the season ending episode but be sure to join us next year.

"I am Jackson Benders, lead investigator, and on behalf of my entire crew, Melissa Sanford, Bryan Chan, Michelle Aysha, Bob

Selson, Tippy O'Hare, Madame Blaze Destiny, and our producer/ director, Matt Capiro, we will officially say:

The ghosts of Winfred Manor are *eliminated*!"

"And that's a cut. Well done, Jackson," called Matt Capiro, from his position beside the camera.

"That was crap," Jackson shot back. "This must have been the most boring case to date. I never had to make so much shit up."

"It doesn't matter. The audience loves it. Our ratings have never been higher," replied the producer/director.

"It's still bullshit. I want to get into a house that is really haunted. Other than a few weird voices in a couple of places, we haven't come across anything that can prove that ghosts exist. Why can't you get us into a place that has a real reputation? Like North Brother Island in New York. They let camera crews in there before."

"What is North Brother Island?" asked Bob Selson, who handled most of their equipment.

"Only reputed to be one of the most haunted places in America," responded Madame Blaze Destiny, who called herself the medium extraordinaire, but who most called the flakiest fake around.

Matt provided more details. "It's located in New York City's East River, between the Bronx and Riker's Island. A thirteen-acre piece of land that became the last refuge for over one thousand people whose passenger ship sank in the river. Later it became home to a hospital for people with contagious diseases. The best-known resident was Mary Mallon, aka Typhoid Mary. She was the first documented person in the country to have typhoid fever, and it's estimated that she infected over fifty people with the disease. Now the island is abandoned—home to a bird sanctuary and off-limits to the public."

"Oh, it's a lot more than that," Jackson put in. "My research shows that some people who went to the island never returned. It would be a ratings bonanza," he added.

"As you know, I've already spoken to city authorities, and they refuse to let any ghost hunters in there. They seem to think we will damage their reputation," Matt rolled his eyes with this comment showing what he thought of that idea.

"We could make it famous—a *tourist* bonanza for them."

"Which is what truly scares them," said Bryan Chan, who had been silently following the exchange between host and director. "They're afraid people will flock to the island, and because so many of the structures are falling down, someone will get hurt, and they will be sued or forced to spend billions of dollars to make the island safe."

Before anyone could comment on his observation, a voice from beyond the group suddenly posed a question. "Would you be interested in a truly haunted house? One that would make anything you've worked on till now seem like a funhouse?"

The person addressing them had entered the front door and passed security without anyone noticing. He was rather undistinguished looking, standing barely five foot seven, thinning grey and brown hair, a well coiffed beard, also grey and brown, close set brown eyes, and wearing a three-piece suit.

"Who are you and how did you get in here?" demanded Jackson.

"My name is Mitchell Cousins. As to how I got in here, well, money can buy you anything."

Before Jackson could go off on the stranger, Matt intervened.

"It's okay, Jackson. I invited him here. He said he had a proposition for us. And yes, he is wealthy, so you had better listen to him."

Mollified—after all rich sponsors were what paid for their show—Jackson held out his hand.

"Sorry about that, we get too many fans breaking in on us as soon as they hear we're in the neighborhood. We were just wrapping up in this formerly haunted house. Matt said you have a proposition for us."

"Indeed, I do. One that I think you will find quite hard to resist."

"You know of a house that is *really* haunted—and you can get us access?" asked Bryan.

"Indubitably," was the reply. He studied their faces for a minute, as if wanting to memorize their expressions before he popped his big news. "I have recently purchased a property with such a reputation. I want to make sure it is cleared of any influences before I move in."

"A reputation? Is it something we would have heard of?" asked Jackson.

"Have you heard of the Vanderbilt mansion?"

"You mean the *House that Peter Built*?!" exclaimed Blaze.

"That's the one. I recently bought it through a tax sale."

"What is the house that Peter built?" asked Tippy, one of the two gifted technicians on the crew.

"It's more commonly referred to as 'Blood Mansion,'" replied Jackson. "Those of us who have been in the profession for many years know the story of how this place was built by Peter Vanderbilt to be a haunted house, which is why we've often referred to it as the house that Peter built. With all the deaths there over the years, though, it's been called Blood Mansion by so many people the name has stuck. It's reputed to be the most haunted anywhere. There have been more deaths and disappearances in that house since its construction in the early nineties than any other place you can name. Rumor has it that Peter actually used parts of other haunted houses to build his mansion."

"How many deaths and disappearances are we talking about?" asked Bob.

"Must be close to a hundred by now," replied Jackson.

"Exactly one hundred that are known. Ninety-two dead, eight missing," Mitchell clarified.

"Aren't the missing people supposed to be the killers?" asked Michelle.

"That's the presumption of the local police and the FBI. However, the first incident took place in 1994, and the three people missing from that time were never found, despite a nation-wide manhunt. The FBI claimed that the bride and groom, with the help of the wedding planner, drugged all the people who were spending the night, then went from room to room slashing the throats of the sleeping guests, sixty-four of them."

"Why would they do that?" questioned Tippy.

"Now that's the sixty-four-dollar question," replied Jackson. "The investigators never gave a reason. Money could not have been behind it since the three disappeared and never claimed any inheritance. The families were well to do, but a financial audit turned up no irregularities."

Mitchell nodded. "If you're interested in taking on this case, I will pay for all production costs, including transportation and food."

Jackson looked at Matt and nodded.

"We are definitely interested," said Matt walking up to Mitchell Cousins and shaking his hand. Let's go to my trailer and work out the details."

As soon as they left, Jackson jumped up, punched the air, and yelled, "*Yes!*"

Michelle was less enthused. As one of the lead investigators it would be her job to go through the premises looking for signs of paranormal activity. "This is not like anything else we've done, Jackson. Are you sure we can handle it?"

"Oh, come on, don't be spooked so easily. So far, every single haunted house has proven to be a nothing burger. Even the few that had unusual happenings turned out to be as soft as kitty cats. Besides, as you know, and most of our viewers don't, ninety-nine percent of all hauntings are easily explainable by logic and science."

"It is not the ninety-nine percent I am worried about. It is the one percent that could hand us our lunch. This may be that one percent, Jackson."

"What do you think Madame Blaze Destiny," asked Bob. "After all you are our psychic and paranormal expert."

"I will have to consult my crystals later, but the vibe I am getting is that this one episode could make us a lot of money."

Everyone laughed, even Michelle, and they began to pack up their equipment. While they finished up Jackson walked out of the house in time to see Mitchell Cousins getting into his limo and being driven away. Matt waived Jackson over.

"So, we have an agreement. Two days and two nights of filming, first class transportation, food catered in advance, and full production costs up front. He did add a couple of conditions, though."

"With terms like that I can accept conditions," replied Jackson, a big smile on his face.

"Don't be so quick," Matt cautioned. "The first condition is that he wants a world-class narrator as part of the team. He said if his house is going to be featured on television, he wants only the best to present it."

"And who would that be?"

"Sir Arthur James."

Jackson snorted. "If he could pull that off, I'd have no problem with it. Of course, I am saying that because there is no way Mr. Uppity James will do it. You remember the one time we asked him to do a small piece because the house we were eliminating was in England and having someone with a British accent would have added some authenticity to it—he basically called us fraud artists before he refused."

"I remember," Matt said. "But I'm glad you have no problem with it because Sir Arthur James has already accepted. Mr. Cousins talked with him while we were in the trailer. I guess money does talk."

"Well, that's just crap," Jackson exploded, his smile replaced by a look that could kill. "You know I narrate my own shows."

"Not this time, Jackson. I agree with Mr. Cousins. Having someone of the reputation of Sir Arthur will not only add legitimacy to our show, but it will also pump the ratings even higher. I bet we can even get one of the British networks to carry it. Sorry Jackson, the decision is made."

Jackson wasn't ready to back away. "You said conditions. What else is there—although I'm afraid to ask?"

"Oh, you'll like this condition even less. There will be another team going through the house at the same time."

"Oh God, no, don't tell me that shitty little outfit, the Spirit Busters has a foot in."

"Not as bad as that. The other crew is actually a renowned group of paranormal investigators, the real McCoy, not a television show crew."

"Anyone I know."

"I am not sure yet, he didn't name them. Just said that they are highly recommended, and well-known in their field."

"They'd better not get in our way, that's all I can say. When is this booked for?"

"Three days from now, so you'd better get packing."

"Before that I want to add a last bit to the episode we just wrapped before it airs tomorrow. Let's get our fans amped for next season."

"We can't say where we're going yet. Part of the agreement. Nothing until after the house is cleared."

"No problem."

Matt motioned to one of the crew who were loading gear into a vehicle. "Bob, bring the camera. We'll add this part in front of the Wilfrid Manor for atmosphere."

Grabbing one of the cameras Bob, who besides handling much of the filming also worked on the technical equipment with Tippy, moved into position as indicated by Jackson. Making sure the angle was just right, he gave the signal and Jackson went into his final spiel.

"Before signing off I want to share some news I've just received. Our team has been invited to eliminate the ghosts of what is said to be one of the most haunted places around. I can't give you more information than to promise it will be our most exciting episode to date—that I can guarantee. And as proof, I *can* tell you that for the first time ever, the Ghost Eliminators will have a special guest narrator, *Sir Arthur James*. So, join us next season and be prepared to be scared!"

"That was excellent," said a beaming Matt, as he signalled to cut. "I'll make sure it gets to the production department before we leave."

* * *

Professor John Samuels stepped away from the podium. "That wraps up this semester," he said, sweeping the lecture hall with an appraising look. "If I have taught you *anything*, it is to be skeptical about *everything*—yet keep an open mind. Ninety-nine percent of all so-called supernatural events can easily be explained by science and logic. And even for that one percent, just because we can't figure out scientifically what is happening, it doesn't mean there isn't a scientific explanation that we haven't yet grasped.

"From our studies of ancient cultures, you have learned that almost all of their beliefs were based on something they had witnessed but could not explain. Today we have the scientific means to explain almost anything we come across. We just have to apply it.

"Now everyone, have a wonderful summer. I will see some of you again next fall, but for the others, go out, learn, and enjoy."

As the students filed out, the professor noticed Associate Dean Jack Watson standing at the entrance. As soon as the last student was gone, the dean came in and closed the door.

"Closed door meeting? Must be serious. Are you canning me?" John quipped, standard banter with his friend of many years..

"Canned, no. Pickled maybe," Jack replied.

"It's not like you to act all mysterious, Jack. I investigate the supernatural, not mysteries."

"That's exactly the reason I'm here. We've had a request for your team to gather and do an investigation, and the interested party is ready to pay the university, and each member of your team, handsomely to do it."

"So, what's the catch? It is what we do, and the university can use the money."

"Regardless, if I had the say I would have said no, but administration has accepted the job and there's nothing I can do about it."

"What is the job?"

"The Vanderbilt Mansion—aka Blood Mansion. I want you to refuse it John. I will find a way to get them to see reason."

"Why would I want to refuse it? This is exactly the type of haunting I have always wanted to get my hands on. Not just creepy noises, and supposed apparitions, but real disappearances and deaths."

"John, people have died there. People have disappeared there. It is like nothing you have dealt with before."

"I can handle this, Jack. Don't worry about it."

"You are the one that always says to be skeptical and also keep an open mind. I hope your mind is open enough for this."

"Always, Jack."

"'Who do you want to bring?"

"I will want Harry Worth for sure. He's one of the best investigators in the field. And for a technician I want Jackson Brown. He's also a geologist and chemist so he can analyze any strange movements or gasses."

"You should also bring Skip O'Reilly. No one knows equipment better than he does."

"Good call. But I would love to be able to find a real psychic, not some fake medium. Any ideas.?"

"Maybe. Let me make a couple of calls."

"Thanks, Jack."

"Oh, and one more thing—but you are not going to like this."

"Please don't say he wants our crew to be televised."

"Not exactly."

"What does that mean?"

"Well, the good news is that you won't have to give any interviews, nor have a television crew hovering over you."

"And the bad news".

"That will all be handled by the other crew that will be there."

"What other crew?" John's voice showing his irritation.

Jack opened the door, turned to John, and practically whispered, "The Ghost Eliminators," before quickly leaving the room. He was not far enough away though to miss the loud "*Fuck!*" that came from John.

CHAPTER THREE

THEY CAME TOGETHER

Ron Harris sat on the edge of the fountain, watching as two sets of vehicles pulled in through the gate at Vanderbilt Mansion. The first was simply a car and a van, with nothing to distinguish them in any way. The van was a simple panel van, the name of a car rental agency marked on the side. The car was even simpler, a Honda Civic that had seen better days. They drove past him and pulled up in front of the house using the inside lane.

The group following behind was quite different. They came strictly in vans, four of them, with huge Casper-looking ghost heads inside rifle targets splashed across their sides. Written in a semi-circle underneath were the words GHOST ELIMINATORS! They pulled up beside the first vehicles and as the two groups started to emerge, Ron could see them glaring at each other. He could almost feel the animosity from where he sat. *Great*, he thought, *now I'm going to have to be a peacekeeper on top of everything else.*

He stood and turned towards the two groups when he spotted another car pulling through the gate. This one was a Mini-Cooper with a racing stripe down the front. There was only one person in the car and as it passed, he could see the driver was a woman with red hair and funky sunglasses but could not make out much more. She parked in a space behind the first two vehicles.

When she got out of her car the place went quiet. Both groups just stopped what they were doing and stared. Ron could not blame them. When he was younger, they would have said the lady was a fox. He did not keep up with today's vernacular, but the word foxy suited her fine. She stood just over five and a half feet tall and had a well-toned body that was easily seen as she was wearing a simple blouse, tied in a knot above her belly, and a pair of shorts. Her face reminded him of pictures of Raquel Welch when she was young, with her high cheekbones, full lips, and bright white teeth. Even her eyes were dark brown like Raquel's, which is unusual for a redhead.

She stood there, regarding both groups, while both groups gawked at her, nobody moving. She seemed to shudder as she walked by the flowers, a distant look on her face, but then it passed.

While everyone just stood there, Ron got up and approached her holding out his hand.

"Good afternoon, ma'am. I'm Detective Ron Harris, recently retired from the force. The new owner of this property has hired me to keep a watch on all of you. May I have your name please."

Grateful that the former officer had broken the silence, and appreciating his approach, she gave him a big smile, shook his hand, and in a resonant voice replied, "I am Jane Wilbury. I am supposed to meet Mr. John Samuels here."

Broken from his trance, John walked over to her and shook her hand.

"That would be me. Jack told me he had a psychic lined up, but he did not mention that you were so—"

"Beautiful," called out one of John's group; probably Skip,

although John wasn't really paying attention.

"Sexy," yelled out one of the crew from the Ghost Eliminators.

Giving that group a frown John completed his sentence. "—so young."

Rather than be insulted Jane just laughed.

"Good genetics in my family. I'm in my thirties—but refuse to say where in that range."

Finally recovering his dignity, John said, "Welcome to our crew. Let me introduce everyone. That tall skinny guy with the brown hair and goatee he combs a hundred times a day is our lead investigator, Harry Worth." Harry just nodded to her.

"Behind him, that short bald guy is our equipment man, Skip O'Reilly."

Skip pushed Harry aside and came over to shake her hand.

"I am a technician, not an equipment guy. Pleased to meet you."

"Finally, that dashing man with the super bright smile is our geologist and chemist, Jackson Brown."

One of the most handsome men Jane had ever met walked over to shake her hand. He had a sculpted short-haired beard and warm eyes. He reminded her very much of the British actor, Lucien Laviscount from the show *Emily in Paris.* But just when she thought she could fall in love with this guy, he opened his mouth, and instead of the cultured voice she was expecting, it came out nasally and irritating.

"Welcome to our little group," he said. "You'll find that we're far more intelligent than that other group over there."

"I am Jackson Benders," said the TV host, as he made his way toward her with his hand extended, "the more cultured of the Jacksons standing near you. You may have heard of me."

"Of course I have Mr. Benders," said Jane taking his hand. "I've seen your show a number of times."

"Being a psychic, you probably watch our show to learn how to control your abilities. Maybe our own Blaze Destiny can give you some tips."

Jane threw her head back and roared with laughter, much louder than would be expected from a lady like her. "I watch your show on nights when I need some comic relief. As for your Blaze Destiny, my cat is more psychic than she is."

The entire university crew burst out laughing, while the Ghost Eliminators huffed and puffed in faux anger—protecting one of their own—even though they thought Jane had her pegged right.

Ironically the only one of them who did not appear upset by this was Blaze herself. She turned to her crew and said, "Don't let that charlatan bother you. People like her are always jealous of people with my abilities."

Although not happy with the situation overall, John realized that the two crews were going to be working in relatively close quarters for the next two days, and it would be best if they could at least get along. He turned towards Jackson Benders and offered his hand. "I watch your show often. I may not agree with all of your methods, but some of your ideas are interesting, to say the least."

Also knowing that getting along for the next couple of days would be preferable to constant battles, Jackson accepted the peace offering. "One can always learn something new, and someone of your reputation would probably have a lot of information you can pass on."

With the shaking of hands, the atmosphere of animosity was broken for the time being.

"Ms. Wilbury, although you have laughed at our show, we are quite serious in what we do. I would like to introduce my crew, but please, no more disparaging remarks."

Jane nodded her head in acceptance.

"The Ellen DeGeneres look-alike there is Melissa Sanford. She is my investigative partner."

Jane thought of her more like a B actress but made no comment, as they nodded at each other.

"My regular investigators Bryan Chan and Michelle Aysha," he continued indicating an oriental man of average height, and a woman of mixed race, and quite attractive. Both waived tentatively at Jane, to which she responded in kind.

"Our technicians Bob Selson and Tippy O'Hare." Bob was a large man in every sense of the word. Probably six foot five and three hundred pounds, with a flock of blond hair. Tippy looked just like his name, short, skinny, very much Irish.

While Bob did not move, Tippy came over to shake her hand.

"If you need anything just come to me. I'm sure I have far more and much better equipment than a group of university dropouts." His Irish accent was unmistakable.

Shaking his hand she replied, "I'm sure I will have no need of your equipment, but thanks for offering."

Not sure how to respond Tippy sheepishly went back to take his position again beside Bob.

"Standing by the truck like he's trying to guard everything is our producer and director, Matt Caprio."

Jane nodded his way, and he nodded back. Jane knew of Matt. He had been a respected director and had worked on several hit movies, but then for some reason became a heavy believer in outlandish conspiracy theories, and now most of the big movie productions would not hire him.

Even though he was in his fifties, Matt had few wrinkles and obviously took care of himself. Little to no fat sat on his six-foot frame. Originally from Australia he had the same rugged looks as Paul Hogan of Crocodile Dundee fame, but she knew he had no trace of an Australian accent.

Before he could mention Blaze Destiny, she was already standing next to Jane. Her outlandish gypsy-like clothes, the large bangles she wore on her wrists, the bandana painted with stars and the moon that she wore on her head, as well as her squeaky voice, just made her appear more fake then if she walked around with a sign hanging on her neck that said, I can see your future. Beneath the getup she was an attractive woman, mid-forties, about five foot eight, long black hair, a round face and a slightly pear-shaped body, yet not overweight.

What got to Jane, though, was the intensity of her gaze.

"You may think I'm a fake, because of my getup, but you would be surprised at what I have seen." She said this almost in a whisper and Jane thought she was the only one to hear her.

Then in a much louder voice, "I will do a reading once we get settled in the house. I want to make sure that a novice psychic like Ms. Wilbury is not harmed by any malevolent spirits that may try to take possession of her." With that she turned away and headed directly to the front door.

As holder of the key, Ron rushed after her, but he had only taken a few steps when a horn sounded, and a small sports car came racing in through the gate. Just before reaching the other vehicles the driver slammed on the brakes. Pushing his door open the driver jumped out of the car, held his arms wide and said, "That is how you make an entrance."

Jackson Benders groaned and turned to his producer as if to say, *you see why I don't want this guy.*

Tall and slim, with a thin face, sporting a pencil mustache, long sideburns, and a Pompadour haircut, the new arrival was as arrogant as the royal lineage he claimed. His saving grace—and what made him one of the most in-demand narrators in the business—was a voice that would charm the pants off a nun.

Walking towards the groups, he pulled down his wraparound shades. "You people are truly blessed that the owner of this magnificent mansion is paying me, Sir Arthur James, a fortune to be here. It gives you the wonderful opportunity to partake of my company, and my presence alone will turn your show into the highest rated ever, even with all your chicanery."

John Samuels turned away from the British narrator and said over his shoulder, "You stick to the show people where you belong and leave us legitimate investigators alone—and we will be okay."

"Ha, legitimate. Anyone who believes in ghosts, spirits, hauntings, bigfoot, or aliens is a crackpot. Yet my presence alone will make people think you nutcases are legitimate."

Ron Harris turned away from the door to face the Brit. "Sir I really don't know, nor care, who you are, but if you come into this house with an attitude like that it will eat you up."

"And just who are you?" the disdain in the actor's voice clear to all.

"I am the only person who has seen the aftermath of every incident that has happened here. From the mass killings in 1994 to the more recent deaths and disappearances a couple of years ago. I watched the coroner pull body after body from this house, and the eight missing people have never been found. So, take that as you will."

Having delivered his message, Ron proceeded to open the door with one of the most unusual keys any of the others had ever seen.

"Now that's what I call a skeleton key," said Sir Arthur. "Is that supposed to add to the atmosphere of that little tale you just told us?"

Ron ignored the jibe, pushed the large wooden door open and waved his arms, inviting the guests in.

"Do you mind if I look at that key?" asked John Samuels.

Ron handed it to the professor.

"This is really heavy," John said, hefting the key in his hand and turning to view from different angles. "Must be solid brass. The skeleton head is a unique design as well. Three dimensional, so it's like holding a skull, with ridges extending back from the ears and jaws indicative of bone protrusions. As well, the brass, although still having the usual yellow base, appears to have shades of red within it. The unlocking portion, though, is shaped more like an Abloy lock. Do you know where it was made?"

Ron shrugged and shook his head. "Like everything about this house, no one knows anything. Even the original plans have disappeared. I only know that a lot of the materials were specially made and imported by the original owner, Mr. Vanderbilt."

All of John Samuels group, as well as most of the Ghost Eliminators, had followed the procession into the house.

"Whatever happened to Mr. Vanderbilt?" asked Tippy, bringing up the rear.

It was John Samuels who responded. "At the time of the first massacre, the wedding party of 1994, Peter Vanderbilt was in Africa on a business trip. When he got the news of what had happened, he hired a private jet to rush him back home. The jet fell off the radar somewhere over the Atlantic and was never found. Fortunately, he had left legal documentation regarding his estate and particularly this house. His assistant, James Neighbors, was the executor and watched over this place as per the instructions—until his own encounter with this house. He and his family were the last known occupants and victims. With no one left to run the trust, the taxes weren't paid, and the property was sold at auction to recover the taxes."

"You know a lot about this place," commented Michelle Aysha.

"When we investigate a supposed supernatural event, the first and most important thing we do is investigate the history of the place. Most unusual happenings can be easily explained through research."

"Research may tell you the official events, but you need to investigate the rumours and suspicions, to get to the truth." Jackson Benders announced this with his own air of arrogance.

"Rumours and suspicions are no better than social media. They just repeat made up stuff over and over until they get enough people to believe it, and then call it fact."

"In normal situations I would agree with you, Mr. Samuels," said Ron. "But in this case, you might want to listen to Mr. Benders. There may be some truth in the rumors that surround this place."

"Like what rumors?" asked Jane her eyes wide watching Ron's face as he replied.

"One in particular, that I believe. That Mr. Vanderbilt did not die in a plane crash but was actually in the house at the time of the murders, somehow directing everything."

"Oh nonsense," said Harry Worth. "If he had still been alive, someone would have seen him at some point in time."

"The story goes that after the massacre he had himself buried somewhere on the estate. Someone working at the hospital found his medical charts showing that he was in the late stages of pancreatic cancer. They say that he built this house, and planned the massacre, so he wouldn't be alone in the afterlife. I only met him a couple of times, but he was definitely a weird character," finished Ron.

"If you are so afraid of this house, then why are you here now?" asked Jane.

"I need closure. I was a mid-level detective when the massacre of '94 happened. I was also the lead investigator for every incident that followed. Each time the FBI took over the case, and each time they declared it a case of murder with the killer or killers getting away and leaving the country. I didn't believe that back in '94, nor in the following cases. People don't kill for no reason, at least not the types that have gone missing in these cases. They had no motive, and no means to disappear out of the country without leaving a trace." He looked around at the assembled investigators, crew, and personalities. "I don't know if, between your two groups, you can actually solve this, but just in case you do, I want to be here."

"Even if it means your life?" asked Sir Arthur sarcastically.

"Even so," was the reply, without a hint of doubt. "Although some of the suites have been prepared with sheets and blankets, I would suggest that everyone stays in groups, even at night."

"You may be a former cop" said Sir Arthur in his condescending tone, "but here you are just a security guard and have no say over us. I personally will find the most comfortable suite and claim it for my own."

Ron didn't actually roll his eyes, but his tone said it all. "Please yourself. But I'm willing to bet that you'll be one of the first to come running to me and begging me to protect you." He turned away and spoke to the others. "Make yourselves at home, but I would *not* get as comfortable as the arrogant aristocrat if I were you."

As the two groups separated, moving their equipment and bags into the house, John Samuels approached the former detective. "Mr. Harris, once we're set up, I'd like to sit and have a talk with you. Since you know more about what has happened here, the information you have could provide valuable clues to help solve this."

Ron looked the professor in the eyes for a moment before responding. "I will answer whatever questions you have, but I don't think it will help much. And please call me Ron."

"Fair enough, Ron. However, one thing I've found in the many investigations I have done is that knowing the history is often the clue to solving the mystery—whether it be a purposely done fake haunting, a situation where the answers are of a natural cause, or some other event."

"Let me go speak with the other group. Apparently, part of my job here is to do an on-camera interview as well as give a tour of the house. As soon as I'm done with them, I'll gladly sit with you." He grinned. "I'll need to have some sanity returned after all."

John laughed as Ron walked away and then turned his attention to his crew. He was helping Skip set up some folding tables and chairs, to place their equipment, and set up an office section in the large entrance area when he heard raised voices coming from the area where the Ghost Eliminators were setting up. Ron's voice was loud and clear.

"I will do your bloody interview, as agreed in the contract, however I will not tell any lies, nor will I modify the truth of what I have seen in any way. You can make of that what you bloody well want to." With that Ron stormed away.

John waited until things had calmed down, and then approached him. "Would you be up to a discussion now, or do you still need a little time to cool down?"

"As I said before, I need to have a sane conversation now, so fire away."

The professor led Ron over to where he had set up his workspace and invited him to have a seat. "I know it's none of my business," he said, when the two men were settled, "but out of curiosity, what did he say to get you so worked up?"

Ron didn't hesitate. "He wanted me to read some stupid script where I point out to him places where I had personally seen ghosts. I tried to explain to him that the only people who may ever have seen anything are not around to talk about it as they're all dead or missing. Then he said I should just make stuff up. You probably heard my reply."

John laughed. "Loud and clear."

"Before I answer any of your questions, could you explain to me how you work? I've seen the Ghost Eliminators on television, so I know what they're about, but how does a real paranormal investigator work?"

"Thank you, Ron."

"For what?"

"For saying that with no sarcasm. We get a lot of people that say we're wasting our time, or that we're kooks, like that arrogant prick, Sir Arthur. I like to keep an open mind. However, to be honest, I have yet to come face to face with a real ghost, although I have debunked a number of supposed hauntings, some of which were enacted by fraud artists."

"A part of me hopes that we don't meet any ghosts, and we do spend our weekend wasting time, since anyone that may have seen a ghost here has probably become one, but there is something inside me that wants to meet a ghost and beat the crap out of it for what it's put me through these last going on thirty years."

John smiled at the image of Ron trying to wrestle a ghost.

"Most likely we will find a natural explanation for everything. That equipment that Jackson, our Jackson I mean, is setting up will measure gas levels. If there is some type of toxic gas seeping through the house that is causing hallucinations, or people to act in unusual ways, it will detect it."

Ron leaned forward in his chair his creased eyebrows showing what the thought of that suggestion but John waived his hand to say just hold that though. "I'm telling you how we work, not what is necessarily happening here.

"There was one case we investigated where a man claimed to have killed his family because demons haunted his house. Testing found that there were large amounts of a substance called silene capensis or what is commonly referred to as African dream root, in the air. Further investigation revealed that his wife had been burning this substance as an incense as she liked the smell. The thing is, African dream root can cause hallucinations and tends to affect people with a dopamine imbalance more than others, which the husband had."

Ron looked sceptical. "Unless this is a gas that only appears intermittently, I doubt it's the cause here."

"We shall see. You asked how *real* paranormal investigators work so I will explain it this way. I set up a series of points, then go over them one by one to fill in the blanks. Here is a synopsis of it, though of course not each situation calls for the same planning, so I tailor my investigation for each separate case. Unlike those TV guys who use the same equipment and the same methods for every single show.

"First, I talk to any eyewitnesses to whatever event precipitated the investigation. I keep them separate if two or more saw the same thing and record their individual stories if possible. If eyewitnesses are not available, I talk to someone who dealt with the eyewitnesses. Of course, here there are no real eyewitnesses, and the closest I have to that is you."

"Unless you can speak with the dead," quipped Ron, his smile showing he was not trying to insult John.

Nodding to Ron's comment John continued. "I take the people making the claim seriously and won't be dismissive or outwardly skeptical. Let them tell their whole story in their own words. I find people are more open if they're talking to someone who is willing to believe their story. I ask them questions like what is their general orientation to belief in spirits? That is, if they hear a sound in the attic, is their first thought ghost—or squirrel? That gives me an idea of whether it is more likely something natural or something unusual. Again, here this won't apply.

"I try to know a bit about the history of the place. Is this the first claim? What is it about the place that leads people to believe it's haunted? Which of course is why I asked to speak with you."

"I'm flattered."

This drew a smile from John. He was coming to like this ex-cop. "When people claim to see ghosts, I ask if the ghost, spirit, demon or whatever they claim to have seen physically interacted with the local environment? Did it make a sound, move anything, etc.?

"I then analyze if there are any other explanations for these interactions? Some could be building-based like noisy heating systems, drafts, slippery windows and so on, or people-based like mischievous kids or adults looking for attention or profit. Could doors be opening because of expanding or wonky floorboards? I create a timeline of reports and look for patterns—like they always happen in the afternoon—which could indicate expansion of joints caused by heat.

"If things are falling off shelves, is it because the shelves aren't straight? I'll use a spirit level and yes, the pun is intended." This elicited a laugh from Ron.

"I find out who else had access to the building on or around the times of the events in question. If there is film or video of the event, I request to see the original whole, unedited, film, tape, SD card, or however it was recorded. Finding out why the recording happened to be made in the first place can be key to deciphering if it's a fraud. Was it organically recorded, like from a door cam, or baby cam, or did someone set out to find a ghost? How easy would it be to stage or fake such a recording?

"Learn who, if anyone, benefits from this claim. Does the claim bring profit, notoriety, visitors, or prestige to a person or place?"

"Much like a police investigation," said Ron.

"Also, if this is happening over a time period, I ask the eyewitnesses to keep a diary, logging every time something happens and the details, since it is often a matter of weeks from when they contact me until I can get there to investigate. Some of the things I want them to keep a diary of are: What were they doing at the time of the incident? What happened? How did it happen? How did they feel? Did they expect something to happen? What was happening before hand? And more. A complete diary can be an important tool.

"These details help build a bigger picture with more context, and it's often here that I find clues."

"That's a lot different than those other guys who just ask leading questions," Ron observed. "I much prefer how your team works," he added with a grin.

"True that. So can I start with you now?"

"Let's get this underway, although I doubt what I have to say will solve this mystery."

"Let's begin with what you know about the house, and its original owner. Tell me any details you can remember. I'm going to record this if you don't mind as my memory is not what it used to be."

"I have the same issues so go right ahead." He waited a moment for John to turn on his recorder and continued. "I know little about the owner, other than he was very rich, and treated everyone that worked on this site very well. He was also kind to the community, contributing millions of dollars for parks, libraries, and so on. You would not have been able to find a single person around here who had a bad thing to say about him during those years.

"It took him a while to build the house. I think four or five years. Most of the workers were people he brought in from out of town, and from what I heard, many were from out of the country. He did hire local craftsmen to do some work, and all were well paid. Plus, the workers he brought here spent time in the town and spent their money there, so everyone here was happy.

"He was here to oversee almost all of the construction, and the odd times he wasn't, his assistant, James Neighbors, took over. That was how I found out one thing that few others knew. You see my cousin was hired to drive this assistant around, and one time, when James got out of the car, he left a file open on his seat. The only paper my cousin saw was an invoice for steel beams, for use in part of the superstructure. My cousin also works in construction and can tell you the cost of every single item needed to build a house. The invoice for the beams was about ten times what he could have gotten the same specs for here. Wondering why, my cousin pulled out the invoice to read the entire thing. At the bottom of the page was a note that said, extra pieces of metal melted down and added to beam, and a cost that looked outrageous. Before he could read further, he saw James coming back to the car so quickly put the paper back and turned the other way. No one wanted to lose their job due to curiosity since it was well paid, and believe me, my cousin was being paid more for driving the guy around for a few days than he made in a month at his regular employment.

"Rumors are that many of the materials used had the same unusual aspects, but of course no one knows for sure. Except of course James Neighbors—should he ever be found."

"His family was the last to occupy the place, correct? What happened to them?"

"I found that one particularly difficult, since I was the one who found the bodies. We had received a call from Neighbors' sister, who lives in California. She said that she had scheduled a zoom meeting with James, but he never appeared at the appointed time. According to her that was very unusual for him since he kept a very structured schedule. She tried phoning him several times, as well as his wife, and got no response. She even tried to reach his kids through Facebook, since they have a family chat set up there. Again, no response. That was when she called our office.

"I knew as soon as I arrived at the house, that we had another incident. Like each and every other time, the front door was open, yet the house, and the surroundings, were strangely quiet. Not even a bird chirping.

"I found the wife first. She was hanging from the chandelier right there." Ron indicated the large chandelier hanging in the entrance. "How she got up there I have no idea. It took a scissor lift for the coroner to get her body down."

John whistled. "I can see that."

"You haven't seen anything yet. I immediately called for backup. No way was I going to keep searching this place by myself. When two more deputies arrived, we carried on. Unfortunately, I was the one who discovered the children. First, I found his eldest son, a thirteen-year-old, at the bottom of the pool. He was lying there with heavy chains wrapped around him. The horror of the last thing he saw was still embedded on his face. The coroner later told me he did not die from drowning, as there was no water in his lungs. His opinion was that the kid had a heart attack, that he had literally been scared to death."

"I then found the younger son, an eleven-year-old, in the theatre room. He was tied, upside down, in one of the theatre chairs. His throat had been slit. He had bled to death, but the cut was not large, so he bled over a period of hours. He had also been stripped and the coroner said his body showed signs of being raped, although there was no DNA evidence left behind since there was no semen found. His facial expression was also fixed in horror."

"And James Neighbors?"

"As had been the case with each incident, he was never found. The FBI claimed jurisdiction again, and their final report says that James Neighbors killed his wife and children, then fled the country. No explanation on how he managed to get his wife on to the chandelier, no explanation of why the older son had no water in his lungs, and no explanation on how he managed to disappear, when none of his bank accounts had been touched. I believe that you have a copy of the report from the FBI."

"Yes, and I did not believe it for a moment. Especially when I saw the picture they have of his wife, hanging from that chandelier. I can understand why your coroner needed a scissor lift to get her down. Also, that she had been tortured in ways that would have been difficult to do without specialized equipment. I also have the synopsis you provided of the incidents, but I only skimmed over them, as I would rather hear them directly from you. Written reports are too static, and don't give the feelings of the person writing them. These feelings are just as important to solving cases like this as the words themselves. Could you please go over all the incidents for me."

"On the first one, you are probably as aware of the events as I am, since it made national news. It was in 1994 and an entire wedding party was massacred. You have all the details, and I really don't want to go over it. It's with the other reports in your file. I will say one thing though, something that has puzzled me to this day, and even had the FBI in a dither.

"Their report said that the bride and groom had put something into the drinks that put everyone asleep, and then proceeded to go through the house, room by room, and slit everyone's throats. So, say that is true, since the coroner did indeed find drugs in the alcohol. Besides the fact that there was no real motive, and that their bank accounts were never touched after the massacre, why would the wedding planner help them do this? She also disappeared, and like the others, her bank accounts had not been touched."

"That is weird, and I saw in their report that they tried to say she was involved sexually with the husband, but my research showed that Betty was gay. She had a partner she loved very much. The FBI's reasoning made no sense."

"I also got to know Betty. We had common friends and even had coffee together a few times when she was setting up her wedding planner business. She was good friends with the bride, but not so much with the groom. She also had to keep it a secret that she was gay, because the parents of the groom, as well as the mother of the bride, would have had her barred from the wedding if they knew.

"Regarding the other events, each incident was seven years apart, seven years almost to the day. In each case it was someone who had only been living here for a year or so."

"I thought the house was always occupied."

"It was. They rented it cheap, that is, cheap for a house like this, so it was always easy to find tenants. Since most years nothing happened, when something finally did happen, it was considered just an unusual event, since a previous family had lived there for years with not a single report of a ghost, an accident, or anything out of the ordinary."

"You say every seven years?"

"Yes. Is there something magical about that number or something?"

"Cults often use numbers that they find magical for their beliefs, and seven is a common theme."

"You think a cult is behind this?" asked Ron, his raised eyebrows showing how little he trusted that theory.

"It is just one possibility. I wouldn't say it is high on my list, but I can't completely discount it yet."

"I doubt you'll hang on to that possibility very long, once you hear about the other ones that followed. In 2001 there was a gathering, a sort of tenants' house party. Some of the guests were local residents. When they didn't return home, we got a call to do a home check. Of course, I was the lucky one on patrol, as even detectives in a small town have to do their share, and was in the area when the call came in. I pulled up to the gate figuring I would have to park out there but noticed it was partly open. The gate has a lock, and back then emergency services didn't have a key, which of course goes against city bylaws. That was corrected after that incident by the way. Anyway, I got to the front door, and it was also partly open. You can read the report, so I won't go into the details of the manner of their deaths other than to say that some were hung, some stabbed, and one had been dismembered; her I found in the chapel—but there were twelve dead and two missing, both men. As you must have read in their report, the FBI again claimed it was mass murder with the two missing people having fled the country. It's only my opinion but I feel the FBI investigator had his own thoughts on haunted houses and was afraid to spell them out in a report, so he took the easy way.

"In 2008, a birthday party. Family had gathered from different places, so it was to be a weekend long party, with people staying overnight. I was driving the area, on patrol because a couple of our officers were ill, and I volunteered to put in extra hours to cover for them. Part of the patrol was a pass by the manor to make sure the tenants weren't causing trouble, an arrangement made with Mr. Neighbors, and which our department was well paid for. The first thing I noticed was that the gate was wide open. As I pulled into the driveway, I saw that the front door was also open.

"I felt like puking, because I just knew it had happened again. I immediately called for backup, but as I said, we were short staffed and only one other car could come, and he was a good fifteen minutes away. I decided to take a quick look around just in case it was nothing except my imagination.

"As soon as I walked in, I saw the first body. It was the birthday girl, a thirteen-year-old. She was stripped naked and lying on the floor, in the middle of a pentagram. Parts of her body had been cut off and were placed at different parts of the pentagram. She had been tortured, raped, and then left to die there. She was the second one to die like that.

"Seven other bodies were found, including her parents and three other teens. One person was missing. The brother of the girl's mother. No trace of him was ever found. The FBI claimed that he was a known pedophile, with mental health issues, and had snapped. They think that he left the home and drowned himself in a nearby lake. His body, of course, was never found, but since it is a deep lake, a proper search was never done.

"Then in 2015, a small family, that had just moved in the week before. Two adults, and their three children, a boy aged fifteen and two girls, twins, aged thirteen. I found the two girls in a similar position as the birthday girl in the 2008 event. The parents were in the sauna, they had cooked to death. The fifteen-year-old boy was never found. You can guess what the FBI said without even reading their report.

"And finally, the James Neighbors family as I said before, in 2018."

"That one seems to be out of the pattern. Do you have an explanation for that?" It was a serious question, as John wanted to see where Ron's mind was at with everything. Ron was the only one in the house right then that knew, intimately, the details of everything that had happened. His response could indicate a bias, or his mental stability.

"An explanation, no. A theory, yes."

He was silent for a while and John did not push, knowing that if he did, he might lose whatever Ron was going to say.

When he finally spoke, he just said numbers. "Sixty-seven, fourteen, nine, five."

"What is that supposed to mean?"

"The number of dead and missing in each incident. You asked for my theory, here it is. The incident in 2015 did not cause enough death to satisfy whoever or whatever is behind this, and yes, I do believe, somehow, that Peter Vanderbilt is the one.

"I'll add one more thing. The last two incidents 2015 and 2018, caused a total of nine dead and missing. The same as in 2008. Now add 2015 and seven. You will get our present date, within days of the incident in 2015.

"I fully expect that this weekend we will get the answers we are looking for. I just don't believe we will survive it to tell anyone."

With that Ron got up from his seat and walked away.

CHAPTER FOUR

THE TOUR

As the two groups were busy with their own work, setting up equipment, preparing interviews and so on, Jackson Benders yelled to get everyone's attention.

"Okay people, and yes, that includes our university friends, please gather around. Ron Harris, the former police officer, and only person who has been in the house and seen the aftermath of every incident, has agreed to give us a tour. To save time and effort, it would be best if we all go together at the same time. Do you agree Mr. Samuels?"

"Completely. I have already had the chance to do an interview with him, so a tour right now for him to point out where the incidents happened would be helpful. On another note, it will be easier for everyone to get along if we go on a first name basis, so please call me John."

"Well said. But since there are two Jacksons, you can call me Jackson One, since I am the older of the two."

Jackson Brown nodded in agreement.

"You heathen can call yourselves whatever you want. I am Sir Arthur and that is how you will address me."

"Whatever makes you happy, your highness," quipped Harry. Although it brought smiles to most of the group, the comment was ignored by Sir Arthur.

"Tippy and I will remain here and continue setting up the equipment," said Bob.

"No. We will need to know the different places in the house where it would be best to set up sensors. Michelle, Bryan, and Melissa will scope out places for effect, but I need you two to make sure that technically the equipment will work where they suggest. Also bring one of the TV cameras. We can film the tour as part of the show."

John was about to protest before Jackson added, "Not to worry. We will edit out any reference to your team."

The group of fifteen made their way through the house, Ron leading and the others following, with some pushing and shoving for position. Feeling a heavy atmosphere Jane stayed close to Ron, protected by his presence. The first stop was the pool room.

They only partially entered the room, with some waiting just outside the door.

"The only victim found in this room was the eldest son of James Neighbors. Like I told John he was found at the bottom of the pool, his body held there by chains. When autopsied, no water was found in his lungs. Decide on your own how that is possible."

"Is the pool always this clear and clean?" asked a voice from the back. Ron thought it sounded like Michelle's."

"A crew came in once a week to test the quality of the water and make sure it was clean. Every other year they would drain the pool completely and scrub it down. If any paint was chipped, they resurfaced it. The last time that was done was after they pulled the body of Mr. Neighbors' son from the pool. They have not been back since."

"It looks like someone was here yesterday. It looks too clean not to have been touched for a couple of years," said Sir Arthur.

"And yet it is so," replied Ron, ignoring the faces that Sir Arthur was making.

They left the pool room and continued on. The next door they came to led to the theatre.

"The last victim in this room was James Neighbors' younger son. According to the reports he slowly bled to death, after being raped."

"I can't believe a father would rape and kill his son, which is what must have happened since the only person missing was the father," said Harry.

"You also can't believe the FBI report. James Neighbors may never have been found, but that doesn't mean he killed his family," replied Ron.

"And what did he do, use a condom, since no semen was found?" added John.

If not for the scene just described most of the group would have found this place a pleasant spot to watch a movie.

"After that description I think I will forego theatre night while we're here," said Melissa.

"On to the next room," said Jackson Benders.

Ron opened a door to a stunning library. Shelves filled the room from floor to ceiling on two walls completely, and partly on a third. The only open wall was the one with the windows, large bay type, letting in plenty of light. The shelves themselves were stacked with books, right to the top, which required a sliding ladder to get to.

"You mentioned how high up the wife of Jim Neighbors was on that chandelier. Could he have used this ladder to get her there?" asked John.

In response Ron walked over to the ladder and pulled. It did not come out, although it could be moved sideways. He then pointed to the rails that passed between the upper two shelves.

"It's built into the wall. He would have had to break it to get it out, and even then, there was no way to balance it. What is unusual is that with all the deaths in this house, none occurred in the library. It was almost as if this room was held in special reverence. Now for the next room where the circumstances are quite different."

A double entrance door led to what proved to be a chapel. The room was spacious with wooden pews to seat at least thirty people. There was an alter at the end, with two large crosses on it, as well as a smaller stand on the side with an unusual looking cross.

"Well, if things start to happen, we can all convene in here where we will be safe," mocked Sir Arthur.

"I would not bet on that," replied Ron in a serious tone.

"Why?" asked Bryan.

"Because one of the victims was found in here, her death particularly macabre," was the answer.

"In what way?" from Michelle.

"A teenaged girl had been dismembered here. A large pentagram had been drawn on the floor, and parts of her body were distributed to various points of the pentagram. Although the coroner could not tell for sure, due to the state of the body and all the blood, he thinks she had been raped before she was killed. He also said that based on the amount of blood flow, she was probably still alive while she was being dismembered."

"Oh, that's disgusting," said Tippy.

"Just about everything about this place is disgusting," responded Ron.

Even though everything had been cleaned, and there was no sign of what had taken place, everyone was happy to leave the chapel.

They passed a large dining room, but Ron did not stop, saying that no bodies had ever been found in there, probably because the room was rarely used.

They arrived at the kitchen. The equipment had all been modernized at some point. None of the appliances could have been older than six or seven years. Pots hung from racks suspended from the ceiling over a counter island with lower cupboards and a dishwasher. There was plenty of other counter space as well, along with many cupboards. Ron led them to the back of the kitchen where there was another door.

"This door leads to the wine cellar. We don't need to go down there as it is temperature controlled and quite cool. Although there were no bodies found down there, one thing of note should be taken into account. After the massacre of 1994, the staff of the caterer was interviewed. One of them said that she had seen Betty go down into the cellar. She assumed that Betty was just getting another bottle of wine for the soon to be married couple. This worker was in the kitchen for over an hour, and never saw Betty come back up. The FBI, of course, just dismissed this, saying that she probably passed by when the worker was not looking. They did send people down there but found no evidence that Betty had been there. Since they had already decided on their own theory, that Betty helped the married couple to murder all the guests, they never looked further into it."

"How could someone go down there and never come back up, or ever be seen again," sneered Sir Arthur.

"That is a very good question," replied Ron, walking away.

He next led them to a staircase off the kitchen.

"This is just one of three staircases that can be used to access the second level. The main staircase you have seen in the entrance lobby."

"Yes, and it is magnificent," said Melissa.

"This staircase here was to be used by guests that wanted to come down and get a snack, without having to pass through the entire house. There is also another staircase further on, used by staff only."

He led them up to the second level. The first door they got to he opened and invited everyone in by waving his arm.

For a suite it was quite spacious. It featured a sitting area, a kitchenette, a small dining table, a full bathroom, and a separate bedroom.

"This was the suite first used by the parents of the bride on that fateful day in 1994. Like all the other guests of that wedding they were found in their bed, their throats slit."

"Okay, I am not sleeping in this room," said Melissa.

"Then you will not want to sleep in any room," replied Ron. "Every single bedroom was occupied the night of that wedding."

"I think it will be fun sleeping in one of these rooms," said Bryan looking over at Michelle. She just rolled her eyes.

"Are all the rooms like this?" asked John.

"No. There are a couple almost as large as this, only without the kitchenette, but there are also quite a few that only have a bedroom, although all of them have their own bathrooms."

"Since the same incident happened in each of these rooms, I really don't think we need to visit all of them," said Jackson Benders.

"I agree," added John.

"I'm anxious to see the third floor. I read that there is a neat observatory there," piped up Harry.

There was only one staircase leading up to the third floor. What was unusual was that the staircase was not located anywhere near the other staircases that led from the main floor to the second floor.

"I see everyone glancing at the placement of this staircase as compared to the others. I was told by one of the workers that helped build this place that according to James Neighbors, Mr. Vanderbilt had requested it be built this way. He said that when he would retire to his own bedroom, the master suite on the top floor, he wanted to pass by the guests' suites and see if anyone would have need of anything before he went to sleep."

"Very kind of him, or very eccentric," said Bob.

"I would use the word strange," replied Ron.

When they got to the top floor, they noticed that there was a relatively small corridor, compared to the other floors, and only three doors. The corridor was semi-circular with one door to the far left, one facing them and one to the right.

"From the outside this floor looks like it should have more than three rooms," commented Melissa.

"It does," replied Ron. "there may only be three entrances, but the master suite itself has five very spacious rooms.

"The door at the end to our left has been locked since the day this house was built, and no one has a key. So, to this day no one knows what is in that room. The center door is to the observatory, and this door opens to the master suite."

Sir Arthur did not follow them to the master suite but instead went to test the door that had never been opened. The others stopped to watch him.

He got to the door and tried the handle. It jiggled a little but did not turn. He tried pushing on the door to see if he could force his way in, but it was solid wood and well barred.

"I guess we still won't know what is in that room, unless we force our way in somehow. Have you tried that skeleton key of yours?"

Ron pulled out the key and showed it to Sir Arthur. "Please find me a way to use this, or any other key, to open that door."

Sir Arthur looked again. Not only were there no key holes on the door, the handle did not have one either.

"That is strange. How would the owner himself get in?"

"Compared to the rest of this house, a locked door with no way to open it is almost normal," answered Ron.

"Why didn't your men, or the FBI force the door open?" asked John. "Shouldn't that have been part of their investigation?"

Giving John a knowing look, Ron answered. "The FBI said that since it couldn't be opened it wasn't important. I think Peter had left certain instructions with his foundation about this room. It would have taken a court order to enter, and the FBI felt it wasn't worth the effort. Someone was surely paid, but whatever the case we were not allowed to force it open."

Giving one last look at the door Sir Arthur turned away and joined the others.

The master suite was enormous. It had its own entrance vestibule that led in to a large living room, that also featured a table for eating. Like the large suite on the floor below it also had a kitchenette with a coffee machine, microwave, small fridge, and a sink. Off the living room was a patio door leading to a spacious balcony. To the far left was a door that led to a huge bathroom, with a Jacuzzi tub, glass shower for two, toilet and bidet. Next to the bathroom was the master bedroom. Inside was a double king size bed, television, two night-tables and large walk-in closet that even had a long rack for shoes. There was also a patio door that led on to the balcony.

The last door led to a miniature theatre, miniature in that there were only two chairs. The projector screen was about fifteen feet away.

Michelle pushed her way through the group and went to sit in one of the chairs. Bryan followed her and plopped into the other one.

"Wow these are comfortable," he exclaimed.

"More than just comfortable. They have the reclining range of a Laz-e-boy and vibrate as well. Apparently, they work with a remote control, that also controls the cinema. The chairs are made to move with the movie, so if the movie is about an earthquake, the chair will shake like you are in an earthquake when that scene comes up in the movie."

"That's so cool," said Tippy.

"So did anything happen in here?" asked John.

"The crime scene analysts say that this is where it all began. The night of the massacre of 1994 they deduced that the bride and groom were sitting in these chairs just before they started killing everyone. The evidence they based this on was that in each of the chair cupholders there was a glass of champagne, only half finished. The glasses also contained LSD, which was also found in the bottle of champagne. The FBI concluded that the husband put the LSD in the bottle, and then hid all the evidence. Of course, in their conclusions they did not put any motive or reasoning behind their deduction."

"Definitely sounds like someone was paid off," commented John.

Michelle and Bryan looked at each other, then down at the chairs and quickly vacated them, almost as if they thought that what had happened was somehow contagious just by sitting there.

"So do you to want to spend your first night investigating in this room?" asked Jackson Benders.

"Oh, no thanks," was the quick reply from Michelle.

"We'll take one of the second-floor suites. Unless there is still blood on the mattresses."

"The mattresses were all replaced after that night, and have also been changed twice more since then," said Ron.

"Wow, they sure must have spent a lot of money maintaining this place," commented John. "Between changing all the mattresses, taking care of the pool, outdoor landscaping and so on, it must cost a fortune every year."

"The foundation that Mr. Vanderbilt created to watch over this place had almost unlimited resources."

"If that's the case, why was this property sold for non-payment of taxes?" asked Blaze.

"That in itself is a mystery. We only know that just before he stayed here, James Neighbors set up a self destruct mechanism for the foundation, that would come into effect if he did not stop it. That mechanism came into effect a month after his disappearance. The assets of the foundation had been sold and all the proceeds donated to various charities, all except this house. For some reason it became the sole asset in the foundation, and then was sold for nonpayment of taxes."

Ron's explanation surprised them.

"How do you know so much about the financial end of things?" asked Melissa.

"I have a friend that works for the city finance department. He told me all about it when they foreclosed."

"Come on, I want to see the observatory," whined Harry, practically pushing people towards that room.

"Oh wow!" exclaimed Jane as they entered.

"From what I have been able to research, the telescope was the most advanced of it's day for a private residence," said John. "A lot of this equipment was tied in to it, but it was never completed. The telescope itself works well, but the computers to download and analyze the data were never set up."

"Any idea why not?" asked Blaze.

John shook his head so Ron picked up on it.

"From what I was told, the computer equipment was custom order and was supposed to be a decade ahead of its time. Unfortunately, the building of it was behind its time. They were months late for most of the parts, and the day of the wedding it was still sitting here awaiting completion. After the massacre, the foundation cancelled the remainder of the order and it was never finished."

"That's a pity," said Harry as he went to sit in the chair beneath the telescope. He looked up into the lens. The telescope was positioned to face the south. He was able to adjust the filters to screen out the effects of the sun and had a pretty good view."

"Okay everyone. Tour is over. Time to get to work," said Jackson Benders. "Bob, Tippy did you get the entire tour on camera?"

"Got it and will back it up once we get downstairs," answered Bob.

Everyone filed out of the room and headed towards the stairs. No one noticed that Harry did not follow.

CHAPTER FIVE

OF MACHINERY AND MAYHEM

Jane walked through the entrance way and into the pool room. It had fascinated her during the tour, so she found her way back there as soon as the group returned. Surprised at how crystal clear the water was, and that the pool was even filled and functional, she opened herself up to see what she would feel. Her experiences of the past had shown her that if there was negative energy nearby, she would sense it right away. The area would cause her to feel slightly nauseous, and if she looked long enough there would be a blackness there, almost like a presence.

It was not only negative energy she felt. If she met a person that was genuinely good, they would emit a yellow aura to her, just like if they were evil, they would emit a black aura. Most people she met were in the middle so did not really emit much of an aura to her.

She'd discovered that sometimes places had auras too. When she was young, she had been terrified of cemeteries. She had been afraid that because there were so many dead bodies there it would be a black place for her. That was when she had first discovered her ability. Then her aunt had passed away. She was thirteen at the time, and her parents had insisted she accompany them to the funeral, and then to the cemetery. The entire experience had been life changing for her.

In the church she had seen both good and bad auras, which surprised her. She expected to see either only good auras, or none at all. At that point her abilities were still weak so she did not sense neutral auras. More surprising though was the cemetery. There she had expected to see mostly black. Instead, she had felt at peace. After the service she had left her family and walked through the cemetery, trying to see if there were differences from one tombstone to the next. By far most of them had no auras at all. A few had a light aura of good. When she read those gravestones, the ones that still had an aura were of those that had died recently. She felt nothing at any of the older gravestones—but one. A large mausoleum. She did not recognize the name engraved on the door, but she felt the blackness around the door's edges, waiting to get out. She turned and ran as fast as she could back to her family. Over the years she had visited many cemeteries and would often lie in the grass and rest, as it was more peaceful than walking through the city where she could feel so much.

Occasionally, though, she would come across a grave, or more often a mausoleum, that exuded the blackness. She never tried to investigate these further.

At one point she went to see a psychiatrist at the university she attended. It was the first time she had confided in anyone about what she felt. Not even her family knew. But she had to talk to someone about it, because she had been wondering if she was going crazy. She had been fortunate in finding the right person. Clarissa Munroe was not only a psychiatrist, but she was also a parapsychologist. Over the following years she helped Jane come to understand her ability and gain some control over it. Now she could block those senses at will, and not *feel* people every time she passed by someone. She did not have the funds to pay Clarissa. Instead, Clarissa helped her in exchange for her help in circumstances like these. Helping university professionals debunk fake hauntings, as that is what almost every case she had been on had turned out to be.

The assault began as soon as she let down her defenses. The blackness was everywhere. Her knees gave way and she fell. Fortunately, she was next to a chair and was able to grab it before hitting the ground. She had never felt anything so dark, and so powerful. Then suddenly it was gone.

"Someone who is still learning their abilities should not be alone in a place like this," said a voice from the doorway, startling her.

Turning she saw Blaze Destiny standing there. The voice, however, did not sound like her squeaky television voice, but like the voice that had practically whispered to her earlier.

"What would you know about my abilities. You are nothing but a charlatan."

Once again Destiny surprised Jane by laughing.

"Because of what you are, I will let you in on a secret. I really am a psychic. Don't let these fake trappings fool you. Nor the nonsense I do on that wacky TV show."

"Then why do you do that show? It makes you look like a fool and a fake."

"The money is good. You can't really make a living as a psychic. As well, the easiest way to prevent people from taking advantage of you because of your abilities, is to make them think you are a fake. But there is also a deeper reason. I have known Jackson Benders for many years. We are good friends, and yes, once we were even lovers. When he told me about his show, and how excited he was about it, I pitched myself as a psychic to be part of it. Not even Jackson knows my real abilities."

Destiny paused as if considering, then continued. "You see I was worried for him. What if he came across a real haunted house? What if it was a place with entities that could cause physical harm. During the show you see me going through the property, calling on spirits to show themselves, doing seances and so on. What I am really doing is opening myself up to make sure there are no evil presences. Of course, to date there never have been."

"Until today?"

Blaze answered the question with one of her own.

"What did you feel when you opened up?"

"Blackness. So strong it knocked me off my feet. Then suddenly it was gone."

"Your feelings come through as colors?

"Mostly yes. Darker is evil, lighter is good. Mainly I see it on people, but sometimes on places."

"How much control do you have over it.?"

"Much more now. I have been getting some training from a parapsychologist."

"You will need much more than some training to survive this house. I suggest you don't open yourself again unless I am present."

"If you have these abilities, what do you feel and how can you control it, let alone help me?"

"I feel many presences here. Some are pure evil, and most are just scared. The foundation of my abilities is emotions. I have been training these for years. They are strictly people based. People can leave impressions behind in many places, not only after death, but during life. I can walk into a house and feel the emotions of past owners going back many years. Here, many of the presences I feel did not die here and have never even been here during their lives. I have never encountered that before and I do not understand it."

Destiny looked truly bemused, pausing again before she turned her attention back to Jane.

"If you open yourself up, then you open up to being possessed. It may be the reason behind some of the murders. If I am with you when you open up, I can guide you and let you know when a malevolent presence might make a move on you. I have one condition, though. No one else is to know. As far as everyone else is concerned I am to remain Blaze Destiny, flamboyant gypsy psychic."

Jane shrugged, willing to humour the other woman. "Sure, but why?"

"I would rather not say, for now. Once we are finished with this house, if we survive it, then I will gladly take you out to lunch and tell you my history and why I am who I am."

"You say, if we survive. That sounds like what that ex-cop, Ron Harris said."

"He is the only one here who is coming into this place with eyes fully open. He is expecting something to happen. It might be wise if we stick close to him."

Before Jane could say anything further, Blaze turned away and left the room. Jane took another look around but did not open herself up again.

* * *

"I want the cameras set up here for a close-up of Sir Arthur, then a scan back to the chandelier. We'll fit in the eyewitness account of Ron Harris right after that." Jackson continued to set up the first scene, turning next to the commentator.

"Sir Arthur, do you have the script that Michelle prepared?"

"Have it and memorized it. I am a professional, unlike most of the people here."

Letting the gibe pass, Jackson turned to Tippy.

"Is the ghost box communicator set up?"

"Ready and already on."

"What is a ghost box communicator?" asked Sir Arthur, his voice its typical sarcastic bend.

Tippy ignored the sarcasm as it gave him the chance to launch into an enthusiastic description of his favorite piece of equipment. Indicating a rolling tray on which sat an unusual looking machine that appeared one part gaming center, one part computer, and one part something from the original Star Trek series, it featured a large seventeen-inch screen, a console with various lights and dials, and a microphone that was shaped like a boom mike from a movie set.

"This piece of equipment was designed specifically for us. It is much larger than the standard issue of this type. This device presents entities with a simple and flexible way to communicate with us. It gives the ability to deliver words, phrases, numbers, emotions and yes or no answers through a uniquely simple, transparent, and documentable method. It scans through a set of diverse choices. While that's happening, there are multiple sensors looking for environmental changes, like suddenly colder temperatures, lack of oxygen, and so on. It also scans for spikes in EMF, that's electrical magnetic fields, but only natural ones. It screens out those caused by phones or other man-made devices. As soon as a spike occurs, it makes a selection with an audio alert, displays it on the screen, and lets us know which sensor was triggered," he said, scanning the machine with the gaze of a proud parent.

"It has a rechargeable, long-life battery that lasts over thirty hours. I keep a couple of spares as well, even though it can be plugged in to an electrical outlet. I can adjust the sensitivity for all the sensors independently. So, if one seems to be acting up, I can turn down the sensitivity when I wish."

"Boring," declared Sir Arthur, waving an impatient hand. "I don't need to know all this minutia."

"Actually, you do," intervened Matt. "As you would have seen if you'd read the entire script—like a professional," he added, unable to resist a dig, "—since you will have to tell our audience what this machine is and what it does."

Sir Arthur gave Matt his standard look of disdain.

"Of course, I have read the script. I have also made changes to it. Your technical descriptions will just bore the audience. I am not in the habit of boring an audience. I will tell them about this piece of fakery in my own way."

Tippy was ready to explode. Destiny walked in at that moment and grabbed him by the arm. "Not to worry. Those who can't understand what you are saying—and its importance—are irrelevant."

Mollified, Tippy went back to making his adjustments.

"Okay, let's do a test run," said Matt. "We'll film Jackson later with the grand entrance. For now, I want Sir Arthur to do his introduction and talk about the chandelier. Tippy move the ghost box closer to Sir Arthur so that we can fit it in the frame with him and the chandelier. Make sure all the sensors are turned on. We don't need to have them go off on the first take, so leave them at their neutral settings, not our special ghost eliminator settings. As well have the screen open with the various sensor icons displayed so that Sir Arthur can describe them."

Fearful of exactly what Sir Arthur was going to say in his modified script, but thankful that this was being taped and not live, Matt gave the countdown as soon as everyone was in position.

"On camera in five, four, three, two, one ..." Then he pointed to Sir Arthur. He didn't have to look at the video monitor to know that Bob would be doing his usual perfect job of tracking Sir Arthur as he walked into frame, past the grand staircase to stand just off center in the massive entrance hall, the grand chandelier above him to his left.

"Good afternoon fans of *Ghost Eliminators*. I am Sir Arthur James. You may have been expecting to see Jackson Benders, but in this episode, the crew of *Ghost Eliminators* will be investigating a special house, said to be the most haunted in the world. Until today, no investigating team had been allowed in here. This mansion has also been unoccupied for the last four years."

Matt silently nodded his approval as he saw the camera slowly sweep the space. He made a mental note to splice in footage of the outside of the mansion as Sir Arthur continued what would become voiceover for this segment.

"I am honoured to have been invited as a guest narrator for this once in a lifetime event. Most of you will know me from the many documentaries I have done. For me, though, this is also a first. I have never before set foot in a genuine haunted house, and though a little fearful, I feel completely safe in the presence of these top-notch investigators."

Jackson Benders had moved over to stand beside his director, whispering to him. "I do have to admit, he knows how to put on a performance. It's not only his voice that catches you. It's the way he presents it, like he really believes every word he's saying. If it weren't for the things he said to us when he arrived, I'd think he did believe it all."

Matt grinned mischievously at Jackson. "Maybe we should have him replace you as commentator full time."

Before Jackson could respond, Sir Arthur moved closer to where they stood, stopping the nasty retort he had in mind.

"Here we are in the grand entrance. Above me you see a beautiful chandelier," Sir Arthur said, the camera following his extended hand up to the extravagant fixture. "There is a story behind it, as there is for many places in this house of horrors. But before I tell you the story of the chandelier, I want to point out to you this unusual looking machine."

Again, the camera tracked Sir Arthur as moved to stand beside something that would have looked natural in a Star Trek episode, but more original series than Next Generation, with it's flashing lights and boxy appearance. "Many fans of this show will already know all about this, but I want to make it known that this machine was especially constructed to the exact specification of the wizard technicians of the Ghost Eliminators. It is set up now and I want to point out some of the special features this marvelous machine has incorporated.

"There are many sensors that can track spirits through the fields they generate, or by the difference in temperature they create when the spirits pass nearby. Those lights you see will flash when a particular sensor is tripped.

"Later on, the crew will be setting up laser lights in various parts of the house and they will also be connected to this machine. Unique to the Ghost Eliminators, these laser posts are crescent shaped, allowing a larger degree of sensitivity, whereas the equipment of other ghost hunters can only point in one direction.

"On the screen you can see a box with an alphabet. If we are really fortunate, we will be able to communicate with an entity that is strong enough to light up various letters. The computer will then quickly put the letters into order to give a sentence, thereby allowing the entity to speak with us.

"Few entities have the strength, or even the ability to spell," Sir Arthur said, with a little laugh. "But this machine is prepared for that. On the next box over, you can see simple emojis. The investigator can ask a question, and the emoji will indicate whether the spirit is happy, scared, angry, and so on. The next box shows a simple yes or no in response to questions asked by the investigators.

"The final box is linked to the sensors. It shows room temperatures, noise levels, laser sensor trips, indicating where they came from., and EMF spikes—or—as explained to me by the tech wizards here, spikes in Electro Magnetic Fields. Every living being, and those that have lived before but never left, emit electricity, including most objects like cell phones, power lines, and so on. Ghosts emit their own form of EMF when they pass through, and this wonderful machine can differentiate between natural, man-made, and spiritual types of EMF, letting the Ghost Eliminators know when there is a presence nearby."

"Kind of a simplified version, and not entirely accurate, but it will make it easier to understand for any new viewers we have," Jackson whispered to Matt, who silently nodded agreement.

"Now let me tell you about this remarkable chandelier," Sir Arthur continued. He lifted his head, and the camera followed his gaze upward. "As you can see, it is quite high up there, a fact of particular importance in the story of the last family to live here—a family of four—husband, wife and two boys, aged eleven and thirteen."

The camera returned to Sir Arthur, zooming in on his face as he looked straight into the lens. "When the police received a call that the family couldn't be reached, they sent a car to investigate. The first officer on scene was Detective Ron Harris, who you fans of the show know will be interviewed later—but I will tell you what he found when he entered the house."

Sir Arthur paused with the dramatic skill of a Shakespearean actor.

"Hanging from this chandelier," he intoned, as the camera zoomed out to include the chandelier in the shot, "almost twenty feet above my head, was the body of the wife, Cindy Neighbors. How she got there no one knows. It took special equipment for the coroner to get her body down."

He paused again, to let the horrible image sink in, then with perfect timing carried on.

"I know this is where the Ghost Eliminators usually ask for the spirits to speak, but I have so wanted to do this since the first time I watched an episode … Cindy Neighbors, if you are here, give us a sign. You can speak with us through our special technology."

"He wasn't supposed to say that," Jackson hissed to Matt. "I guess this is part of the adjustments he made to the script."

"Don't worry we can edit it out later."

Sir Arthur made one more appeal. "I'm sure you must have something you want to tell us Cindy …"

Matt was just about to call "Cut" when lights suddenly started flashing on the Ghost Communicator—even the lights that were supposed to be disconnected until the lasers had been installed. Every sensor was beeping. A loud noise sounded in the background, almost like a growl. The emoji flashed—*scared*. The alphabet box lit up one word—*RUN!!!*. A wind blew through the entrance.

The machine started sparking and caught fire. Bob ran over with an extinguisher and quickly put out the flames, fortunately quickly enough to prevent any major damage.

"Okay, that was amazing!" Sir Arthur exclaimed. "I don't know how you guys set that up, but it will look great in the show. The timing was perfect—coming just after I asked Cindy for a sign."

Jackson looked over at Tippy and Bob, but they both just shook their heads.

John Samuels had been watching the scene and was ready to give them hell for making stuff up, but seeing their reactions, he realized their surprise was genuine.

"Ah, Sir Arthur. That was not us," said Tippy, his voice trembling.

"Oh, come on. Take credit where it is due. It was downright brilliant, and I rarely give that compliment."

"Mr. James, I don't think that was planned," said John.

"It is Sir Arthur, and how could that not have been planned?"

"Because you actually communicated with a ghost," answered Blaze. "They were not expecting that to happen."

"What, you are behind this nonsense, too?"

This time it was Ron who intervened. "I would suggest you get used to this Sir Arthur," he said emphasizing the Sir. "This house is just waking up. It's true seven-year cycle is now. This is only the beginning."

"Oh, come off it. Even if you did not set that up, all that happened was an equipment failure, nothing more and nothing less," said Sir Arthur.

Melissa, cut in before anyone could respond. "Has anyone seen Bryan and Michelle?" she asked, a frown creasing her forehead as she looked from one to another.

"I saw them leave a few minutes ago, just before the Sir Arthur show. They said something about checking out the garage," said Jackson Brown.

"That is not wise," said Ron. "I suggest you get them back. From here on it's best if everyone stays together."

"After what just happened, I'm inclined to agree with him," said Matt. "From what I've read there have been no incidents at the secondary building, so I'm sure they're fine, but still, Bob, contact them on the walkie-talkies and tell them to regroup. They do have them I hope."

"Yeah, I made sure they were equipped earlier. They know the routine. On a shoot everyone remains in communication."

Turning to John, Jackson asked, "What about your investigator?"

"Harry's probably somewhere snooping around for secret passages or something, and no, we don't have walkie-talkies, so we'll check for him later. He's a professional and will know not to be separated from the main group for too long."

"More likely checking out the telescopes," put in Chip, looking up from his computer screen. "You know how he is about 'scanning the sky' as he puts it. He'll get it out of his system and join us soon, knowing him."

Bob continued to try to reach the other two investigators, but only static replied.

"And I guess you think the walkie-talkies are not working because of spirits, too," quipped Sir Arthur.

"Probably just some interference," said Bob. "If someone goes outside it will probably be fine. Talkies are finicky like that. Doesn't take much to cause interference."

"I'll do it," said Tippy. "Don't worry I won't go far, just out the front door and in view of everyone."

Tippy picked up a walkie-talkie, tested it with Bob, and left the entrance hall. But as soon as he exited the front door, he lit up a smoke. That was his real reason for volunteering. Smoke or not though he made sure he could see the group from where he was, though with all the haunted places they had visited where nothing supernatural happened, he wasn't really taking Blood Mansion seriously.

It would not be long before the house taught him fear.

"Do they have any equipment with them?" asked Skip. "After that demonstration I'm beginning to believe your equipment may be worth something after all. That demonstration we saw was not equipment malfunction. I've seen enough equipment malfunction to know that."

Bob was practically beaming with pleasure. He had heard of Skip's reputation in the science technology field, and to have someone of his stature acknowledge the usefulness of his equipment could be monumental in getting his patents to sell.

"Most of what you see here was designed and built by me and Tippy. Oh, there are other ghost shows that claim to have the same equipment, but our equipment is custom, and been thoroughly tested.

"Looking at our equipment desk I see they have taken a portable EV recorder, a video camera, an EMF meter with sound, a laser grid pack, and a full spectrum light, which we call an APL."

"What do these pieces of equipment do?" asked Ron. We may have to depend on this assembly of tech, and I for one want to know what it's about.

"What are the specs?" asked Skip. "Our cop has the right of it. Before we go wandering any more, we should be properly prepared. After that demonstration we just saw I'm willing to give your equipment the benefit of doubt as to its usefulness."

There being multiple pieces of each device Bob walked over to the table and lifted them up one at a time to describe them.

"This is our own, adapted, portable EV recorder. Other ghost hunters have EV Recorders but nothing like ours. This here can be plugged directly into a computer for fast file transfer. The sound quality is the tops in the industry, clear no matter what the surrounding area holds, be it echoes, open spaces, whatever. It has ten gigs of internal memory with hundreds of hours of recording. It has live EVP listening capacity, either using speakers or headphones, and an extra SD card slot for even more storage. It uses AAA batteries which are rechargeable and can last up to a hundred hours. Here hold this."

He handed the device to Skip.

"Very light. Will be handy for any further investigations."

Turning back to the table Bob picked up what looked like a square box with eight rows of eight buttons on one side, an on-off switch with various dials, and a small computer screen on the other side.

"These aren't buttons. They are special light emitters. We call this our All-Purpose Light or APL. There are various settings. On normal it can light up a large room like a search light. However, it can also work in UV, infrared, and wide angle spread, and has temperature change detectors. It can show if one part of the room is at fifty degrees Fahrenheit, and another is at thirty. It can also be attached to a camera and the camera will film in whichever setting you want."

"So kind of like a ghost detector," remarked Ron. "This will come in handy." So far Ron appeared to be the only one there who was taking the situation seriously. Although the scene with Sir Arthur and the machine had elicited some worry, their past experiences of non-haunted hauntings had lulled both investigating groups into a sense of apathy towards the house.

"A laser grid pack is used to track movements. We usually set it up with a camera so that if a laser senser is tripped we can film the event. The sensor posts are placed in areas that are likely to have the most movement. There is a built in Wi-Fi system that connects to a main junction that then sends a signal to our ghost machine. The system of lasers has a short range, maybe twenty to thirty feet, but the junction box has a booster so it can emit up to two miles. Each pack comes with ten laser posts and one junction box."

"We should set some of these up as soon as your two team members are back," said John.

"That's a ten four," yelled Tippy from outside letting everyone know he was following instructions and keeping close.

"Put out your smoke and call Michelle and Bryan like you are supposed to be doing," yelled back Bob with a grin, then continued with his information session.

"Finally, this last baby is an EMF meter. Yeah, it looks like something out of the movie *Ghostbusters*, the Bill Murray original, not the, all girls remake, but this has far more features, and is far more powerful than what they pretended to have back then. It detects the smallest of changes in electromagnetic energy and alerts us with lights and sound. It has been fortified to reduce outside interference and false readings. It can detect both man-made and natural EMF, and signals the difference depending on which side of the detector lights up.

"They also took stakes for the laser array systems. I guess they wanted to set it up while they were there, preparing to place some outside.

"So, if they have this equipment with them, they should know if something is headed their way?" asked Jane.

"If they've turned them on, then, yes."

* * *

The secondary building had various entrances, including two large garage doors, two side doors to enter the garage, and a front entrance with a covered driveway to enter into the reception area. From the reception area one could head back to the garage, or upstairs to the offices. Michelle and Bryan entered through the main entrance, Bryan putting down his bag of toys as Michelle called it.

"So where do you want to start?" asked Bryan.

"Let's check the offices upstairs first. We can decide from there where to set up equipment. I haven't read of any activity related to this building, but I'm sure using the APL we can make it feel creepy. Maybe we can set up sleeping bags and spend the first night here."

"Just you and me," whispered Bryan.

"You can keep your pecker in your pants, at least for the first night," laughed Michelle. "I'm willing to bet those beds at the mansion are quite comfortable for just about any position."

Bryan swiveled his hips in a suggestive manner, but then got down to business.

"Before we go upstairs let me set up a camera aimed into the garage. It should give a creepy vibe. We can use the handheld one for the upstairs visit."

Camera prepared; they headed up.

The top of the staircase opened on to a landing with another reception desk. Straight ahead was a large conference room. There was very little wall, and more window facing into the reception area, so it gave them a clear view of the room. Other than a conference desk with a dozen chairs the room was bare. The interior walls had no decorations, and the outside walls were similar to the walls in the reception area, mostly windows. To their left was a hallway down which they could see more doors leading to offices, although these were more private.

It was the area to the right that fascinated them the most. A door led to a spacious open room, square in shape, that had to be a good thirty-five feet along each wall. As soon as they entered the room, to their left, was a massive, floor to ceiling, stone fireplace. Beyond the fireplace was a bar, and two doors, one leading to a bathroom, the other to a storage area.

The height was a good twenty-five feet at the apex, the room having a pyramid shaped ceiling, completely in wood. There were many windows in the room, letting in much light.

"I guess we'll have to wait until this evening to test the APL," said Michelle. "Switch on the EMF reader. Let's see if we can get any readings at all."

Reaching into his pocket he pulled the EMF reader out. As he did so, the walkie-talkie also came out, but not into his hand.

"Damn," said Bryan as it hit the floor. Michelle, who had already turned away, jumped at the noise it made.

"This place has a creepy enough atmosphere as it is Bryan. You don't have to add sound affects to scare me."

"Ha, ha." He bent down to pick up the walkie-talkie and saw that the back cover had come off and the batteries had come out. There were supposed to be two batteries, but he could only find one.

"Okay, this is weird. The talkie only had one battery in it."

"Not possible. Bob and Tippy are always very careful about making sure the equipment is working and ready to go."

"Well, this is the first time we've done a show in a place that has a real reputation of death like this property. Maybe in the excitement they dropped a battery without realizing it. Not a problem. In my bag I have some spares. When we're finished up here, I'll get them out." Bryan was trying to put a logical explanation to it, after all they had never encountered a real haunting before. Even as he said it, he knew it was not likely, but let the thought pass in the excitement of the investigation.

They tested out the EMF reader. It appeared to be in working order, however, other than a quick beep when turned on, it gave no indication of any activity.

"Does it usually beep like that when you turn it on?" asked Michelle. "Because it never does when I do."

"No that's a first for me as well. Still there are no readings on it now. Everything is flat line."

"You know this place really is beginning to give me the creeps. I'm not sure I even want to spend a night in this building. Let's just set up the equipment and get back to the others."

"That's fine with me. I am anxious to test out that bed, since you mentioned it."

"Time to think with your big head, not your little one. We have work to do."

"Hey, neither of my heads are little."

"Well, the one on your shoulders sure is oversized," Michelle responded, completely pan-faced. Before Bryan could respond she left the room, leaving him standing there. Looking around he started to feel creeped out too, so he quickly followed her.

At the other end of the hallway, they came across four more offices, mostly about ten by twelve in size. Two had desks in them, one room, a bit larger, had a photocopy machine, a center island with drawers and shelves that held paper and other office supplies, and a wall where the electronics were installed, including the internet wiring, and a fuse box. Bryan opened the box and saw only a few breakers.

"This must only be for the upstairs. There have to be more breaker boxes in the garage."

After checking out each room they decided that they only needed to set up laser lights in the hall, reception area, and the large room for the upstairs area.

"Let's check out the garage and then start setting up the equipment," suggested Michelle.

Back on the main level Bryan grabbed his bag and reached into the side pockets for more batteries. Problem was the side pockets were empty.

"Okay, someone is playing with us. I know I had a handful of batteries in this pocket. I bet it was Tippy playing games again."

"I'm not so sure about that," replied Michelle. "Even Tippy wouldn't want to jeopardize a big shoot like this by acting like his normal juvenile self. Check one of the laser posts. They use AA just like the talkie."

Bryan handed the EMF reader to Michelle so he could have both hands to open up a laser post. As soon as Michelle grabbed it, the reader beeped again, then went quiet. Looking at it, she saw there were still no readings.

"Okay, that is weird."

"So far everything here is weird. I got the batteries. I'll put them in, and we can contact the others."

Michelle headed into the garage section. Bryan followed, trying to insert the batteries as he walked, but stepping over a wood strip separating the two areas, he tripped and dropped one. As soon as it hit the floor the battery rolled away and out of sight.

"Damn, something doesn't want us to contact the others," he laughed as he bent down to look for the other battery.

"Don't even joke about it," replied Michelle.

Just then the EMF reader beeped again.

"Yeah, something is trying to tell us something," she said. Opening the back case of the EMF reader she pulled out a battery.

"Use this."

Bryan grabbed it from her and very carefully inserted it beside the other battery and put the cover back on.

Michelle had walked over to the oil pit while he was doing that. The oil pit was a recess in the floor large enough for someone to stand in while a vehicle sat above, to drain oil and do other mechanical work. The pit stretched twenty feet long and was two and a half feet wide. Above one section of the pit was a hydraulic lift.

Michelle stood at one end of the pit and looked down its length.

"Looks like there is a recess about halfway. You're the mechanic. Any idea what that would be for?"

"I have no idea why there would even be a lift over the pit. Kind of redundant. Ah, finally," he said, as the walkie-talkie came to life.

"Michelle, Bryan can you hear me, over." It was Tippy calling.

"Loud and clear," answered Bryan.

"It's about time. I've been trying to reach you for over five minutes. What are you guys doing anyway? There's time for nookie later."

"Very funny. We just had a battery problem is all. What's the panic?"

"We had an incident at the house. Jackson wants everyone back so we can discuss it. The ex-cop recommends we all stick together, and even the professor leading the other team thinks it's a good idea."

"What type of incident?'

"I'll tell you all about it when you get back, but just say our ghost box went a little crazy when Sir Pigeon decided he wanted to play Ghost Eliminator while doing a first run on the documentary."

"Bryan you've got so see this." Michelle was down in the pit and looking into the recess she had spotted earlier. "It looks like there's a door back there."

"Hold on Tippy. Looks like Michelle has spotted something. I'm going to check it out. Get back to you in a minute."

Two minutes passed, and then Tippy heard a loud crash coming from the direction of the secondary building.

"Bryan, can you hear me, over."

He repeated several times—with no response.

CHAPTER SIX

IT WAKES UP

Harry heard the group leaving but didn't care. An astronomy buff, he was now sitting in front of a telescope that was more powerful than any other that he'd had the chance to use on his own. Occasionally at the university he would be allowed into the observatory, but usually was only given a few minutes on the scope, and even then, he wasn't given permission to chose what he could look at.

This telescope may have been over twenty-five years old, but it was almost as advanced as the one at the university, which was only ten years old. It had filters to screen out the sun, a twenty-inch aperture, a focal length of 78.7" with a highest practical magnification of 1016x. He had not thought they made telescopes this powerful for personal use back in the early nineties. The optical design was a Truss tube Newtonian reflector. He knew that these designs were being developed in the nineties, but he had not realized any were even available back then. This was even more advanced than the Sky-Watcher Stargate-500P Synscan he had been looking at recently for his own home.

Since the telescope was already set to face the south, Harry did not need to move it. Most astronomy buffs know that during the daytime the best way to view any stars is looking south. With minor adjustments he was able to view the primary stars of Orion including Betelgeuse, Rigel, Bellatrix and Alnitak along with Iota Orionis, although its binary companion was not viewable. He also tracked down Capella, Procyon, and Aldebaran.

He had no idea of the passage of time and didn't move from the telescope's chair until he heard a noise in the hallway. Looking around he realized that everyone was gone, but still that noise kept coming from the hall.

"Okay, time to join the others. I'll come back later." The sound of his own voice startled him for a second. Then he heard the noise again. It sounded like a door opening. Thinking that maybe not as much time had passed as he thought, he expected to join the others in the hall. But when he left the observatory room, there was no one there. What did surprise him was that the door to the far room was open.

"Hey guys, how did you get that door open? I thought it was locked, with no keyhole."

Getting no response, he walked towards the door. The entrance was dark, so he stuck his head inside and called out again. Still no answer.

"Okay everyone, stop with the games." He passed through a small vestibule and the room opened up for him. Although dimly lit, it was bright enough to see that no one was there. But as he looked around, he saw what *was* there.

"God, no!"

He turned to run out of the room, but the door had shut, with no way to open it, not even a door handle. He heard a noise behind him, but was afraid to turn and see what it was. Terrified was more the word. Harry felt something touch his shoulder—and started screaming.

* * *

"While everyone mopes around trying to decide if we actually are in danger, how about you pick up one of those gadgets and we go check things out around here?"

Melissa looked at the striking Jackson Brown and thought, you say the word and I would go anywhere with you. She finally managed to get out "Sure" then headed to the equipment table, picking up both a portable EV recorder and an EMF reader. Turning them both on she handed the EMF reader to Jackson. She then picked up one of the portable cameras.

"Where do you two think you're going?" asked John.

"Just going to check out a couple of the rooms on this level. We won't be far, and we won't separate," replied Jackson.

"I don't think that's a good idea," said Ron.

"If they want your advice they will give it to you," quipped Sir Arthur. "You rent-a-cops think you are so smart."

"They can do as they wish," replied Ron. "But when strange things start, remember what happens in horror movies to those that go off, even in pairs. This house will make a horror movie seem like a comedy."

Sir Arthur just laughed.

While the cop and the Brit were paying more attention to each other, Melissa and Jackson of the university team left the main area.

"Let's check out the theater first," said Melissa. "The story about the younger son of James Neighbors was weird. Maybe we can find a clue to this mystery there."

"Sounds good to me," Jackson responded in his squeaky voice. Although it would have bothered most people, Melissa thought he sounded quaint.

She turned the camera on and filmed as they walked. Seeing the look from Jackson she answered his unasked question. "Jackson, that is, our Jackson, insists that whenever anyone walks around during an investigation, they always have a camera with them and operating, just in case."

"Why, if he just plans on making stuff up?"

"Jackson believes in ghosts. Yes, he fakes stuff for ratings, but he keeps telling the crew to always be prepared because one day we will come across something science can't explain, and he would hate to miss capturing it on film."

They reached their destination and pushed open the door to the room. Melissa reached over and pointed to the EMF's lights.

"If these light up it is supposed to indicate that there is a presence nearby. To be honest I was never sure if any of this stuff worked. Oh, we had a few beeps and lights go off in some of the places we investigated, but not once were we ever able to prove for sure that there were ghosts present, despite what our Jackson said during the shows."

"I did watch a few of the episodes. If your group had actually been serious, you might have come across something for real. But it looked like your producer was looking more for effects than reality."

"Yeah, Matt's like that. His only concern is ratings. In your investigations, did you ever uncover anything supernatural?"

"Mostly what we uncovered were fraud artists, or completely natural phenomena. We had a couple of cases, though, that we were never able to explain. One was a haunted restaurant in Toronto.

Usually, we can explain all noises and so-called sightings quite easily with science. But this place had some very unusual noises and we could never discover the source. As well some of the witnesses were hard to discredit. Towards the end though the owner asked us to leave. His explanation was that none of the ghosts were causing harm, and they brought in lots of patrons. John still thinks that the owner was behind it, but I have my doubts.

"How did you end up being a part of this television crew anyway?"

"I'm a website designer by trade. I was approached a few years ago by Jackson Benders. He wanted something flashy and dazzling to reflect his show. As I started work on it, I realized that to achieve what he wanted I would need to go on one or two ghost hunts with him. After the first show I was hooked, and he hired me on as an, I quote, *investigator*. I still did their website, but now I join them on their quests, as Jackson calls them. And you? How did you end up being a real paranormal investigator?"

"Kind of a twisted and convoluted story." Jackson frowned at the memory, wanting to present it in a way that did not make him look like he was smarter than his friends, but still wanting to impress the lady he was attracted to. "My first fascination was as a teen. Near where I lived there was an abandoned mine. Everyone said it was haunted. I went there one day with a group of friends. There was nothing out of the ordinary so after exploring for over an hour we decided to have our picnic lunch in the mine. It was about a half hour later that we all started seeing things. Soon we were running out of there as fast as our legs could carry us, screaming that ghosts were after us.

"I have a very scientific mind and once I had time to think about it, I decided to do a study of the mine. I found it strange that we all started hallucinating at the same time, and only after we sat in one place for some time."

He hesitated a moment to place his thoughts in a way that would not make him look like he was a juvenile delinquent. "I 'borrowed' a chemistry kit from the school and went back to the mine alone. I went to the spot where we sat. Along one of the walls there was water dripping so I took a sample of that and using the kit I analyzed it. Sure enough it had traces of nitrous oxide. I took my findings to the school, and they contacted the government, who sent a team in. After a full analysis of the mine, they closed it down and made sure it was sealed. I decided after that to major in chemistry and geology. Now I teach at a university but go with John on expeditions to out fraudsters. Haven't really come across anything that I could genuinely believe was paranormal, and we have done over a dozen of these investigations. Oh, there were a couple that left questions we could not answer, like that restaurant I mentioned, but that does not mean there wasn't a scientific answer."

"Do you think this house has a scientific answer? If so, what would it be?"

"Most likely yes. I'm leaning towards gases, like in the mine. That case you saw me with has a full kit to analyze for gases. Once everyone is set up, I'll start analyzing the air. According to the reports I read, in the first incident each body that was autopsied had traces of Benzodiazepines, but they were not able to figure out which one. Depending on the type it can induce a heavy sleep. Now I believe that there may be a gas caused by natural sources that is seeping into the house and causing hallucinations."

The EV recorder gave the first indication of something unusual. It had a mini speaker built into it and it emitted a short squawk, causing both of hem to jump.

"It's never done that before." Melissa's voice quivered.

"What does it usually do?"

"Well, we would ask if there was a spirit present and ask it a question. If there was a spirit present, and it felt like speaking, we would hear words. Of course, most of the time it was Matt from the other room."

"Isn't that what your big machine that just caught fire is supposed to do?"

"Kind of hard to wheel that around. This is for touring around a place."

The squawk repeated, twice more. They were both staring at it when the lights started flashing on the EMF. Then They heard a voice coming from the EV recorder. It sounded far away, but the message was clear.

"RUN!"

As they both spun back towards the entrance—the door shut.

"Do you think gasses caused that?"

* * *

Sir Arthur sidled up to Jane Wilbury.

"Let's do a little exploring of our own. I heard this place has an extensive wine cellar, temperature controlled, with bottles that have been stored here since this place was built. There should be an amazing selection to chose from."

"How would you know that?"

"Those yahoos that hired me may think of me as just a voice, but I research every subject I am asked to narrate. Of course, certain subjects fascinate me more than others, and one of those subjects is wine. I am somewhat of a connoisseur."

Even Jane was not immune to the charm of Sir Arthur. Plus, during her years of learning to cope with her abilities, she had turned to drinking and had acquired a taste for wine. With the help of the psychologist, she had managed to turn away from her dependence on alcohol, but she had kept her taste for fine wine. She took a look where Ron was standing, discussing the situation with John, wishing he would come as well, but realized he would just insist she stay there with the others. She made up her mind. While the others were focusing on the missing Jackson Brown and Melissa, they slipped away.

"I studied the layout of the house. The wine cellar is reached through a door in the kitchen as Ron said during our tour."

"You really did research this place."

"I must admit I lied a bit when I arrived. I have watched every episode of *Ghost Eliminators*, even before I was offered this role. I still don't believe in this stuff, but their show is entertaining. I would never say that in public, since I have a reputation to keep, which is why I once turned down a spot on their show, but my agent told me this could get me more lucrative American contracts, so alas money can pay for damaged reputations. I trust you not to mention it to anyone."

"Of course not. Still if you don't believe in this stuff, I don't see what we would have in common, other than wine."

"Make me believe. Tell me about your psychic abilities."

Not sure if he was humoring her, making fun of her, or really wanted to know the truth, Jane decided to act as if it was the last of these.

"I started to notice I was different when I was a teen," she began. "Before that I always thought that everyone could see what I see. To put it bluntly, I can see evil. I can also see what is truly good. It manifests itself as colors, almost like auras. I see it mostly on living people, but sometimes also on places. Occasionally I even hear voices, but fortunately that is rare. It was hearing the voices that drove me to finally see a psychiatrist. I was lucky. The psychiatrist I met with was also a parapsychologist., who helped me realize I was different, not crazy."

"So, when you look at me, what do you see?" Sir Arthur was expecting an answer that would match his own perception of self worth. He was to be disappointed.

"Not much of anything. Don't take that as an insult in any way. Unless a person is considerably evil or exceptionally good, it doesn't show me a lot. Just sort of a neutral-colored aura."

Somewhat mollified Sir Arthur asked, "So what do you see in this house?"

"I only tried to open myself once. That was in the pool room. I saw black. A black so intense it knocked me off my feet. If Blaze had not come in, I'm not sure what would have happened."

"That fake?"

Jane was about to defend the other psychic, but then remembered her promise. She decided to word it carefully.

"When she entered, it brought me out of my trance. Probably just the sound of her voice. After that the blackness was gone."

"Yeah, I guess her voice will do that to someone," laughed Sir Arthur. The more he talked, the more Jane noticed his aristocratic voice changing.

He noticed her look and laughed.

"I see my Yorkshire accent is slipping back in. No, I have not always been a stuck up noble. I was born and raised on the streets of Sheffield. After my parents died in an accident, I was forced into a boy's home, but was later adopted by an elderly couple, who really did have noble blood. But they were more than nobles. They were the nicest people in the world. I was only with them for ten years, before they both passed, about a year apart. I was twenty-one then, and found out I had inherited their estate, which was more than substantial enough. I parlayed that into acting, and then narrating. I was knighted at the age of thirty, five years ago, after saving the life of a friend of Prince William. I wish I could say it was something heroic, but it was just a simple application of the Heimlich maneuver.

"However, the knighthood elevated my status, and since then I've had to live up to it. Hence all the dramatics when I arrived."

"Like most Americans I am not really up on British tabloids, but I would think a story like that would have made it into American news."

"The Royals like to keep their secrets. They would not want a simple thing like what happened to be thought of as knighthood-worthy, so it was kind of kept quiet. You know I am rarely this upfront with someone I just met—but for some reason I feel like I can be open with you."

"They say, Sir Arthur, that knowing when you can be safe with giving secrets away to someone is a psychic gift," replied Jane, with only a hint of a smile.

Sir Arthur laughed.

"It will take more than that to convince me that psychic powers exist. Also please call me Arty when the others aren't around. That's what my real friends back home call me. But when the rest of the group is around, I prefer Sir Arthur, to keep up the reputation."

Jane laughed. "Sure, Arty, why not."

They had passed through the kitchen and arrived at the door leading to the wine cellar.

"Once we get down there, open yourself up and tell me what you see," Sir Arthur suggested.

"I'm not willing to do that. Not here, not now."

"You must be terrified of cemeteries then."

"Not at all. I find them quite peaceful, for the most part."

Sir Arthur gave her a quizzical look.

"Sounds strange right? The truth is, that good spirits do not stick around for long, unless they've been tortured, or suffered a painful death, and then they usually stick to the place they died, not the place they are buried."

Sir Arthur's face told her he was following—and interested. "Often the same is true for those who are evil," she continued. "Occasionally I do come across a grave, usually a mausoleum, that emits evil, and those I avoid. Mostly there's nothing, so I find it more peaceful than being in a city. Although I have to open myself up to sense anything, that has not always been true. If I let my guard down, I can be overcome."

"The way you explain it almost makes me believe. Almost. Are all psychics like you then?"

"Those who are truly psychic, and not fakes, have different ways of feeling their abilities. For some it's emotional. They feel emotions. For others it can be physical. I've met some who will get attacked by those they sense through their abilities. I have seen marks, like bites and whip marks, appear on a psychic while they are in a trance. Some can only access their abilities through the use of psychedelics."

"So, fakes like Blaze Destiny just don all that paraphernalia to make it look like they are psychic, but all their hand waving is just for show, or do you also do the hand waiving thing and calling out for spirits when you work?"

Doing her best not to give away Blaze's secret, yet wanting to defend her at the same time, was twisting Jane's insides. Why couldn't it have been Ron instead who accompanied her to the wine cellar, she thought. She felt more comfortable around him.

"As I said, my ability works mostly with colors. I do not need to call out and waive my arms about. I just need to concentrate on opening myself up. One should also remember never to judge a book by its cover."

"You're defending that fraud? Or do all of you psychics defend any who claim to have abilities, whether they do or don't?" Sir Arthur barely kept himself from saying that frauds defend frauds.

"I have never met Blaze until today, so I know little about her. However, I have met a legitimate psychic that hid behind being a fake, because she got tired of countless people coming to her to communicate with their dead, and expecting it to be for free, or making fun of her."

Not wanting to insult Jane, Sir Arthur accepted this possibility with a nod of his head, then turned and opened the door. There was a light switch at the top of the steps. When flipped on it revealed a wooden staircase heading down to a darker area.

"Hopefully there is another switch at the bottom," said Sir Arthur. "I didn't think to bring a flashlight."

"Neither did I, but if worse comes to worst I have my cell phone," replied Jane to Sir Arthur's back as he led the way down.

"It's getting cold," she said, as they descended.

"The wine cellar is supposed to be temperature controlled. That is why it feels so much colder here." Sir Arthur had reached the bottom and feeling along the wall came across a light switch. He flipped it and the level lit up.

"Oh, wow!" was all he could say.

They faced a corridor that had alcoves off to both sides, each alcove holding shelves of wine, each shelf named with the type of wine it held.

"There must be hundreds of bottles here," said Jane in awe.

"Maybe thousands," replied Sir Arthur.

They started reading the shelves. The alcoves were divided into sections. Each section denoted by a color. Red wines had red colored labels. Rosé was light pink. White wine had white labels, Dessert wines had brown labels and sparkling wines had silver labels.

Within the alcoves the wines were further separated by type. In the white wine section were shelves labeled Riesling, Pinot Gris, Sauvignon Blanc, Chardonnay and so on. The reds had Pino Noir, Zinfandel, Cabernet Sauvignon. Further divisions were based on regions, like Chianti. Among the champagnes, that were also divided into chardonnay, pinot noir, arbane, etc., and they found brands like Dom Perignon, Moet, and others.

"I don't think I can say wow enough," said Sir Arthur. "So, what shall it be my lady, a nice champagne?"

"I'm more of a riesling girl myself."

"Here's an Erdener Treppchen Riesling Auslese 1976," he said, pulling a bottle off the shelf.

"I'm not familiar with that brand. Do you think it's still good after forty-five years?"

"This place is set at a perfect temperature, and the way the shelves are set up, giving just the right tilt, I am willing to bet it is. Shall we?"

"Shouldn't we bring back a couple of bottles in case the others want some?"

"Who said anything about going back right away?"

"What, you're going to break the top of the bottle and we drink it like that?"

Showing his other hand Sir Arthur produced a wine opener and two glasses.

"Where were you hiding those?"

"I wish I could take credit for being that creative. I found them on the shelf next to the bottle."

"Suspiciously convenient."

"Someone probably came down here and got sidetracked. The glasses are a bit dusty, so it has been a while."

Sir Arthur popped open the bottle while Jane held the glasses, having first used a tissue she had in her pocket to wipe off the dust. He filled the two glasses, then sat in the corridor, his back to a wall. Putting the bottle beside him he patted the floor on the other side.

"Time to take a load off. We can have a glass or two and then rejoin the others."

"Take a load off? Spend too much time in America and our expressions rub off on you, I guess."

Sir Arthur just laughed.

Jane handed him one glass then sat beside him. They drank the first glass in silence, then Sir Arthur refilled the glasses. It didn't take long for Jane to feel a flush from the wine.

"This is really tasty," she said. "You know I don't usually start to feel wine's effects until the third or fourth glass, but this stuff must be stronger than I'm used to."

"It's not so much the wine as the temperature. The cooler temperature will make you feel the effects sooner."

Jane shivered. "Yes, it is cool down here."

"I'd offer you my jacket, except I am not wearing one," laughed Sir Arthur. "Would you like another glass to warm you up," he added when he noticed hers was almost empty again.

"Maybe one more, then I think we should head back. Between

the wine and the cold, my control over my abilities might begin to slip, and I really don't want that to happen here."

He topped up their glasses and sat back. Looking around he noticed something unusual. "From what I understand, no one has been replenishing this wine cellar. Yet with all the people that have lived here over the years the shelves are still almost full. I see very few empty spaces. Don't you find that strange?"

"Maybe they kept the cellar locked so that any tenants couldn't access it."

"Could be, yet I did not see any special locks on the door. That simple door handle lock would be easy to pick."

"Not everyone has your sense of morals," said Jane.

"Oh, come off it. If you were paying thousands of dollars a month to live here, and knew about this wine cellar, are you telling me you would not try to access it? Maybe there would be a tenant who has no taste for wine and no curiosity, but to have a number like that I would find unusual."

"I guess you're right. The dust covering on the bottles would indicate that they don't usually replace missing bottles. Could be that people were afraid to come down here because of the reputation of the house."

"Do you think that people that will live here for two years would be stopped by a so-called reputation? If they disbelieve enough to live here, why would they believe enough to avoid the cellar?"

"Well, that's a weird way to put it, but I see your point. So do you have a theory?"

"No. Just pointing out that it is strange." Lifting his glass in a toast Sir Arthur said, "Here's to strange things not being harmful."

He looked at Jane when she did not respond. Her eyes were focused on a point down the corridor, against the back wall. She was just staring; her eyes open wide.

"Jane did you hear me?" He waived his hand in front of her face, but no response.

Suddenly the lights in the corridor went out. The only illumination left was from the stairway. Sir Arthur would have pulled out his phone, but it was of no use since he still kept his old Blackberry which did not have a flashlight. He could barely see Jane's silhouette.

"Jane, get your phone out. I can hardly see."

Still no response from Jane.

Then the light in the stairway went out.

"Damn. Jane, we need your phone!"

He reached over to give her a shake.

Jane was no longer there.

* * *

"No one listens. That's why horror movies are more realistic than people think."

"What are you talking about, cop?" asked Jackson Benders.

"If you hadn't noticed, two more of our company have left. Also, I haven't seen that other investigator, Harry, since we returned from the tour."

That was when Jackson noticed that both Sir Arthur, and the gorgeous psychic were missing.

Hearing them Blaze, looked around and noticed the same thing.

"I told that girl not to use her abilities here. She had better listen."

John looked over at her. "When did you tell her that, and more importantly, why?"

"In the pool area. She had opened herself and suffered for it. I hope she didn't go back there."

"Where do you think you are going?" demanded Ron, seeing Blaze heading away.

"I am the only one here who has the ability to protect that girl."

"Not alone you don't," said Ron, moving to join her.

John intervened. "I'll go with Blaze. Get the rest of the crews back if you can. Use the walkie-talkies but keep everyone else here." Grabbing one of the radios off the table he added, "They are more likely to listen to you, than to me."

"As if that has worked until now," was the reply, yet Ron let them go and turned to those remaining.

"Blaze, don't forget a portable camera," called out Jackson.

John gave him a dirty look, but Blaze responded by picking up a camera from the equipment area and said, "Policy. On a case we document everything."

After they left the area, Ron tried to get the remaining crew organized while trying to clear his mind of thoughts of Jane in trouble. *Damn, why am I letting a woman get in my head like this*, he thought. Since his divorce he had avoided getting involved with anyone.

"Bob, can you call everyone on the walkie-talkies and try to get them back."

"I don't think Sir Arthur or Jane have one."

"They must have cell phones. Try calling them." Bob looked at Jackson Benders who nodded his approval.

"I have Jane's cell number," said Skip. "I'll try her."

Matt pulled out his cell phone. "I have Sir Arthur's number programmed into my phone. I'll give him a try. Bob, you try Michelle again. Maybe now her talkie is reachable, or call out to

Tippy who may have a better signal from outside. He can take time for his smoke later."

Pulling out his phone Matt saw that he had no service.

"Hey Skip, do you have service on your phone?"

Skip had just found Jane's number on his computer, so he checked his cell phone.

"Nope. But I'm not surprised. There are no cell towers near here."

"But I had service before we came into the house," said Matt.

"Then go out front and call them. But since they're in the house, they probably don't have reception."

"It's why we always bring the talkies with us on cases. We never know with some of these places if there will be cell reception.," said Bob.

He grabbed one off the desk. Turning it on and squeezing the talk button, he put out the call.

"Round up everyone. Report in, then return to base of operations."

He repeated the call three times, with no response.

"Tippy should have replied; he's just out front," said Matt.

"Hey, Tippy, did you hear the call?" yelled Bob as he walked towards the entrance. He couldn't see Tippy from his angle of approach, but knew he had to be close.

Before he reached the door, it closed.

"Stop the games Tippy," his voice even louder. He got to the door but was unable to open it. He tried banging to get Tippy's attention, but no response. Bob turned to look at Matt, who looked back. Jackson Benders, who had sat quietly through all of this got up and went to try the door—without success.

Screw this he thought, picking up one of their chairs and

slamming it against the window. The chair broke to pieces in his hand, but the window was unchanged, not even a crack.

Skip looked at Ron and asked, "What now?"

"Now we pray that we survive."

* * *

John followed Blaze down the hall. He had to hurry his pace to catch up to her.

"What was this you were saying about Jane not opening up?"

"She has only recently learned to control her abilities. If she loses that control something will be able to take control of her."

Blaze quickened her pace until they reached the pool area. The door was partially open, even though she was sure that Jane had closed it earlier. She rushed through the door calling out to Jane. There was no response. As soon as she entered, she realized that the room was empty. John followed her in.

"Why did you think she returned here?"

"She had an encounter here. I thought the British peacock had convinced her to show him her abilities. Since she had one experience here, it would have been the natural place for her to come."

"What type of encounter?"

"Her ability manifests itself through colors. She said that something really dark had knocked her down. I found her sitting on the floor. But right after, she said it was gone."

"You seem to know a lot about this for a fake," said John, eyeing her in a knowing way.

"My abilities show as emotions. I can feel presences through the emotions they emit."

"So, you pretend you're a fake because you don't want people to know that you're for real?"

"For a skeptic you seem to accept things easily," she replied, turning to face him, her eyes boring into his like she was searched the depths of his psych.

John laughed, then flashed her a big smile, her intense gaze not phasing him. "Oh, I am a believer in many things, psychic abilities being one. I have always believed that human brains have abilities that remain mostly untapped, except for a remarkable few. Why certain people are able to access these abilities is one of the studies I perform at the university. Where I am skeptical is in hauntings. I have investigated dozens, hoping to find a single legitimate one, but so far, they have all been either frauds, or explainable by science, like gases, wind tunnels, etc. By the way is Blaze your real name?"

"It is now. I had it legally changed several years ago."

"Why?" The puzzled look on his face making Blaze grin.

"If I told you what my birth name was you would understand."

"It couldn't be worse than Blaze Destiny."

"That's what you think. My surname was Belt."

"So? What's wrong with Blaze Belt. It isn't that bad."

"Unless you know that my father named me Chastity."

John put the two together and groaned. "Oh, that's just mean."

"That was my father. It's all you need to know about my childhood to understand my reticence when it comes to letting people know about my abilities. If my father had known my capabilities, he would have used me like a circus freak. If I am going to be thought of as a freak, it will be on my terms. Now, getting back to what you said before, you're about to get your wish. This house is waking up."

"Your abilities are telling you this?" asked John, raising his eyebrows.

"No, the evidence around us. That machine of the Ghost Eliminators acting like it did for one thing. I have seen it in operation many times, and it never did that before. I can also sense things, presences trying to get my attention. It is why I told Jane not to open herself up. She is not strong enough, and if she is open to the wrong entity, it can take her over." The concern in her voice quite evident to John.

"Are you strong enough, if you open yourself?"

"If this were a normal haunting, I would say, yes. But this house is something else. There are many presences here. Presences that don't belong."

"What do you mean, don't belong?"

"Just that. The presences I feel are of people who never visited here, which means they didn't die here. There are also too many of them. According to what the ex-cop said, there were a total of a hundred possible victims if you include the missing. I feel like there are many hundreds in here, maybe even thousands." Blaze spread her arms as if to encompass all that was there. "It makes no sense."

"Could you be feeling everyone that passed through here, including workers, tenants that stayed with no issues, even people that walked on this land before the house was built?"

"My abilities don't work that way. I only feel those who have died in the places I visit—or resided there for a long time. And yes, I have felt presences in a number of the haunted places the Ghost Eliminators have investigated, since most of those places have stories behind them. But in none of those cases were the spirits able to manifest in any way. As I mentioned to Jane, I accompanied them because Jackson Benders is an old friend, and I wanted to make sure he came to no harm. At the same time, I did not want to make my true ability public. It was just safer to make everyone think I was a fake."

"Why? What is wrong with letting people know that these abilities do exist. Some people will even accept the possibility and want to know more. Maybe even develop their own."

"Because it will most likely be the wrong people that will accept this, and I prefer my freedom." Seeing the look on John's face Blaze explained.

"I know others who have abilities. One was a good friend named Henry Watson. I see by your face you recognize the name. You would have read about him in the news. The real story though did not come out."

John nodded in understanding, having never really believed the story provided by the authorities.

"He approached the CIA back in 2001. The exact date was August 15th. His ability was precognition, although he only felt events that would be catastrophic. He told them that on September 11th, in New York City, there was going to be an event that would cause the deaths of thousands of people, and that it would happen at the Twin Towers. They didn't believe him, until it happened. September 12th they arrested him as a co-conspirator.

"That was the story they released to the press. What they did was use him for scientific experiments. They force-fed him LSD, thinking they could enhance his abilities, and use him like a crystal ball to see what their enemies were doing. Long story short, they loaded him up with so much stuff that he went crazy. He somehow got out of the room they had him locked up in, climbed on to the roof, and jumped. Eleven stories down. I learned most of the story afterwards from his sister who had been able to visit him once. They wouldn't let her back in after that visit, afraid she would figure out what was happening, and of course she did."

The lines on Johns forehead creased, a sign of his disapproval of how the authorities had acted.

"The press said that the stress caused him to commit suicide, and the government ended up clearing him of all charges, saying it had been a terrible mistake. They did that because they did not want his sister to investigate what really happened. Yes she had figured it out but had no way to prove anything, but if they left the memory of her brother as being a terrorist they knew by her previous actions that she would not let it go.

"He was not the only one I know of who has been taken by government agencies when they show any type of psychic abilities. It happens all over the world. That is why I, and many others I know, keep our abilities quiet."

"I can understand and sympathize. I promise you that I will repeat none of this to anyone."

"Not even as a peer reviewed paper to enhance your reputation," replied Blaze, her manner suggesting that she was half serious.

"My reputation in that domain is already settled." John laughed. "Now back to why we are here. Do you feel these presences now?"

Blaze stood for a moment saying nothing. Then her eyes went wide.

"It is happening. We have to get back to the others. *Now!*"

She ran towards the door, but it was too late. The door slammed shut, locking them in the pool room.

CHAPTER SEVEN

SEPARATION ANXIETY

Tippy started running toward the garage, yelling back to the others that something had happened to Bryan and Michelle. He had only taken a few steps when he heard the door close behind him. He froze, not knowing what to do. Then reluctantly he turned back to the house. He might need help if Bryan or Michelle had been hurt. When he reached the door, he turned the knob and tried to push it open, but neither the knob, nor the door moved. He hammered on the door with both fists, but no response.

"Come on guys this is not funny. Bryan and Michelle may be in trouble." He banged on the door again. He thought he heard someone banging back but could not be sure. He went over to the window to look in just as a chair flew against it. He jumped back, but saw that the chair had done nothing to the window.

"What the hell!"

He saw Jackson take another chair and slam it again against the window, to no effect. Tippy picked up a rock and threw it with all his strength at the window. The rock bounced back and hit him in the face, taking a gouge out of his cheek, but doing no damage to the window. Holding his hand to his bleeding face he tried to get the attention of Jackson, but he had already turned away.

Tippy banged on the window with his fist, but no one inside seemed to notice.

"Shit! Shit! Shit!"

Realizing there was nothing more he could do there, he decided to go over to the garage to see if he could help Bryan and Michelle—then the three of them could try and figure out how to get into the house.

That was when he noticed the two deer standing a few paces away. They were almost motionless, just watching him. He moved to the side to give them a wide berth and continued towards the garage.

That was when he felt the bite. Looking down at his leg he saw a fox latched on to him. He kicked it off and started running towards the garage. One of the deer moved in front of him and rammed him over. As he got back on to his feet, he saw more deer coming his way.

"Fuck this can't be happening." Looking around he spotted a large tree about halfway to the garage. Hoping he could make it, he ran as fast as he could, the deer coming at him from behind. He reached the tree and was grabbing on to the closest branch to pull himself up when the first deer reached him. It bit on to his leg and pulled him off the tree. Soon he was lying on the ground surrounded by deer, biting him, and pulling his arms. A fox ran up and bit his stomach.

Yelling, he managed to throw the fox off, push the deer aside and jump for the tree again. This time he was able to pull himself onto the first branch. But the deer were still grabbing at his feet with their teeth, so he climbed higher. Finally, he was able to sit on a large branch, well out of reach of the animals. He was bleeding from multiple wounds, and felt like he might have a separated shoulder, but for the moment he was safe. Looking down he saw that he had dropped his cell phone, which one of the deer was busy chewing on. He put his hand into his pocket and thankfully the walkie-talkie was still there. He tried again to reach someone, but all he got was static.

"This is just great. Here I am treed by deer and I can't tell anyone, or even take a bloody selfie."

* * *

"You say there is a door in that recess?" asked Bryan. "I've never heard of that before in a garage. Maybe they use it for supplies to keep the pit clean."

"I'm going to check it out."

"No. Wait for me. We don't know what might be behind that door."

Michelle moved further in to leave space for Bryan. Instead of entering the pit from the end where the stairs were, like Michelle had, Bryan walked halfway down to see if there were any other recesses. From where he was, he would not even have known there was any recess at all. If Michelle had not entered the pit, they never would have found it. Lying down on the floor Bryan passed his cell phone light along the walls of the pit. He was able to see the recess then, but just barely.

"The way this is designed, and how the lighting is, the only way to ever see that recess is by entering the pit," he said to Michelle. "That is strange. Why would they want to hide it?"

Michelle came out of the recess, wanting to see what angle Bryan was at in relation to the recess. She saw him getting back to his knees when she heard a crunching noise, like metal breaking. Looking up she saw the lift collapsing.

"Look out," she yelled as she dove back into the recess.

Bryan heard her cry and looked up, but it was too late. The lift fell on top of him. Because of the position he was in, the lift landed in the middle of his back, crushing him, and leaving half his body hanging over the edge of the pit and the other half still on the garage floor. The lift broke into pieces and fell part way into the pit. By diving back in the recess Michelle managed to save herself, but was now blocked from getting out. After everything settled, she tried to push away the lift to escape, but it wouldn't move. From where she was positioned, she could see Bryan's arms, but not much else.

"Bryan are you okay?" There was no response. "Bryan!" she yelled again. Still nothing.

She tried again to push the lift with no success. She was able to squeeze her head through part of the lift and saw what had happened to Bryan. His lifeless body hung only a few feet from where she stood, close enough to see the devastation, but not close enough to touch him.

She pulled her head back into the recess, sat on the floor, and cried.

* * *

"Yeah, gasses definitely did not cause that," said Jackson as he pulled on the door, to no avail.

"Could gasses be causing that?" asked Melissa, pointing to the screen at the other end of the theatre. Habit made her turn on the camera and point it in that direction.

Jackson looked at the screen and saw images playing. Scanning the room, he saw no sign of any projector, nor did there seem to be any working electronic equipment. Turning back to the screen he watched, with Melissa, the story unfolding there.

First, they saw a house. It was a simple ranch style bungalow, with a large picture window and multi-colored bricks, looking like something from the sixties or seventies. A man opened the front door. He had a mustache and intense eyes and was dressed in a dark colored suit, with a white shirt and a strange looking tie, like something from an old western. Then the scene shifted to the same man in a clown outfit.

"Oh my god, I know who that is," said Jackson.

Melissa looked at him, the question on her lips, which he answered before she could ask.

"That is John Wayne Gacy."

"The notorious serial killer?"

"Yes. And if I remember correctly that is the house where he killed over thirty young men and boys."

They continued to watch the scene unfold. As John Wayne Gacy stood by the open door to his house, a line of boys and young men paraded through.

"Those must have been his victims. I saw pictures of them posted on a forum once, when we were asked to investigate the land where his house once stood. Apparently, the owners there thought it was haunted. We found nothing out of the ordinary. Still those faces haunt me to this day. But this movie is impossible. Some of his victims were never identified. Some of the pictures they have of them were only artist drawings, others were black and white photos. This film is in color, the faces are clear and the features match perfectly the drawings and photos I saw."

They continued to watch as the last person entered the house, forty-five in total. John Wayne Gacy then smiled at the camera, entered the house, and closed the door.

"They only found thirty-three victims, but the killer had indicated that there were forty-five. This movie shows that."

"Could this have been made later on, using Hollywood effects?

"I guess it is possible, but the images are so good it would have taken a major production to do it, yet I have never heard of a film like this. I also don't think it would have been possible at all in the early nineties, which would mean it would have to have been done by James Neighbors, and that makes no sense."

The movie started up again. Now the victims were marching down to a basement. Along the way John Wayne Gacy would point at one of them and say something. Although there was no sound, Melissa had learned to read lips. Five times he mouthed the word "river." Another time "BBQ pit." She passed this information on to Jackson who nodded in return, knowing the context of each location. In all, twenty-two marched down and into a crawl space. As they approached the crawl space their appearances started to change. Some had socks sticking out of their mouths. Some had large amounts of water coming out instead. Many had ligatures around their necks. All of them had their hands handcuffed behind their backs. As they got closer to what could be seen as trenches, their clothes started to disappear. Melissa saw then that they had various instruments protruding from their anuses. She had to turn away.

"Don't turn your head young lady," commanded the first voice they had heard. "You must watch my art in progress. Then I will have you perform these acts on your gentleman friend."

Jackson looked at her. "We have to get out of this room before the movie is finished."

Melissa put down the camera, which was still running and pointing at the screen, went to the door and tried to open it, Jackson beside her lending his weight. No matter what they did the door would not budge.

"Maybe we can find the projector and stop the film," said Melissa.

Jackson ran over to the screen and stood in front of it. If there had been a projector his presence would have distorted the image on the screen. He looked behind the screen expecting to see some wiring. There was nothing. Looking around, Melissa spotted one theatre chair that was not bolted to the ground. Despite its weight she was able to lift it and smash it against the door. Although the door did not budge from its frame, she had managed to make a small hole. Encouraged she picked up the chair again and slammed it against the door, calling for Jackson to help her. When he didn't respond she looked back at him. He seemed frozen to the spot, but was fading.

"Since you do not want to play with him, then I will claim him myself," said the voice she realized was that of John Wayne Gacy."

"*No!*" she yelled. She ran over and tried to grab Jackson's hand, but her hand passed right through his. Not knowing what else to do she ran back to the door, picked up the chair and kept slamming it against the door, hoping that by opening it up she could stop the movie from taking Jackson. But as she slammed the chair against the door, Jackson continued to fade away.

* * *

"It won't open," said John, desperately trying to pull the door open. "Can your abilities help with this?"

Blaze put the camera on the floor, not even realizing she had turned it on and pointed it at the pool.

"I have never come across something like this before. I'm afraid to open myself. Even with all my training and practice this house is so strong I might lose control and be taken over."

John looked around for something heavy with which he might be able to smash the door open, or into pieces. There were a few chaise lounges, a number of Styrofoam boards to help those who could not swim, and the usual "spaghetti" pool strips. Nothing that would damage a person, let alone a wooden door. Then, hanging on a wall, he saw, a pool skimmer. He grabbed it off its hooks. It was heavier than a standard skimmer.

"Maybe this might do something."

First, he tried swinging it sideways. It made a bit of a gouge in the wood frame, but that was about it. Turning it, he thrust it into the door like a javelin. I good sized chunk came out.

"A few dozen more times and I might be able to create a hole large enough for us to crawl through. Give me five minutes and I think I can have us out of here."

"I seriously doubt we have five minutes," said Blaze, her voice trembling.

Turning around John followed her gaze. Marching out of the pool were human figures, but they were formed from the water itself.

Then they heard the voices.

"Purser, purser. Why did you do this to us? Now you must pay. We will take you to join with us."

It was obvious that they were counting Blaze and John as the mysterious "Pursers."

John turned back to the door, doubling his efforts. But he knew he would never get through the door on time.

"Blaze, can you use your abilities to stop them. Maybe try telling them we are not who they think we are."

"I have never been able to do that before. I doubt I can now."

"You've never had a situation like this before, so you don't know what you are capable of."

"I'm afraid if I open myself, they could take control of me. If that happens, we are finished."

"If they get a hold of us, we're probably finished anyway. We have nothing to lose."

"You have nothing to lose. I could lose my identity, maybe my soul."

"If they take your soul, I will offer up mine as well in exchange for your release."

Blaze looked at John in surprise, realizing he was serious. It gave her the courage to try.

She backed up, nearer to John, to give herself more time to work. Looking directly at the figures coming towards them she raised her arms and opened her psyche.

"We are not the pursers you are looking for. Turn back now."

She poured all her will into her words. It was working. The figures stopped and then slowly started losing their forms and sliding back into the water.

That was when she sensed the blackness that Jane had told her about.

"I am the Purser," said a voice. "Unless you go and claim these two for me, I will torment you far more than I already have."

His words had an effect. The figures reformed and once again started advancing.

"John, you'd better hurry!"

* * *

"Jane, where are you," called out Sir Arthur. He heard no response. He also did not hear any other sound, not the sound of movement, or even breathing. It was like she had never been there.

He strained his hearing further. Still nothing. Then—a movement from the opposite end of the corridor from the stairs. The area that ended in a wall.

"Jane, is that you? What are you doing down there?"

Still no response.

Then the sound of bottles breaking.

"Jane, are you okay? Did you fall?"

Putting his hands in front of him, he made his way towards the sound, holding on to the wall and then grabbing a shelf as he passed an alcove. As he shuffled his foot forward it brushed against something. Reaching down he touched what appeared to be a cell phone. He quickly picked it up realizing it was probably Jane's. Her cell phone, he remembered, had a flashlight app. Fiddling around he was able to engage it. Bright light lit the darkness. He shone it down the corridor to where he had heard the noises. Sure enough, there was Jane, her back turned to him.

"Jane what is wrong? Why aren't you answering me?"

Jane turned around and faced into the light. Her eyes glowed red. In each of her hands was a broken wine bottle. Blood dripped from her hands where she had cut them when breaking the bottles.

"It's okay, Jane. You can put the bottles down. We are safe here."

"That is what you think." The voice that spoke was male, had a German accent, and was definitely not Jane's.

"Who are you?" asked Sir Arthur, not really sure he wanted to know the answer. He was finally starting to believe that he should have listened to the ex-cop.

"You do not make demands of the doctor. It is the doctor who makes the demands. Now come over here. I want to find out what makes a knight tick."

Between the accent, the fact he referred to himself as a doctor, and what he wanted to do, made Sir Arthur realize who he was speaking to. He turned and ran to the steps, mounting them two at a time. He arrived at the door, but could not get it to open. He started pounding on it. He heard steps behind him and turned to look back. Jane the doctor was approaching, the bottles raised in the air.

"My experiments must proceed. Come back here right now," said the voice.

Sir Arthur returned to pounding on the door and yelling for help, as the doctor approached.

CHAPTER EIGHT

OF MAYHEM AND MACHINERY

"Do you hear that?" asked Jackson Benders of those still in the entrance hall.

Ron was the first to respond. "Yes, it sounds like pounding."

"More like desperate banging," said Bob.

Looking around Jackson spotted a part of the chair he had broken against the window. The back piece was made of metal and when he picked it up it was heavier than he had thought.

"So, this is why those chairs are so bloody heavy to carry."

He turned to the others.

"Matt, keep an eye here. Skip and Bob. Do you think you can somehow use these machines to help us?"

Looking at each other they both nodded. It was Skip who replied.

"Maybe we can adjust the machine to emit its own EMF. That might break some of the control of whatever presence is holding us hostage."

"And maybe clear the interference of the talkies," added Bob.

"Then get to it. Ron would you be willing to come with me and see if we can help those who are in need?"

"Don't just stand there gabbing. Let's get moving." Ron walked over to the table with all the equipment. Expecting him to pick up a piece of detecting equipment, Jackson was surprised when he picked up a U-joint for the camera tripod.

"This is a strong piece of metal. It might come in handy."

The two left the entrance area, heading first towards the pool where the loudest banging was coming from. They got to the door and saw a small hole—with water coming out of it. The banging had stopped.

"Use that piece of metal like a crowbar where the hinges are. I'll use this near the lock."

They both got their levers in place.

"Now push!"

With both using all their strength the frame cracked, and the door popped open, releasing a flood of water, followed by two very wet people and a still functioning camera.

John immediately started sputtering and spitting. Blaze, though, was blue, and not breathing. Ron started CPR. Within seconds she coughed up a lungful of water, then opened her eyes.

"Hi handsome."

Ron stared at her in amazement, then started laughing.

"What the hell happened here?" asked Jackson.

"You wouldn't believe us if we told you," replied John. "But I don't ever want to have a purser serve me again."

Before anyone could respond they heard more banging.

"The theatre!" exclaimed Ron. Jackson hesitated over Blaze, but with a look John let him know that he would take care of her.

The two men left Blaze in John's care and ran towards the theatre. Using the same method as they had with the pool door, and with help from the other side, the theatre door burst open.

"Hurry," Melissa screamed. "John Wayne Gacy is trying to kill Jackson." Seeing Jackson Benders in front of her she added, "The other Jackson."

Rushing into the room they saw Jackson Brown lying on the floor. Ron ran over and knelt beside him trying to get a response. He felt for a pulse and couldn't find one. There was no blood anywhere, and no marks on him. Ron tried CPR. As soon as he blew into Jackson's mouth, blood shot out of a hole in his throat.

"What the hell just happened," yelled Jackson Benders.

"I have no idea. I've performed CPR many times with nothing like this. It's not possible unless there was already a hole in his throat, and I can promise you there was no blood on him when I started."

Jackson Benders came over to stand beside Ron. As they watched they saw ligature marks appear on the other Jackson's neck.

"That is definitely not possible," said Ron.

"It was John Wayne Gacy," said Melissa, through her tears.

"John Wayne Gacy has been dead for a long time," observed Ron.

"Since 1994," came a voice from the door. Blaze was standing there with John beside her holding the dripping camera. "The same year this cursed house was built."

"Didn't you tell me that dead presences haunted only where they lived, died, or committed heinous deeds?" asked John.

"Yes, that is what I told you, and that has always been what my experience has shown."

"Oh, come on Blaze. You and I both know that you're a gifted actress but far from being a psychic," said Jackson.

"It would appear that there is more about hauntings than you ever knew, even about your own crew," said John. "Of course one thing you said is true. Blaze *is* a gifted actress. She fooled you for many years."

"Yes Jackson, I really do have psychic abilities," Blaze added, giving John a look as if to say please don't rub it in. "It is not something I want the world to know about, so I play the fraud on your show. In reality at each one of your investigations I search for possible malignant spirits to make sure you don't get yourself into trouble."

Jackson was dumbfounded. Before he could respond they heard more pounding.

"That's coming from the kitchen," cried Melissa. "Who could that be?"

"Still missing are Sir Arthur and Jane, as well as Harry. It must be one of them," said Ron.

The group rushed into the kitchen, deciding that there was safety in numbers.

The kitchen was empty. They were looking around when the banging happened again. It was coming from a door at the back of the room.

"That's the wine cellar," said Ron as he ran over with Jackson right behind him. Once again, they put their tools to use. However, this door was much heavier and better sealed than the others, and their efforts were unsuccessful.

"This is almost like a refrigerator door, to keep the wine cellar cool," said Blaze.

"Change of tactics, Ron. Both of us on the same side this time."

Jackson leaned into the metal bar. Ron pushed on the U-joint that he had set on each side of the lock. Finally, the door popped open and Sir Arthur fell at their feet.

"Quick close the door," he yelled at them from the floor. "It's Josef Mengele. He's trying to kill me."

The two men looked at each other and then into the wine cellar. Climbing the stairs was Jane. In each hand she had a broken bottle.

There was blood on her hands and her clothes. They looked down at Sir Arthur and saw that he was bleeding from multiple wounds.

"Look at her eyes," yelled Melissa.

She had almost reached the top of the stairs. Her eyes stared back at them, red and glowing. Blaze pushed the men aside and slammed the door shut. Since they had not broken the jamb, the door clicked.

"Move that fridge in front of the door," she told them.

"But that's Jane," said Ron. "We have to help her."

"Not right now it isn't," replied Blaze.

The door handle started to jiggle. Sir Arthur had managed to regain his feet and was already standing beside the fridge.

"Are you guys going to help or what?"

It was John who grabbed the other side of the fridge and helped push it over. Ron tried to stand in their way, refusing to give up on Jane.

Blaze put her hand on his arm. "There is nothing you can do for her now. She is possessed. The best thing we can do is to make sure she can't hurt anyone else right now. If she comes out of this knowing she killed someone it could seriously harm her mentally."

"Can you help her?" asked John.

"Maybe. First, we need to know what in hell is going on here."

"It's a damn real haunted house, that's what's going on!" yelled Jackson.

"Pull yourself together Jackie."

Using a name she hadn't used since they were lovers reached through Jackson's fright and calmed him. He looked her in the eyes and then nodded.

"We've been in haunted houses before. You always thought it was part of the show, but some of the things were real. Although none of those presences were evil like this house is. Each one that I encountered had a reason for being there. But none of what is happening here makes sense."

"Maybe there is something," said John.

"What are you thinking?" asked Jackson.

"Let's regroup with the others in the staging area. It will give me time to form my thoughts better."

"Maybe your tech guys have come up with something as well," said Ron.

* * *

Seeing Bob and Skip busy at work on a machine Blaze and Jackson decided not to disturb them. They put the two cameras near the equipment table then gathered around the desk that John had been using. He opened his laptop.

"Do you have a satellite connection? Does the internet work?" asked Melissa, her eyes puffed and red from crying, but trying to use work to deal with what she had seen. "Maybe we can get a message out and get some help here."

"Yes, to the satellite, but no to the internet. But for what I'm looking for I won't need it."

"What are you looking for?" asked Jackson.

"One of the hauntings I've been called to investigate was the former site of the residence of John Wayne Gacy. No, not the original house. That was demolished after they pulled out all the bodies. It was the house that was built on that lot. I keep a copy of all the files on my laptop."

He found the file he was looking for and clicked it open. There were various word docs of notes he had taken. Locating the one he was looking for he opened it.

"As I thought. His house was demolished and all the materials from it were taken to a dump. Apparently, though, some bricks were unaccounted for. More than some. When one of the dump trucks arrived, it was half empty. Yet when it left the house, it had been full. The incident was noted in a log, but no one questioned it at the time," he said, looking up from the screen.

"Blaze, you had mentioned that the only way a presence could be here would be if they had died here or committed horrible acts here. What if parts of the house where the acts were committed were moved elsewhere. Could the spirits, or whatever follow those parts?"

"It may be possible," she replied, hesitantly, a frown on her face as she thought of the implications. "I never really thought about it. But how could they have ended up here, hundreds of miles away?"

"My research has shown that rumours persisted during the construction of the house that Peter had brought in parts of other places that were supposed to be haunted," said Jackson. "Ron, you mentioned the same thing when we did your interview, and that the construction crew often didn't know where the materials came from. Would you happen to know how these got here—or what was brought in?"

Ron shook his head. "Peter Vanderbilt was very secretive about much of the materials. The only thing I know for sure is what I told you. That some metal beams were custom made at an inordinately high price, as my cousin mentioned. What are you getting at?"

"Blaze told me that she feels there are far more presences here than can be accounted for by the number of people who have died in this house. What if these presences were brought in purposely by Vanderbilt?"

"To *what* purpose though?" asked Sir Arthur, his aristocratic air, and accent, all but gone.

Melissa stared at this change but before she could mention it Blaze spoke up.

"There have always been people who believe they could somehow open a portal to the other side using the spirits of the departed. Maybe Peter Vanderbilt was one of those? Maybe he sought immortality through the use of a portal."

John clicked open another file. This one titled Peter Vanderbilt.

"I always start my investigation with the original owners. I haven't really read much of this file since Peter was supposed to have died before ever living here. Let's see if anything here can tell us something."

The files contained mostly news and magazine articles. Much of it financial news and a lot about his philanthropic work. They read through a few articles, but very little was mentioned about the man himself. As they were skimming, Michelle spotted something.

"Go back to that article there."

"This is just another of his philanthropy endeavors," said John.

"Yes, but look what it's for."

The title read: Billionaire Gives Indian Mystic $10 Million to Build Sanctuary. Reading through, they saw the connection.

"Does anyone know about this Indian mystic, Swami Shankar?" asked Jackson. "It's not like we can look up stuff on the internet about him."

Skip heard mention of the name and joined the group. "Yeah. He was a mystic who claimed to have found the secret of eternal life. He had a cult following for a while, but once his sanctuary was built, he went very quiet. Some time in the early nineties a group of hikers came across his sanctuary and found a lot of dead bodies. The Indian authorities investigated and declared it a mass cult suicide."

Seeing everyone staring at him Skip self-consciously explained.

"I took a class in university on cults. You remember that professor, John; he spouted this stuff about cults having special knowledge or something. It fascinated me at the time. I ended up quitting the class when he got all weird. But I remember this was one of the cults he talked about."

John looked at Blaze again. "Is it possible that he found something?"

"Or he thought he found something," was her response.

"Ron mentioned that there were rumors that Peter Vanderbilt had cancer and was dying, based on someone seeing lab reports," said John. "Say that was true. What if he thought he could build a house that would focus spiritual energy somehow giving him another chance at life? Maybe he did learn something from that Indian mystic."

"Even if all your guesses are true, how does that help us?" asked Bob, working his way over to the others.

"I'm not sure yet" was John's reply. "We need more information and time to work this out."

"I don't know how much time we have. The house has woken up and already claimed one life and maybe more," said Blaze.

"Who died?" demanded Skip.

"Sorry Skip," she responded. "Of course, you haven't heard because we didn't disturb you and Bob when we got back here—but Jackson Brown is dead. He was killed in the theatre room. We think it was the ghost of John Wayne Gacy."

"That's not funny."

"It wasn't meant to be," said Ron.

"Oh shit. This can't be happening."

"It is and there is nothing we can do about it," declared Sir Arthur.

"Maybe there is," said Bob.

"You two were able to do something?" asked Jackson.

"We think so," replied Skip. We rewired the ghost machine, since it's the most powerful piece of equipment here. We've set it up to emit an EMF field. We think that as long as we stay within its operating field, we should be safe."

"How big is that field," asked Melissa.

It should cover this room and outwards as far as the kitchen, part of the pool room, and in general, a good portion of this floor. It won't go as far us the upstairs."

Sir Arthur raced to the front door and tried to open it.

"Your machine doesn't work. I can't open the door."

"It won't reverse what has been done already," replied Skip, "but it will stop anything else from coming into this room—in theory."

"How can we know for sure?" asked Ron.

John turned to Blaze. She looked him in the eyes and then nodded.

Closing her eyes, she opened herself up, reaching out. She remained in a trance for almost three minutes.

"Yes, I think it is working. I can feel the presences at the edge of the field. They want to enter but appear unable to. I do not know though how long it will last."

Bob stared at Blaze.

"Yes Bob, it turns out our Blaze really is a psychic. She's been fooling us for years," said Jackson.

Ron looked at Sir Arthur, expecting another of his quips. He was conspicuously quiet.

"We still don't know what has happened to Tippy, Michelle or Bryan. Can you work any magic on the talkies?" asked Jackson.

Bob smiled and waived his hand at Skip. "The master has an idea."

Skip walked over to the equipment table and picked up one of the walkie-talkies. He opened the back, pulled out some of the wires and then connected it to one of the EMF sensors. He then taped the two machines together and turned on the EMF. He handed the mangled contraption to Jackson.

"I don't know what range it will have, but give it a try."

"Tippy, Michelle, Bryan can you read me? Over …"

There was no immediate response, however, they were hopeful since the static was gone.

"Hello, can anyone here me? Over …" he repeated.

"Damn it's about time someone called." came Tippy's voice, his fear coming across as anger.

Bob grabbed the machine from Jackson's hand.

"God I'm glad to hear your voice. Are you okay, partner?"

Wondering at Bob's reaction John looked at Blaze. She whispered, "They're a couple. Go figure, huh. They look like polar opposites."

John whispered back, "Well you know what they say, opposites attract." Blaze answered with a smile.

"If you call sitting in a tree, bleeding from countless bites, with a herd of deer and some foxes watching you from below—okay—then I'm just peachy."

"So, the phenomenon extends beyond the house," said Blaze.

"Not surprising," said Ron. "Even the tiles he used for the driveway and the water fountain were imported."

Jackson took the walkie-talkie away from Bob.

"Tippy we can't reach Michelle or Bryan. Have you heard from them?"

"I was talking to them when I heard a crash—and then silence. I was heading over to check on them when everything went to shit."

"We can't reach them. Bob and Skip jury rigged the walkie-talkie to filter out EMF interference. That's how we were able to reach you, but we don't think it extends far enough to reach the other two."

"Sometimes they switch to another channel, so their private talk won't be heard by the rest of us. You would think after a year of dating they would have got beyond that by now. Maybe from here I can reach them. Let me try. I'll get back to you."

Tippy switched channels and called out to Bryan and Michelle.

Inside the garage Michelle heard Tippy's voice calling. At first, she ignored it, lost in grief and fear. But when she heard it a second time she looked around for the source. She put her head through the section of the lift and saw the walkie-talkie lying on the ground. She was somehow able to contort herself enough to reach the floor and grab it.

"Tippy this is Michelle. Can you hear me?"

"Thank God. Are you two, okay?"

It was silent for a moment and then she answered. "Bryan is dead. A lift collapsed on him and crushed him. I'm trapped under the lift in an alcove. I can't move the lift to get out, but other than that I am physically alright."

"Is that the alcove I heard you telling Bryan that had a door? Maybe there's a way out through it?"

"I don't think I can move right now."

"Are you stuck under the lift? You said you aren't physically hurt but are you pinned?"

"No. It's just that Bryan is dead, and I'm so afraid."

"Look, let me get back to you. Switch your talkie to the standard channel. I'm going to try to connect us with everyone in the house."

"If you aren't in the house, where are you?"

"Stuck in a tree with a bunch of animals underneath looking to make a meal out of me. It's no better at the house. Things have happened there too."

"What things?"

"Let me call back Jackson and let him know your situation. We can talk about what has happened at the house later. Switch channels now so we can see if they can hear you too." He switched his own device back and keyed the mike. "Jackson, I spoke with Michelle. She's okay but trapped. Bryan is dead."

"Fucking shit. Did she say what happened?"

Michelle's voice answered in response. "The lift over the pit collapsed and crushed him. I'm trapped in an alcove inside the pit."

"I'm so sorry about Bryan. How are you holding up?"

"Terrified. There's no way the lift should have fallen like that. And I keep hearing noises, like a car revving."

"Hi Michelle. This is John. I'm really sorry for your loss, but now is not the time to mourn. We need to work together if we want to get out of this mess."

"How bad is it there?" Michelle's voice got stronger as she managed to put aside her fear for the moment.

"I won't hide anything. It is bad. Jackson Brown is dead and Jane and Harry are missing." He gave the others a look to say not a word about her real condition. "We are trying to figure out a way to stop this, but we need your help."

As John released the talk button, Jackson quizzed him. "How can she help us? She's trapped. What are you doing?"

Blaze answered. "He is calming her down. Panic will not help her."

"It's more than that. I've been in enough garage oil pits. There should be no alcove. Maybe it's hiding something. Something that can help us figure this out."

"You want me to check what is on the other side of the door, is that it?" Michelle responded.

"What door?" asked John.

"At the end of this alcove is a door. I don't know where it leads. I was thinking of trying it to see if it offered another way out."

"Do you have an EMF sensor with you?" asked John.

"I do but it's missing a battery. I'd have to take one out of the talkie if I want to use it."

"Do you have your cell phone with you?" asked Bob after taking the walkie-talkie out of John's hands.

"Yeah, but no signal."

"You don't need a signal. I installed an app on your phone during our last investigation, remember? It emits a limited EMF signal. Turn it on. We think it can protect you."

A minute later she got back to them.

"Yeah, it looks like it is working. I don't hear that car revving anymore."

Bob gave John a big smile and handed the walkie-talkie back to him.

"Okay, Michelle, it's John again. Keep the EMF working and try to open that door. Maybe there's a clue behind it, or at the least a way out for you."

"Tippy can you still hear us."

"Loud and clear."

"Bob says he put the same app on your phone. Turn it on and see if it drives away the wild fauna."

"I'd be happy to, if only the wild fauna hadn't eaten it."

"Okay, I'm at the door." Michelle's voice broke in. "Turning the handle. The door doesn't seem to be locked, but it's as if there's something else on the other side, preventing me from opening it. Let me give it a push."

Everyone held their breath, waiting to hear what would happen, hoping for the best and fearing the worst. The worst happened.

Michelle let out a scream.

"Michelle!" Jackson yelled into the mike. "Are you, okay? Michelle, please answer."

Nothing … then …

"I'm okay." Michelle sounded breathless, shaken. "But when I was finally able to push the door open—a body fell through."

"A body?" cried Tippy.

"I should say bodies. There are several. Funny thing is, they don't stink."

"Bodies? How many?" asked Tippy.

In the house they heard Ron say, "Eight" before Michelle said, "Seven."

"The missing people," said Blaze. "It's starting to make sense. Except we're still missing one. Ask Michelle if she can tell how many men and how many women."

Jackson relayed the question.

"There are six men and one woman," Michelle responded. "The woman has on a wedding gown and the man beside her has on a tux. One of the bodies is clutching a piece of paper. Other than that, except the one that was partially blocking the door, they're all just sitting here in the same position, like they were having a meeting or something."

"Michelle, can you reach that piece of paper? Maybe it's a message of some sort."

"Not that I want to, but yeah I think I can get it—I have to crawl over a couple of them."

"So, Betty is still missing," said Blaze. "And for some reason the original couple put their wedding clothes back on before starting their killing."

A minute passed then they heard Michelle again.

"Okay, got it. It's a letter, signed by Jim Neighbors … Oh my God. You guys listen to this."

For whomever finds this note.

This is our third night in the house, and the feeling of evil has begun to pervade everything. I had honored my benefactor's request for many years, and as we hit the 25th year of his plan, I was unable to find new tenants within the required limits. This being a down year for spiritual activity I felt it was safe to move my family into the home until I was able to find a new tenant. Until now the pattern set out by Peter had been exact. Still, I had taken some precautions that I had thought would keep us safe.

Now though something has changed. I fear for my family. I have tried this night to keep us all together, but things keep happening to separate us. My wife has disappeared during a simple bathroom break. I sit here with my two children knowing that what is to come will mean the death of us, but I don't know if I can prevent it.

We tried leaving this morning, but the house would not let us. The doors will not open. The windows will not break. I have tried appealing to Peter but whether or not he can hear me I do not know. I will make one more appeal, using a ceremony he taught me; however, I think he is too far gone now, and no longer controls what is happening here.

Whomever finds this note, please take heed. It may be your only chance of survival. Peter built this house so that his spirit will be able to see everything that happens, and he can manipulate not only people but objects. I have discovered one kink in his armour though. In the chapel he built, even though he consecrated it using the ceremonies he was taught and filled it with objects he acquired from places of evil, he put in one unusual wooden cross he had thought was filled with the same type of energy since it came from a reputedly haunted house. What he did not know, and I discovered through research, is that inside the cross are three bubbles that contain soil from the holy land, holy water, and pure silver. The cross had been consecrated by Pope John Paul II, and any evil it may have absorbed was cleared. Therefore, any objects placed beneath it are invisible to Peter and untouchable by him.

In the mini alter this cross was placed on is a small compartment. I have put inside this compartment some of the original plans of this house, the few that I could find, and a copy of the diary Peter wrote explaining how he built the house, and maybe in this diary can be found a way to destroy him. There may be enough clues in the plans to help find his "sanctuary" but the plans are incomplete. The only way to end his reign is to find his sanctuary and destroy everything it contains, including his body. Then the "sanctuary" must be opened by consecrating it with holy water or burning it out completely. You can make holy water using the same cross I mentioned in the chapel.

I am hiding this note in a place that I hope someone can find. I feel Peter is occupied right now and not paying attention to me. Unfortunately, that means he is busy terrifying my wife.

Once I finish this note I will place it where you have found it, assuming anyone does. Then I will call for Peter to come and let him know that the copy of his diary is no longer in his bank vault, and that unless he releases my family, I will make sure it goes to people who can do something to stop him, that I have left instructions for this to pass if I do not survive this house. God willing, he is not too far gone to listen to me, but I fear that the evil he has absorbed now controls him. Then again I probably should have realized the extent of his own evil when he had that hotel burned down, causing the deaths of dozens, just to make sure that wedding in '94 took place here.

If you find this note it means I was not successful, and I pray that whoever finds this note will be able to use it to end the evil that Peter has created. Since I had arranged for the trust to be annulled should I not survive this, eventually the property will be sold at auction and hopefully they will demolish this place. I am truly sorry for the part I have played in this. I did try to pick tenants that had done wrong and escaped the law for the times of sacrifice, but that doesn't mitigate what I have participated in. I tell myself that if it wasn't me, Peter would have found someone else, but I know that is just myself trying to justify my actions.

I wish well whoever finds this note.
Jim Neighbors

CHAPTER NINE

THE DIARY

"It looks like he didn't have the time to find a place to hide his note," said John.

"But however Peter is controlling people it isn't foolproof," said Blaze.

"What makes you think that?" asked Ron.

"The fact that Jim Neighbors still had the note on him when he went to that room in the garage."

"Wouldn't that say he had good control, since this guy was not able to hide the note somewhere it could be found?" asked Bob.

"I get what Blaze is saying," answered Jackson. "If Peter had full control of Jim, he would have known about the note and destroyed it."

"Yeah, but putting him in that room was just as good," said Sir Arthur.

"Not really, considering that we found it," piped in Michelle. Jackson had been holding the talk button during the conversation so both Tippy and Michelle could hear.

"Peter does not seem like the type to take any chances," added

Blaze. "He would have made sure that note could never be found, not even by a fluke. He would have turned it to ashes."

"You would think the guy could have left us more information than he did," said Matt.

"He may not have had the time," replied Ron. "If he knew that Peter, or whatever, was coming to get him soon, he probably wrote as much as he felt he had time for. The fact that he placed the diary and plans in the chapel shows he did what he could."

"Michelle, do you see any other way out of there?" asked Jackson, returning to the most pressing problem, getting Michelle to safety.

"No. It is not a large room. Barely enough to hold the bodies that are here."

"I know this may be gross, but can you check the bodies to see if they have anything that could be of use. Maybe one of the other bodies has a note."

"Ahead of you on that. The wedding couple have nothing. What is strange though is under her wedding dress she has on a negligee, almost like she got into her wedding dress after getting changed into her sleepwear. Same goes for the groom. I can see pyjama bottoms sticking out of his pants. It also looks like the clothes were put on sloppily, like they did not know what they were doing. The buttons on his shirt for example are all misaligned. They are both covered in blood, so it does look like they did the massacre, but no reason as to why."

"The why would appear to be Peter Vanderbilt," whispered Blaze.

"The next body has no note, but he carved a message into his hand. Yes, I said carved. I'm going to use his jacket to wipe the dried blood off and try to read what he wrote. Here goes."

The dried blood easily came off.

"Just one word all in capitals. *SCARED!* With an exclamation point."

"He carved an exclamation point into his hand?" questioned Jackson.

"That's what I said. Okay, next two bodies have no notes or anything, but their faces look like they'd been frightened to death. Other than the wedding couple they all look like the last thing they saw frightened the shit out of them. The wedding couple just looks like they went to sleep. And one more thing."

Silence for a minute.

"Michelle, are you okay? What is one more thing/" asked Jackson.

"I accidently moved one of the bodies, and well, I took some medical training a long time ago. I can tell a separated shoulder when I see one. The body I just touched looks like it had both shoulders separated."

"Both?" from Tippy.

"Yes. Now looking closely, it would appear that other than the wedding couple every other person here had been tortured. I'm seeing cut marks, bruises, even a broken bone or two. These people were most assuredly tortured before being placed here."

"You think they were placed there?" asked Jackson.

"Unless someone can walk over here, get down into the pit and crawl through this small access door with a fractured leg, than yes. I see now that one of the bodies has the bone coming right through his leg."

"Can this get any worse?" asked Sir Arthur in the background.

"Shut up," replied Ron. "In every horror movie I have watched as soon as someone says that it gets worse."

Sir Arthur gave him a look meant to say, *stop being a sissy.*

Then.

"Oh shit."

"What is it Michelle," called out Jackson, thinking something bad had happened.

"Nothing. Just dropped my cell phone. Damn now hearing that revving again."

"Michelle, when you dropped the phone, the EMF app must have disconnected. You need to turn it back on right away," yelled Tippy into his walkie-talkie.

"Having a hard time getting at my phone. It's under the leg of one of the bodies."

"How did it get under a leg?" asked Jackson.

"Don't know. It's almost like the leg moved or something. I'm trying to push the leg and if feels like it is resisting. Now something just grabbed my pant leg!"

They could hear the panic in Michelle's voice.

"Michelle, get out of there," yelled Jackson.

There was no further response.

The look Ron shot at Sir Arthur said, *I told you so.*

* * *

"Tippy, do you still have that iron nail hanging around your neck?" asked Bob after taking the walkie-talkie away from Jackson.

"Yeah, why?

"Because with it you can create your own EMF field, using the talkie. It won't be as powerful as the one emitted by the phone app, but it should be strong enough to get you out of that tree."

"Why didn't I think of that. Okay, give me a minute."

"How can he make an electromagnetic field with an iron nail?' asked Matt.

"And why would he have an iron nail around his neck anyway?" asked John.

"I gave it to him a few weeks ago to mark our first year together. The meaning behind it is personal between Tippy and me.

"As to how to make an EMF generator with an iron nail, it's simple physics and engineering. By wrapping a wire around an iron nail and running current through the wire. The electrical field in the wire coil creates a magnetic field around the nail. In some cases, the nail will remain magnetised even when removed from within the wire coil. He can use the battery and wiring from the talkie to do it."

"But then we won't be able to keep in touch with him," pointed out Ron.

"If he can get to Michelle, he can use her talkie."

"If she is still alive—and if her talkie wasn't destroyed by those zombies," said Sir Arthur.

"Zombies?" questioned Matt.

"What else would you call dead bodies that are brought back to life," he snapped.

"I don't believe they're being brought back to life," replied Blaze. "Instead, they're being controlled by ghosts sent by Peter. That's why they only started moving once Michelle dropped her phone and the EMF app shut down."

"Okay, I'm ready to do this," called back Tippy. "I will be able to hook it all through the talkie, and the field I can generate should be almost as strong as the one on the phone app. Once I do it though, I will have to be quick. Hooking it up like this will drain the battery fast."

"Take care of yourself partner," said Bob.

"Will do. Signing out, for now."

"All we can do now is wait to see if he can get to her," said Skip.

"No that is *not* all we can do. We can go to the bloody chapel and get that diary and the plans," said Ron.

"And just how do you expect to do that?" asked Sir Arthur. "Or don't you remember that the tech guys said their machine has a limited range, and our only present psychic has said she can feel the presences waiting for us."

"Bob, did you set up that app on any other phones?' asked Jackson.

"Yeah, it's on Melissa's.

Melissa pulled her phone out of her pocket. "Oh crap, I only have like five percent power left. I must have forgot to plug it in."

"Will that be enough?" asked Ron.

"It will have to be," replied Jackson. "We need that diary as fast as possible. Who knows how long it will be before Peter figures out a way past our defenses. It is a short trip there so hopefully it will be enough."

"Bob, can you download the app to another phone?" asked John.

"Well, we have no Wi-Fi here and the codes are on my computer back at the office, so I have no other way of doing it."

"Why don't you build one out of the talkie like Tippy did?" asked
Sir Arthur.

"No can do unless you have a piece of iron on you."

"No, but you can blame the airlines for that."

"Huh," responded Skip.

"I usually carry around a small iron magnet as a good luck charm. Don't ask why, as it is a long story. Anyways when I got to the airport and was going through their security I beeped. It was the magnet. I took it out and put it in the bin as they asked. When I went to get my stuff out of the bin later it wasn't there."

"Can you jury-rig one of the EMF detectors, like you did with the big machine?" asked John.

"Probably, but it will take time, and we only have two left.

"Time is not something we have a lot of," said Ron. Our tech gurus said that they don't know how long their machine will keep those ghosts out, and we don't know how long it will take to figure out a way to stop this once we have the diary. We have to go now."

"Are you volunteering?" sneered Sir Arthur.

"Since it takes a backbone, we certainly won't expect you to," replied Ron.

"I'll go with you," said Blaze. "I should be able to sense when we get to the end of the field generated by the big machine. That way we only turn on Melissa's phone when we have to."

"I'm coming too," said Matt. "Three together stand a better chance."

Melissa handed Ron her phone. "You just need to swipe. There is no code required. The app is on the front screen. The glance I just had shows it is shaped like our EMF detectors."

Bob grinned. "Yeah, that was Tippy's idea."

"Take a camera," said John.

The others looked at him, questioning this suggestion.

"The Ghost Eliminators have the right idea about this. Document everything. The camera may pick up something we could use."

Blaze picked up a camera, and with her leading, to use her abilities, the three left the entrance area.

"Bob, you and Skip get to work on converting the two EMF detectors to emitters," said Jackson. "We still have two people in the house who are missing or taken, Harry and Jane. We will need those emitters if we want to find them."

"Are you seriously going to divide our group even further by sending more people out there?" demanded Sir Arthur.

"So, if it were you out there you wouldn't want others to come and find you?" asked Melissa.

"If it were me out there you would already think I was dead, so wouldn't waste your time, nor risk your lives," he replied.

"Jane is not dead," shot back Bob. "Maybe the EMF emitter can chase the ghost out of her, and she can be saved."

"Besides, the only reason Jane is where she is now is probably because you talked her into going with you to sample the wine," hissed Melissa.

That one hit home for Sir Arthur. He knew Melissa was right. He looked down at his feet, refusing to look the others in the face.

Jackson quickly settled the issue.

"No one is going anywhere yet. Not until the chapel party gets back and we can have a look at that diary. Maybe something in it can help us."

"If they get back," muttered Sir Arthur.

"Keep your bloody blimey comments to yourself," yelled Bob, getting in Sir Arthur's face. "They must knight anyone in England, even those without balls."

John intervened, pushing himself between the two.

"Look we're all on edge. Let's not take it out on each other. We need to pull together if we want any chance of surviving this. Bob, please go work with Skip on those emitters. Sir Arthur, if you don't have anything positive to add, could you please not say anything."

Bob turned away and went to join Skip at the equipment table. John gave Jackson a look and he nodded in return. They joined each other in quiet conversation.

Melissa gave Sir Arthur another dirty look and went to join Bob and Skip to see if she could be of help. Sir Arthur sat in one of the chairs, head bowed.

* * *

They had just reached the door to the chapel when Blaze held up her hand.

"I can sense presences on the other side of this door. How far into the room I am not sure. Time to turn that phone on and see if it will work here."

"Why wouldn't it if it worked for Michelle," asked Matt.

"Because she only had a few presences to deal with. What I feel on the other side of this door is many of them, some of which are quite evil."

"In a chapel?" asked Ron.

"As a cop you must know that evil people often hide behind religion. Just think of all those boys raped by priests," said Matt.

Ron started Melissa's phone, found the app, and opened it.

"It's working," said Blaze. "I feel the presences moving away from the door. I still sense them but not quite as close. Let's go in and see if we can make it to the alter."

Pushing the door open, Ron led the way, holding Melissa's phone tightly in his hand. After hearing what happened to Michelle, he didn't want something to somehow knock the phone away from him.

The three stayed close together, not sure how much range they had with the phone.

"Back there, I see it," said Matt.

He pointed to a smaller stand beside the altar. On it was one of the most unique crosses he had ever seen. Carved of wood, with a distinctive carving of Christ, at it's base it had three plastic bubbles. One contained dirt, one contained a liquid, and the last one contained what looked like silver filings. The lower part of the stand contained a small cabinet door.

"We had better hurry. The phone just dropped to three percent power."

They made their way towards the back of the chapel as quickly as the presences would allow them. It was obvious that their little EMF emitter was not nearly as powerful as the big machine. The presences moved reluctantly, but they did move. It took them a few minutes to cross the near thirty feet.

While Ron kept watch with the emitter, and Blaze used her senses, Matt got down on his knees and opened the cabinet. As promised in the Neighbors letter, he found a black, leather backed diary, and a rolled-up wad of papers that were most likely the plans.

"Got them. Let's get the hell out of here."

"That may be a problem," said Ron pointing towards the door.

Standing between them and the door, and closer to them than any of the other presences had managed to get, was what had to have been a ghost, even if it looked as solid as they were.

The figure looked familiar to Matt, but he couldn't place it right away. Then it spoke.

Pointing at Blaze it said in a strong voice, "I have come for you Charlotte Shelby. You murdered me. Now you must pay the price."

Ron moved to put himself between the ghost and Blaze, holding out the phone. As he watched the power on the phone dropped to two percent. And it was not stopping this ghost as it continued to get closer.

Matt grabbed Ron's arm and shoved the documents into his free hand.

"I can handle this. I know who this ghost is. When I wave my hand grab Blaze and run as fast as you can out of here.

Matt moved in front of Ron and started talking to the ghost.

"Bill Taylor, she is not the one you are looking for."

The ghost ignored Matt, still looking at Blaze and advancing.

Matt moved a little to the side, walking between the pews.

"William Cunningham Deane-Tanner, you will listen to me," Matt used the ghost's full birth name this time.

That name caught the attention of the ghost.

"I no longer go by that name. Who are you to speak it."

"My name is Matthew Capiro. Like you I am a producer and director. I have studied you for years and seen all your film, both as an actor and as a director. You are my idol."

"Ghosts of former Hollywood stars are often easily flattered as they lived for adoration in their lifetimes," Blaze whispered to Ron.

Hearing her voice, he started to turn back to her. Matt waved at her to keep silent.

"I know all about your murder case. I have studied the file extensively. I know who killed you."

Pointing at Blaze the ghost of William Desmond Taylor said, "Charlotte Shelby killed me. I was looking in the mirror and saw her pull the trigger before the bullet hit my back."

"She pulled the trigger, but she was acting on someone else's orders."

"Whose orders?"

"My orders," said Matt.

Blaze and Ron looked at each other, realizing that Matt was going to draw the ghost to him, in order for them to get away. Ron looked at the phone. Down to one percent.

He showed it to Blaze and shook his head. They realized they had no choice but to let Matt do what he was going to do.

"I have never heard of you. Why would you want me killed?" The ghost had shifted position and was now advancing on Matt.

"My real name is Buron Fitts. I was the L.A. district attorney, so I was able to make sure your case was never solved. I was also the lover of Minter Shelby, daughter of Charlotte, who you deflowered with your lofty promises. We got our revenge on you."

"That is a lie. I never slept with Minter," raged the Ghost. Now its attention was fully on Matt, he signalled Ron.

"I have pictures of it, you pedophile you. From when she was fifteen."

Now the ghost roared and rushed at Matt. Ron grabbed Blaze's hand and ran for the door—just as the phone went dead.

"They're coming," yelled Blaze as they hit the door. They rushed through it and into the protection of the EMF emitter from the big machine. They heard Matt yell in pain behind them but could do nothing.

* * *

Blaze, Melissa, Jackson, Ron and John, with a subdued Sir Arthur were gathered around a table where the plans had been rolled out, and on which lay the diary. They were standing close enough together that their shoulders were touching, all wanting to see the diary and plans for themselves. Bob and Skip continued to work on the emitters.

The plans themselves did not show much, so they were hoping the diary would indicate something. It was a smaller black leather notebook, like something that can be easily bought at an office supply store but embossed on the cover was Property of Peter

Vanderbilt. As John read aloud to the group no one moved or made a sound.

If you are reading this diary, it most likely means that I have succeeded, and that I am travelling the world as the most powerful being around. It is now too late for you to do anything about it. But I will tell you my story here.

It has taken me years of work, and plenty of research, but the time has almost come. I am writing this diary so that a hundred years from now people will be able to see how great I was, even back in those days. Until then I have left instructions with my will that this book will be kept in a prepaid bank vault for that period of 100 years.

Why 100 years? Because by that time my spirit will have absorbed enough psychic energy that I will no longer need this house to survive but will in fact be free to travel the world.

This all started two decades ago when I met a mystic from India named Swami Shankar. He claimed to know the way to eternal life. He came to me because he wanted funding to build a sanctuary for mystics. I made a deal with him that if he taught me the secret to eternal life, and shared his mystic knowledge, I would donate $10 million for him to build his sanctuary. It was the best money I have ever spent.

I was with him off and on for the next decade, as he showed me the way to capture and hold spirits, and then how to harness their strength to build my own psychic power. The fool however did not understand what I did, that the strength of good spirits is finite, but those that are evil, or who continued on in anguish after their deaths, hold the most power.

With this in mind, I contracted one of the top architectural companies in the world to design a house, but to certain specifications. The materials to be used were ones that I was to choose, and the layout would be made to focus the energy of the captive spirits directly to me. It had to be one way only. As well I would have to be buried within the house, at the exact point where the power would be focused towards me, but using materials that would allow the power to enter my place, but not reflect outwards. To be clear, the architectural firm I hired had no idea of what some of the materials to be used would consist of. Nor were they aware of certain changes and additions I made along the way. So going to find the original plans will not help anyone.

My inner sanctuary, where my 100-year rest would take place has walls of mirrors reflecting inwards, the backing made with pure silver.

The walls of the remainder of the rooms of the house are laced with lead, specially prepared so as not to leach out. Every thirteen inches there is a small 2-inch square that does not have lead, but instead aluminum, to capture the power of the residing spirits, with the back painted with a special plutonium paint that will siphon that power to my chamber.

Of course, when I say rest, that does not mean I will not be active. My studies have shown that for my strength to grow I will need to have a sacrifice occasionally. Only deaths that are fueled by fear and pain can give this to me. So, my instructions to my assistant are to make sure that the house is occupied at all times. It is to be rented out, from time to time to tenants he is to choose for sacrifice, for me to get the power I need. To ensure that tenants can always be found there will be periods where I will be at complete rest, with no spiritual activity within the house. Of course, even with this the house will get a reputation and I will need to have certain investigators downplay that part. It is amazing what money can buy. Even federal agents if you know who to talk to.

Over time the house will still get a reputation and it will become harder to find tenants. However, it is only for the first 30 years that I will need the sacrifice, and even then, only once every seven years. Should the house only be rented for a maximum of two years at a time, with nothing untoward passing between sacrifices, then the skeptics will keep coming for the cheap rent. My assistant will make sure that the house is never vacant for more than a month or two between tenants to keep this façade going. After that time my strength will continue to grow without this. The spirits I have captured by building the house with the materials I used will guarantee this.

I have taken pieces from many of the most haunted, and evil places in the world. In each case, using a ceremony my mystic accomplices have developed, the spirits of the most tortured and evil spirits of each place were trapped into the part I took and then were added into the construction of this mansion.

Further in this diary, I will list some of the pieces I have acquired, at least the more famous, or should I say infamous, where they came from, and the type of spirit or entity that was trapped within.

I am not foolish enough to think that it is guaranteed this house will stand for 100 years. My sanctuary is sufficiently hidden that even should this house be torn down, burned to the ground or otherwise destroyed, my place of rest will remain undiscovered. For that reason, I will not divulge that final piece of the puzzle. For that is the key to me rising again. Only from within can the passage to my new home be opened.

As long as this house stands for 30 years my future is assured. As I said, I have paid my assistant well to handle all the details after my "passing," as well as making sure that if he doesn't, he knows I have made arrangements for him and his family to suffer greatly.

This copy of the diary has been kept in a safety deposit box that was prepaid for 100 years. That way, once I have risen again, I can prove that I arranged this well ahead of time, and my greatness will be confirmed to everyone. The original will be with me, as the final notes must remain hidden until I rise again.

Soon it will be time for me to take my place in my sanctuary. My doctors have informed me that my cancer is spreading quickly and that I have only a matter of months.

The wedding is set to take place next week, and the events at that wedding will set in motion all that will come thereafter. I will be in my chamber before then and will be able to see all that transpires. Once it is complete,

I will take the pills that will put me to sleep, and my spirit, or soul if you prefer, will be released from the prison of my body. It will rest in the chamber as I gather strength, and I will be able to watch all that goes on in the house and direct my spirit army to perform the tasks I assign them so that the sacrifices required will come to pass.

Now for the design of my magnificent home. It was the Pritzker Prize-winning architect, BV Doshi, in his book, Paths Unchartered, who said, "A building is created out of memories, associations, sounds, forms, spaces and images, and many other related and unrelated encounters. Through these, he reconstructs his image to connect to the world around." However, he did not begin to grasp what can be done with memories and encounters.

Here is a list of the materials I used and the reasoning behind them. Where I could not obtain actual materials, I was often able to obtain pieces of the person, be it bones, clothing they wore, or something else. Not as powerful as a piece of their home or where they committed their evil, but enough to draw their spirit here.

"Connection to the outside, to go deep within."

The idea behind this is that the outdoors can communicate with us—all we must do is listen. They tell us how we can engage with a site or its history (history is the most important aspect of this) or convey the spiritual context through which we can experience the place, to the point of eliminating any sense of humanity. These spaces, by the language that they speak, engage with us and evoke a sense of dread and fear, when used correctly.

For this reasoning, the grounds themselves begin the focus of spiritual energy. These grounds were the site of an ancient Native graveyard, but one that was all but forgotten even before the first Europeans came to North America. The land where this house sits was said to be the burial site of a powerful, and evil shaman. Although little was known about him, I was able to speak to an elderly Native who may have been the last of his tribe who had this knowledge passed on to him. He mentioned that what was passed down to him was that the stories of the twin brothers, one good the other evil, were true. The evil one became known as a shaman and caused much harm before he was finally trapped and destroyed, on this land. Yet even though the actual history of it has been forgotten, even to this day the local Native tribes refuse to walk on this land. When we started digging, some ancient bones were found, and these have been placed with me in my sanctuary. Whether they are the bones of this shaman

I know not, but just the fact that they rested on these grounds gives them power.

The gardens out front were grown using earth removed from grave sites around the world, mainly from places that were said to be haunted. The shrubs and flowers may look lovely, but for those who can feel the psychic power, they will feel ugly.

For the road and path leading up to the house, I have had my workers make special stones, fitted like a uni-pave driveway. Even my workers though, did not know where the stones came from.

In the city of Edinburgh, Scotland, there rests a graveyard called Greyfriars Kirkyard. Its history of evil goes back to the 1670s when a merciless judge named George Mackenzie presided over the trials of the Presbyterian Covenanters. Basically, it was described as the first-ever concentration camp, with hundreds dying from malnutrition, executions, and even torture. But what really sealed its fate was when George Mackenzie died and was buried with his former prisoners. Over the centuries his control over the spirits grew, and when his vault was broken into in 1991, his spirit was released, and attacks started to happen. Visitors often left the cemetery with bruises, scratches, bite marks and burns, and there are rumors that some were even killed, but that knowledge was suppressed by the authorities. Even exorcisms failed, with one of the exorcists dying. No research will show when this began, however eventually the story will come out and you can be assured the authorities will modify dates as they will not want it known that this has gone on for a long time and they did nothing about it for many years.

It will get to the point where the City of Edinburgh will close off the Covenanters' Prison from the public. Plans are already in the works for this. So, I stepped in. I made a deal with the city and the grounds were made temporarily off-limits to the public. I had my people go in and remove many of the gravestones, as well as the entire vault of George Mackenzie. These were replaced by new stone, made to look aged, so no one knew what had happened. I used a ceremony taught to me by the swami to keep the spirits contained within these stones. Although the hauntings continued afterward, the inherent evil of the attacks subsided.

The garage, where cars are to be repaired, held a special interest for me. Built into it are pieces of The Number 7 Bus. Yes, the bus itself did exist. Always thought to be just a ghost story or a phantom, the city of

London believed it enough to widen and modify the intersection where the bus was said to appear causing accidents and death. My researchers found the original bus in a scrap yard near Stonehenge. It was disassembled, melted down, and the steel was used to make the steel beams that support the second floor of the building. Furthermore, I was able to acquire the oil from the Golden Eagle 1964 Dodge 330 Limited Edition, which was said to have caused the three police officers who drove it, to kill their families before committing suicide, and was also said to be responsible for many deaths thereafter. I was able to get the oil following oil changes, shortly after each death, from 1980 through to 1993. Ironically there were no deaths on record attributed to that car, but off record there were many. This oil was used to anoint the oil pit in the garage after it was completed.

At various places surrounding the property are hidden pure quartz crystals. They are positioned so that all psychic energy points inwards, towards my sanctuary, focusing all the power to me.

And now we get to my pride and joy, the place that will become known as The House That Peter Built. It would take more pages than I have in this notebook to list where every part was placed in the house. Instead, I will list what was used, since by the time anyone sees this diary the house itself, most likely, will no longer exist as I have made arrangements for that. After all, I can't have anyone else following simple instructions to build what I have. There can only be one like me, as I want no competition in my future "life."

Before I provide the list, when people read this, the first thing they may ask is why there is nothing from The Darvaza Crater or The Gateway to Hell in Turkmenistan. The reason is simple. There is no psychic energy coming from there. People call it the gateway to hell because of the fires in the pit caused by mining. But no deaths or anything of that nature have happened there.

Something else that people should be made aware of. Psychic imprints are not just where people died. It is often where they enacted their worst sins, and on death, their spirit is drawn back to that place. Of special note is that when they have terrorized and killed people in these places, they return to take control of the spirits they imprisoned. I will then control the controllers. They will be my spirit army.

Unfortunately, I will need one more sacrifice to complete my preparations. This time I will have to get my own hands dirty. I also need one spirit to keep me company. The day of the wedding I will lure one person out of the party to spend the next hundred years with me.

Now read my list, and marvel. It is amazing how money can buy you almost anything.

<u>Houska Castle, Czech Republic</u>: Folklore considers this castle to cover one of the gateways to Hell, built to prevent demons (trapped in lower levels) from reaching the rest of the world. During World War II, the Wehrmacht occupied the castle until 1945. The Nazis were said to have conducted experiments into the occult in this place. According to one source, there were "multiple myths about their supposed occult involvements there." Another source states locals believed that the Nazis had been using the "powers of Hell" for their experiments. I will leave it to whomever finds this book to do their own research, as I am sure the tales of this place will long outlast it.

From this place, I have acquired wood that used to surround the portal to Hell, as well as metal used by the Nazis in their medical experiments conducted in the room where the pit to Hell is located.

<u>Poveglia Island, Venice Italy</u>: Where plague sufferers were sent to spend their final days. They were greeted by

a doctor who wore a mask that looked like a terrifying bird. I have acquired one of these masks, said to have been used by one of the first doctors to run the island during the time of the plague, and afterward it sat in the office of a corrupt doctor in the 1930s who performed evil experiments including lobotomies. The spirits of the people he killed haunted him, and he eventually committed suicide by jumping off the Belltower/Lighthouse of Poveglia.

<u>112 Ocean Avenue, Amityville, Long Island, N.Y.</u> more famously known as the Amityville Horror. Despite recent stories, my research proved that it was haunted. When they renovated and replaced some windows, I acquired the glass, which was used in the making of some of the windows of this house.

<u>Tower of London, England</u>: Hidden away for years were stones taken from the tower when it was renovated and upgraded with gun platforms in the mid-1700s. I found them in part of a house that was built using those stones and which was reputed to be haunted because of it. I bought that house and tore it down to make use of the stones here. A portion of the spirits of the souls that were tortured and executed in the tower still reside in these stones.

The Catacombs, Paris: What haunted house would be complete without something from the most famous burial place in the world. There are several stone crosses within the catacombs. One that is there now is not the original, as it sits prominently in my little chapel.

Auschwitz Concentration Camp: Steel taken from the cremation ovens has been used in various parts of this house. The spirit of Josef Mengele has been brought with the steel.

8213 W. Summerdale Ave. Chicago, Illinois: Best known as the house of John Wayne Gacy, where he murdered at least 33 young men and boys. Bricks from that house were used to make some of the fireplaces. In addition, I was able to obtain a finger of John Wayne Gacy after his death in May from the warden of the Stateville Correctional Center, which is incorporated into one of the fireplaces. Money can buy anything.

Notre-Dame-de-Bonsecours Chapel in Montreal: The stained-glass windows at the entrance come directly from there. It cost a fortune since I had to have someone make copies and then replace the windows in the actual chapel without anyone knowing. The people there thought my crew were window cleaners. The church itself is shrouded in mystery. The bodies of many nuns are buried in the crypt, and many did not die of natural causes. Some of them were still alive when they were buried. The psychic energy from these is especially strong.

<u>Château de Brissac, France</u>: One of the main chandeliers which now hangs in my entranceway. Once again, I acquired the original and replaced it with a copy. Although there were many incidents there of murder and mayhem, the most famous one was when Jacques de Brézé murdered his wife and her lover when he discovered them doing it in his own bed. His wife was King Louis XI's half-sister Charlotte de Valois.

<u>RMS Queen Mary</u>: Tiles from the first-class pool are embedded in the bottom of my pool. I uncovered an old diary written by one of the captains of the vessel. The rumors of drownings are true, even though the official records do not show it, and only the rumors exist. Two of the drownings were deliberate. A purser, whose name is lost, murdered two women in that pool and then committed suicide. According to the captain's diary, the purser had affairs with both women. When they demanded he choose between them he could not decide which, so he decided he would have both, forever.

<u>404 S. Alvadaro Street, Los Angeles</u>: I acquired the only piece that still remained of the home where William

Desmond Taylor was murdered. A section of one of the front pillars. I used it to make some of the decorations in the chapel. He was a well-known Hollywood director with various vices, most of which I believe were true despite the general belief that they were only rumors. He was murdered by one of the many enemies he had, and his spirit is still looking for revenge.

<u>Voergaard Castle, Denmark</u>: The lady of this Renaissance castle had the architect thrown into the moat and left to drown so that he could never build another one like it. It had an infamous dungeon without light, ventilation, or room for a man to sit or stand, always in the dark with limited air holes making breathing difficult, which the ruthless noblewoman, Ingeborg Skeel, made much use of. An exorcism was done, moving her spirit to a nearby swamp after her death. My ceremony returned her spirit to the castle and then into the doors which now adorn the front of my home.

As a final word. People reading this will think that I am an evil person who wants to have an evil afterlife. This can't be further from the truth. I have used these materials because of the psychic energy they emit. When people die peacefully whatever psychic presence they may have had is quickly dissipated. Only those who have died in pain and fear, and those who have caused it, leave behind a psychic energy that lasts for long periods of time, sometimes even millennia. With the ceremonies I have used I believe—make that—I know that I will be able to use these psychic energies, while at the same time cleansing them and helping these tortured spirits along their journey to eventually find peace. Unfortunately, more will have to die in fear and pain along the way. But I feel little guilt as the thousands of spirits that I will help to find peace more than justifies these actions. Still, know this. When I rise again, I will be powerful. Any that try to oppose me will be made to suffer, those who choose to follow and worship me will receive treasures beyond what they could imagine.

The list of names of those people of evil that I have acquired parts or personal possessions from is long. I will give here a brief list of some of the more notorious ones.

John Wayne Gacy

Josef Stalin

Pol Pot

Adolf Eichmann (The number of evil Nazis was probably the largest of any ruling group in modern history.)

Charles Manson

Genghis Khan (This one was especially difficult to obtain.)

Jeffrey Dahmer (Although his ghost is not here yet, with him still being alive, I am sure he won't survive long in prison for what he has done. My ceremonies will draw his spirit here in his passing.)

Ted Bundy

Vlad the Impaler (Another difficult piece to locate.)

Dr. H.H. Holmes (America's first known serial killer.)

Amelia Dyer (I was so happy to locate a locket she had worn to add my first female evil ghost.)

Ingeborg Skeel (The doors from her castle have her spirit embedded in them, thanks to my swami's ceremonies.)

Elizabeth Bathory (Another piece difficult to obtain, but a necklace she once wore is in my collection.)

Thomas de Torquemada (What collection of evil ghosts would be complete without the first grand inquisitor.)

Jim Jones (Maybe I can help him find his peace with God.)

The one name I would have loved to add to this list

is Jack the Ripper. Unfortunately, there are no known artifacts connected to him that exist.

There are more, but as I said too many to mention here.

Again, know that what I am doing will be considered one of the greatest acts in human history. By cleansing these spirits of their evil it will usher in a new world and new world order. Where everyone will live in peace and evil will be eradicated. I will oversee all and ensure that it does. Yes, many lives will be lost, but the spirit of humanity will not only survive this, it will thrive.

Peter Vanderbilt

They all stood there in stunned silence.

CHAPTER TEN

THE SEARCH

"What a narcissistic, evil asshole," said Melissa backing slightly from the group, but keeping close for comfort.

"The level of his arrogance makes Sir Arthur appear humble in comparison," added Ron still staring at the diary on the table.

Surprisingly Sir Arthur made no comment.

"Well we do know that Peter can't see the future," said Chip.

"How's that?" asked Bob.

"He said the place will be referred to as The House that Peter Built. Yet it is more commonly referred to as Blood Mansion."

"Be that as it may it does explain a number of things," said Blaze a thoughtful expression causing her forehead to crease.

"But how does it help us?" asked Jackson.

"To start with we're getting an idea of what we're facing," replied Ron.

"How's that?" asked Bob, who had made his way over to their table, along with Skip.

"In the Chapel Matt addressed the ghost as William Desmond Taylor. We know now that part of his house was used here."

"He said he took bricks from the house of John Wayne Gacy, and that is who was on the screen in the cinema when Jackson Brown was killed.," said Melissa.

"Jane has become fucking Josef Mengele," added Sir Arthur. His language caused the others to pause and look at him. Not only was it not what he had portrayed since his arrival, but neither was his accent. However, no one commented.

"It explains the car revving that Michelle was hearing as well." said Ron.

"But how does that explain the bodies coming back to life?" asked Skip.

"His spirit army," replied John. "He says in his diary that he can command them."

"So, we are facing the most evil army in history," commented Bob.

"But is he really in control?" asked Blaze.

"After what we have seen why would you question that?" asked Ron.

"Because of what James Neighbors said in his note. That he thinks the evil that Peter has absorbed now controls him. So, he would be the general, but there would be something behind him giving him his orders."

"He also says in his diary, that these grounds were said to be the burial place of an evil Native shaman. Is it possible that it's the shaman who controls things now?" asked John, looking at Blaze.

"I would say that is a distinct possibility. Native Americans are amongst the most spiritual, and nature-knowledgeable people in the world. If it is true that this shaman's spirit has occupied these lands for hundreds of years, then his strength would be much more than that of Peter. He could let Peter get control of the spirits, and all he would have to do is get control of Peter."

"So in essence it is a Manitou," said Bob.

"A Manitou?" asked Jackson.

"You mean like in that hokey movie from the '70s with Tony Curtis?" replied Sir Arthur.

Ignoring Sir Arthur's quip, John responded to Jackson's question. Opening his laptop, he scanned to another file.

"A couple of years back I was asked to check out a supposed haunting on land that had been used by the residential school system in Canada. If you are not aware, this was a system where Native children were forcibly removed from their homes and sent to live at these schools. There they were punished if they spoke in their Native language, or in any way discussed their Native heritage. It was the government's and church's way of enforcing cultural integration. Many children died at these places, and there are reputed to be many undiscovered graveyards. The owner of this parcel claimed that he was being harassed by spirits, that he said local Natives were calling Manitous and were sending them against him. So of course, I had to research Manitous.

"This is from a website called Manitou Legends. An article titled "Background on Manitou: The Native American Religion," by Franklin Andrews. I won't read the entire article, but here are some notes I took.

"Manitou is the belief of Algonquians meaning 'mysterious being,' or simply 'mystery'. An Algonquian word that represents the unknown power of life and the universe.

"Common among many Indigenous peoples of North America, it is related to the concept of mana, which is a personal supernatural force, and connected to the worship of the sun. A supernatural force that according to an Algonquian belief permeates the natural world.

"It is universal and manifests everywhere: the environment, events, organisms, etc. When the world was created, Aashaa monetoo meaning the 'good spirit' or 'great spirit', gave the land to the Indigenous peoples, specifically to Algonquian-speaking ethnic group Indigenous Shawnee. In some Algonquian traditions, it was also called Gitche Manitou.

"Native Americans acknowledge traditional healers and spiritual leaders who used manitou to see the future, heal illness, and change the weather. Ojibwe traditional healers used their spiritual connection to cure patients since the illness was believed to be caused by spirits and magic.

"In tribes that practice shamanistic rituals, Manitous are often connected to an inanimate object or animals to achieve the desired effect. A buffalo manitous for a successful hunt or plant manitous may be connected for healing. It involved the belief that shamans had the power to communicate with spirits, heal the sick, and help bring souls of the dead to the afterlife.

"Also, some believed that if a shaman was evil he would use these spirits in an evil way. So yes, it could be considered the Manitou of an evil shaman. And no, it is not about to be born again through a tumor on someone's back. Yes, Sir Arthur I also saw that hokey movie."

"So, what happened with that investigation?" asked Melissa.

"There was no Manitou. It was a group of local Indigenous people that wanted the land investigated for potential grave sites. The owner had refused to allow it. So, they scared him with the Manitou tale, and certain effects. In the end though it worked. The owner realized how serious they were and decided to let the investigation go forward. It is a slow process though."

"Is there any way to know for sure if it is a Manitou?" asked Skip.

"I could do a seance," Blaze offered. "But that might be quite risky, since it would mean turning off the machine."

"That's a nonstarter for sure," said Jackson. "Right now, that machine is the only thing keeping those monsters away from us."

"What we have to do is find the room where Peter's body is and destroy the body, like James Neighbors says in his note," said Ron. "I'm assuming that once the general is gone, the army will disperse and the shaman will be powerless."

"Most likely," replied Blaze.

"The question is how," said John. "Where would we start? Do we go through the place room by room?"

"We can probably narrow that down a lot using logic," replied Skip.

"How?" asked Melissa shifting position from one foot to another, a nervous habit she had.

"First, it's highly unlikely that he would have made access to his resting spot through one of the bedrooms on the second floor, so we can eliminate those rooms for the time being. Second, the pool room is unlikely since it's mainly poured concrete. Even if it is there, there would be no way to get at it, and no way for him to get out to secure his 'resting companion' before he died. Remember he said in his diary that he would be taking someone from the wedding with him to keep him company. And third, I am discounting the theatre, kitchen, and dining room for the same reason. He might have been seen if he lured his companion from such a conspicuous place." Skip looked around the group and saw nods of agreement.

"Narrowing it down would leave the chapel, the wine cellar, and the top floor. Personally I would think it has to be the closed room on the top floor, since no one ever had access to it."

"Using your logic, it can't be that room," commented Sir Arthur.

"He said in his diary that even if the house was destroyed, his resting place would not be found."

"Shit, I didn't think of that," said Skip, acknowledging the point with a tip of his head toward the actor. "I guess the wine cellar then. After all, that was the last place Betty was seen."

"We shouldn't discount that third-floor room," said John. "His resting place is not likely to be there, but maybe a passage to it might be."

"Also, what about outside?" asked Melissa. "What better way to protect his resting place than having everyone trapped in the house whenever something happens."

"Except this time not everyone is trapped inside," replied Bob. "I just hope that Tippy makes it to Michelle and they are both safe."

Melissa could hear the tremble in his voice and see the tears in his eyes. She went over and gave him a hug. "Bob, you know Tippy is one tough son of a bitch, and never quits. If anyone can figure out how to do it, he can."

Trying to cover for his new, emotional friend Skip jumped in. "We now have two portable emitters. Bob and I were able to adapt the last two detectors. How long they will last, we can't say for sure, but it should give us a good hour of search time, and the range should be sufficient to protect anyone using it."

"How many feet around?" asked Sir Arthur.

"I would think an area of about ten or twelve feet in diameter, so roughly the size of an average bedroom."

"We have three emitters," said Melissa. "I plugged my phone in when Ron and Blaze got back, and it's already at forty percent power."

"That should also give about a half hour of time," said Bob.

"There may be three machines, but there are eight of us, and I don't think the groups should be any smaller than three," said John. "Also, we need to leave someone here to coordinate everything. I suggest we start with the room up top and the chapel. Once we have checked those out, we can meet back here, make sure the emitters are charged enough and then check the wine cellar."

"I think Bob should stay here. We need at least one tech guy near the equipment," said Melissa. Bob gave her a look of thanks, knowing that she said it so he could be closer to Tippy.

"I will keep the tech guy company," said Sir Arthur.

"Not surprised," replied Ron.

"Okay, two teams. I'll go to the third floor with Skip and Melissa. Maybe Skip can figure out how to get in to the locked off room."

"I want to know what happened to Matt, so that works for me," replied Jackson. Ron and Blaze nodded in agreement.

"Since we have only an estimated time for the emitters, I suggest that everyone is back here in no more than forty-five minutes," said Bob. "Meanwhile Sir Rubie and I will go through the diary again and see if there are any clues in it that we missed.

Skip went to the equipment table and grabbed a couple of screwdrivers and the metal bar Jackson had used on the pool and theatre doors. He also picked up two walkie-talkies, handing one to Ron.

"Keep the volume low. They may know we are coming, but only Blaze has the ability to sense them, the rest of us will have to rely on our eyes and ears."

The two groups of three were soon ready to leave, with Melissa holding the emitter for one group, and Jackson for the other.

Bob grabbed two cameras and handed one to each group.

"I have already downloaded the videos on to a portable drive. As

John mentioned before, document everything."

"Okay, everyone stay as close as you can to the one holding the emitter," said John. Then they all made their way toward their destinations. As soon as they left Bob went back to the table to study the diary and the plans.

"Hey Sir Arthur, why not be useful and come give me a hand. Maybe your Limey eyes will see something I don't."

Getting no response, he turned to where he had last seen Sir Arthur. He was no longer there, and neither was Melissa's phone.

* * *

"Okay you crazy critters. Let's see if you like this." Tippy turned on his new-fangled emitter.

At first there was no reaction. Then the herd of deer below him looked around as if dazed, saw the foxes, and turned and ran. Then it was the turn of the foxes. Soon there were no animals below him.

Tippy cautiously climbed down. He gave a good look around and then ran for the garage.

As he approached the main entrance, he saw a couple of cougars standing by the door. Even with the emitter working, he feared that once he got close to the door the cougars might attack him anyway. He noticed a side entrance to the garage area that was not covered by animals.

"I sure hope this is just a mistake on your part, Peter, and not a trap." He got to the door and tried to open it. It was locked, but Tippy figured he would be able to pick the lock. Pulling out a mini screwdriver he kept in his pocket he managed to jiggle the lock and get it open. Just as he accomplished that he saw the two cougars standing behind him. They looked a bit dazed, like the deer did after they came under the affects of the emitter, but then they saw Tippy standing there, fresh meat.

Tippy pushed the door open, squeezed through and then slammed it shut, just as there was a heavy bang on the other side. Looking around he saw a two by four and was able to use that to jam the door shut.

Turning around he studied the garage. A few feet away was one end of the oil pit. About halfway down he could see the collapsed lift. At the far end of the garage, he saw three large electric boxes and another lift. Then he heard the screaming.

Pulling his home-made emitter from his pocket he made sure it was still working and went to the area of the pit that held the collapsed lift. Bryan's body was lying underneath part of the lift, his arms and head hanging over the pit. Blood had dripped from his mouth and formed a pool underneath him. Trying not to look at him Tippy crouched at the edge of the pit, and gave a shove on the lift, making sure it could not collapse on to him as well.

"Michelle, can you hear me," he yelled. The screaming had stopped.

"Tippy is that you?" her voice came through clear, but shaking.

"Yes. Are you okay?"

"I think so. The bodies stopped moving when I heard your voice."

"Listen to me Michelle. My emitter must have sent the spirits away, but it's power source won't last much longer. You need to get your phone and engage your app. Can you do it?"

"I … I think so."

A minute later.

"Got it. App is back on."

"Good. Make sure you don't drop it again. It's the only thing keeping us safe. I am going to try and find something to help move this lift."

"Wait a sec. Let me get out of this room and into the alcove where I can help you."

"Don't forget the talkie."

"Fortunately, when I dropped it, it landed near the phone, so I have both."

He heard her moving things around and assumed it was the bodies that surrounded her. Soon after he saw her hand waving out from the alcove.

Looking around he spotted a small portable jack on wheels.

"Okay, I see something that might do the trick. Be right back."

"Please don't go. I'm scared."

"Hang in there Michelle. I'm just going a few feet."

Fortunately, the jack was easy to move and he placed it into a position under part of the collapsed lift. It was a manually operated jack and he started pumping the rod until it was touching the lift.

"I'm going to start moving it. Let me know when you have enough space to get out. I'm afraid to move it too much as it might collapse further and completely block you in. Are you ready?"

"Just get going Tippy. I don't want to be here a minute longer."

He pumped the jack a few times. Although the heavy steel section that was blocking the alcove moved, the remainder of the lift shifted.

"Shit. If I pump this thing any more the lift might collapse and block the alcove completely. I don't know if I will be able to get you out if it does."

"I think I can get out now, with your help."

Tippy moved to the edge of the pit and saw what Michelle meant. It would be tight, but she might be able to squeeze through. The only problem was that if she pushed against the lift, even a little, it might fall on her. He looked back to where the jack was positioned. Taking his emitter he went and placed it beside the jack, hopefully ensuring that no spirits could push it while he was helping Michelle, then went to the edge of the pit and lying on his stomach reached out. He was able to grab her hand.

"We may only get one shot at this. When I grab your hands and pull you will have to push with your feet. We must be quick about it. Oh, and make sure the phone app remains on and is secure in your pocket."

Michelle adjusted the phone and then reached and clasped Tippy's hands. Tippy had moved to a crouching position to give himself more leverage.

"On three. One, two, three!"

Tippy pulled with all his strength, Michelle pushing with her legs against the edge of the alcove. With their combined strength she popped through the opening, over the edge of the pit, and on to Tippy who had collapsed backwards. Before they could move, they heard a screeching sound and the lift collapsed into the pit. If Michelle had not come out on the first try, she would have shared the fate of Bryan.

She looked Tippy in the eyes and then gave him a huge, wet kiss on the lips.

"Yuck. Bob kisses better than you do."

Michelle punched his arm but was laughing as she rolled off him.

They looked where the lift had collapsed. Sure enough, if she had not been able to get out on that try it would have been almost impossible to move the lift again, and it completely blocked the alcove now.

Then she saw Bryan's body and started crying. Tippy gave her a big hug.

"There, there now. Let it all out."

Instead, Michelle pushed him away and got to her feet.

"No, now is not the time to mourn. I will cry for him later. We have to get back to the others."

"That's not so easy. Between here and the house are a couple of hungry cougars, as well as a herd of possessed deer and some possessed foxes. Also, we can't get into the house and the rest of our group can't get out."

"So, what now then."

"Give me your talkie. I want to let Bob know we're okay, and then see if they have any ideas yet."

Michelle handed Tippy the radio.

"Bob, can you hear me?"

"Tippy!" Bob yelled back through the talkie. "Glad you're okay partner. How about Michelle?"

"We're both fine, other than some cuts and bruises. Had a close call with a couple of cougars …"

"I told you to watch out for those when you go to the bar."

"Very funny—not. These two were huge man-eaters."

"So were those two we met that time in Boston."

This time Tippy couldn't stop the laughter from coming out.

"The look on their faces when they found out we were gay was priceless, but enough of the jokes. We have to figure out how to get back to the house. Is everyone there still okay?"

"I wish I could say. They left in two groups of three. I'm staying near the equipment. We lost Matt though, and now Sir Arthur has disappeared."

Bob proceeded to fill them in on the diary, and why the others had gone out searching.

"Shit, this just keeps getting worse. So, they're trying to find the resting place of the spirit commander. What should we do?"

"You have to figure a way to get out of there without being attacked by the animals. I was going through the diary again and I might be able to figure out the location of the resting spot with your help."

"How?"

"Triangulation. Peter said in his diary, and I quote, 'At various places surrounding the property are hidden pure quartz crystals. They are positioned so that all psychic energy points inwards, towards my sanctuary, focusing all the power to me.' If you can find where those crystals are, we should be able to follow them back to where his lair is. I wish the rest of the group had stayed here longer. They might not have had to go searching if they knew this."

"They still might have. Knowing where his lair is still might not tell us how to get into it. Maybe they'll find the access route."

"Possibly. Although I wish at least Blaze was with me. Being psychic she might know how many crystals Peter would have needed."

"You keep doing research. Michelle and I will see if we can find something here to arm ourselves with. Should be something in this garage we can use. Then we'll go searching for the crystals."

"Be careful Tippy. You know that I love you and want you back."

"Love you too. Will contact you when we can. Out."

* * *

"Blaze, when we were last in the chapel, I remember something that struck me as odd at the time. Matt was able to distract the ghost of the movie director to the point that it came inside the range of our

EMF emitter, although briefly, since the emitter shut off not long after. How was it able to do that when none of the other presences could?"

"I think it was because Matt goaded it. He kept making accusations, and the ghost got angrier and angrier. I guess at one point its anger overcame its fear or pain or whatever the emitter causes."

"So that would mean that maybe other spirits could also get around our emitters," said Jackson.

"Possibly, yes," replied Blaze. "Though I think the key is emotions. Not the emotions of Peter, but of the spirit he's trying to control. I'm wondering if it's possible that when a spirit gets personally emotional it causes Peter to lose control of it."

"Or maybe the emitter blocks Peter's control of the spirits, so he won't let them get in range," said Ron.

"Either way, I think we should avoid making any of the spirits angry," said Jackson.

"I concur," said Ron.

They arrived at the chapel. Everything was calm outside the door. Although the hall still had a spooky atmosphere, there was no evidence of anything untoward.

"What do you sense, Blaze?" asked Ron.

"Not much of anything. I feel presences, but oddly nothing from inside the chapel. It's like our disturbance before caused most of the spirits to leave."

"Can you two handle this? I've seen the aftermath of an attack in this place, so I'm somewhat immune to its affects. You two, not so much—and add in that the victim this time is someone you know."

"Let's just get this done with," replied Jackson. Blaze nodded in agreement.

With Jackson operating the video camera, Ron pushed the door open.

The daylight was getting dimmer so the light from the chapel windows was not illuminating much of the room. Ron found the light switch. Although the lights were not overly bright, they were sufficient to show what was before them.

Lying on the ground near the altar was Matt's body. It had been partially dismembered, like someone had started cutting him up but had been interrupted.

Standing near the body of Matt was the spirit of William Desmond Taylor. Although his form was clear it was also translucent and fading. "I would not let them desecrate his body any more than they already had. It is my fault he is dead, so I would not allow the indignities they were trying to perform. His accusations were false, but in causing me to anger as he did, he also allowed me to escape my imprisonment. I will guard his body as long as I can, but I will not allow myself to be imprisoned again."

"Can you help us destroy Peter?" asked Blaze.

"I can do no more than I have."

"Do you know where his body is?" asked Ron.

The spirit looked at him. "I know you. You have been here many times before. He laughs every time you come here, but now he just thirsts for blood. You will become another victim soon. I can't help you any further, except to say there is no route to his body in this room, but there is a means here to destroy it, should you find his body."

With that the spirit faded away.

"What do you think he meant by that?" asked Jackson.

"It means our search must focus not on a way to find Peter's body, but on a way to destroy it," replied Ron.

"It is staring us right in the face," said Blaze. The two men followed her gaze.

"That's the cross that James Neighbors mentioned in his letter," Jackson almost whispered, afraid of alerting Peter's spirit army.

"More than just that," said Blaze, as they made their way to the altar. She pointed to a small bottle of liquid under the cross.

"Is that holy water?" asked Jackson.

"Better than that. We can use the cross to make holy water, but in the jar is holy oil, used to consecrate people on Easter Sunday. And you know what oil does."

"It burns," answered Ron.

"Exactly. Jackson, you grab the cross, I'll take the oil and the matches and candles on the other altar."

She reached for the candles and then hissed and pulled her hand back.

"These have been consecrated using an evil ritual. They won't help us. I was hoping we could use them to make sure the fire gets good and hot. But Peter will probably be able to control them."

"Not to worry. We have some candles with our equipment. You remember we always have some available for atmosphere for our shows. We can use the cross to bless them or something."

"Yes, that would work. I forgot about that."

"Is everything about your show fake?" asked Ron.

"Mostly yes," replied Jackson, whose honesty surprised Ron. "Not out of choice. Almost every house we went to that was supposedly haunted didn't really have any ghosts. We needed the effects to keep the show going. But *we* are not fake. We *do* believe in what we're doing and were waiting for the day when we had a real encounter."

"And now that you've had one, what do you think?"

"I'm thinking that if I had known it would be like this, I would have stuck to unhaunted houses and fake effects."

Ron laughed. "Let's get this stuff back to the staging area before something happens."

* * *

John led the way with determination. He would not let fear rule him now. For once in all his investigations he knew there were ghosts here. He tempered his fear with excitement. Yet he felt some trepidation when he thought of his friend Harry Worth. Would they find him when they got to the third floor? If so, what condition would he be in?

Melissa followed right behind as they mounted the stairs, making sure the three of them were close enough together to be protected by the emitter. At this moment she was more afraid of seeing another body, like Jackson's in the theatre, than of something happening to her.

Coming last Skip gripped the tools he'd brought so tightly his hands were red. He'd been on a few investigations with John but had always thought it was a lark. He never expected to come across a ghost any more than he expected to bump into Bigfoot while shopping at Walmart.

When they reached the third-floor landing, John first took a quick look into the observatory. That was the last place they had seen Harry. The room was empty. He turned and headed to the other end of the landing. The door there was the same as before. A handle that didn't turn and no other visible locks. He tried to push on it, but it didn't budge.

"Okay, Skip, work some magic for me."

"I do wish Blaze was with us. She might be able to sense what's on the other side of the door," said Melissa.

"Is it true that you worked with Blaze and thought she was a fake the entire time?"

Melissa laughed. "Funny thing, huh? She would go through the house, waving her arms and muttering for the ghosts to be respectful, and we would respect them, and I would be laughing along with Michelle and making faces and mocking gestures. Not once did I think she was the real thing. But I look back now and remember times when there was a bit of fear in the air, and she would go through, and it would feel okay after that. I always chalked it up to her being comic relief. What about you, though? You're the skeptic and yet you accepted her abilities from the get-go."

"I have always believed in psychic abilities. I have never believed in ghosts. At least not as they've been projected to be by most literature or film. If anything, I thought they were just what people believed were left behind, the feelings, the emotions, etc., or maybe even thoughts sent out by psychics, like telepathy, to fool people, but nothing physical, or visible in any way. This house has taught you about psychics. It's taught me about ghosts."

"Nice philosophical chat," said Skip, who had been examining the door while they talked. "But we need to concentrate here, now. John, give me a hand. I think I found the right pressure point. I need you to push on the metal bar, as I have it, while I work with the screwdriver here. Get a good grip."

John took a position standing over Skip, legs apart, both hands solidly gripping the metal bar. Skip, on his knees, had the screwdriver pushed partway into the door frame. "Okay, and push!"

As John pushed on the bar, Skip pushed on the screwdriver. Suddenly the screwdriver went fully into the frame next to the door handle. With John pushing on the metal bar the door popped open.

"Well done, Skip."

Skip stood up, and holding the screwdriver in front of him as a weapon, advanced into the room. The light was fading outdoors as the sun was beginning to set, so Skip reached into his pocket for his cell phone, wanting to use the flashlight app.

"Not necessary," said John from behind him as he reached to the right of the door and flipped the light switch.

When the light came on Melissa screamed.

The room was almost as spacious as the observatory, but unlike the observatory, it was crowded with equipment—not exercise equipment.

It wasn't the devices that made Melissa scream. It was that most of them were covered in blood.

John grabbed her and pulled her to him, smothering her cries. "Shhh. Don't look. Skip and I will do the search."

She pulled away.

"No, we're all in this together. We must all pull our weight. I will not be thought of like Sir Arthur. Also, this room is kind of large, and we only have a guaranteed radius of about ten feet with the emitter. We need to stay close. Besides someone has to document this room," she said, lifting the camera. "I'll shoot if either of you can describe what all this stuff is. I recognize the stocks and the rack, and I think that's an iron maiden," she said, scanning the macabre scene, "but that's about it."

"I guess I can do it," said John. "One of the *benefits* of so much research," he added with a twitch of his brows. He pointed at a nearby device. "That's a Judas chair—the suspended victim's orifice is slowly impaled on and stretched by the pyramidal tip of the seat. And beside it is a brazen bull. The bronze statue is hollow inside. A person would be locked in it and then a fire was lit underneath, slowly roasting the person to death."

He stopped to see how Melissa was doing, but she just motioned with her hand for him to keep going. He ran his fingers through his hair and looked around. "That triangular board is a Spanish donkey. A person is forced to straddle it, putting their full weight right on the crotch. Weights are then added to their feet until it splits them up the middle. And on the table here," he said, pointing out individual items, "a thumbscrew, a Spanish boot, the pear of anguish, a breast ripper. Various knives, as you can see."

Skip let out a soft whistle. "Most of the blood is old, but some looks more recent," he said. "You don't think—?"

"Unfortunately, I do," replied John.

Melissa looked at them and then it hit her what they were talking about. Her eyes went wide as she scanned the room. "Oh my God! Over there!" She pointed to the iron maiden.

Now looking more closely, they could see blood still dripping from the sarcophagus-like iron case. They stuck together as they made their way over to it. When John undid the clasps on the side and pulled it open—out fell the body of Harry Worth.

This time Skip screamed.

John got down on his knees and lifted Harry's head. He could see the pain and horror Harry had gone through written on his face. Feeling for a pulse he found none. In a way he was glad. Given the condition the body was in, there would have been nothing they could do for him.

John almost screamed himself when Harry's arm raised up and pointed to a wall behind the table holding the smaller pieces of torture equipment. Harry was clearly dead, but there was his arm in the air. It stayed there for a few seconds, then dropped back down.

John looked again in the face of his friend but saw no other signs of movement. He lowered Harry's head to the ground and stood up.

"What just happened?" asked Skip in a quavering voice.

"You tell us," Melissa shot at him. "You're the tech guy who built the emitter."

John held up his hand to calm them. "I don't think Peter has as full control of all the spirits like he thinks. Especially when one is close to an emitter. Harry was trying to tell us something."

He headed towards the table that Harry had pointed at, the other two following. Behind the table he could see an area where dust had been disturbed. "Give me your screwdriver."

Skip handed it over and John bent down near the dust disturbance. He drove the screwdriver through the wall, then picked up the metal bar and rammed it through the hole he had made, twisted it, and pulled. A section of the wall came out, revealing a small tunnel.

"Too small for a person to fit through," commented Skip.

"Maybe not for Peter, or whatever he has become," said Melissa.

"But if Peter is a spirit, why would he need an access tunnel at all? Couldn't he just pass through walls?"

"His spirit, yes, his trophies, no," replied John.

"Trophies?"

Melissa grasped what John meant first. "Oh, that's just sick!"

John pulled out his phone, made some adjustments, and dropped it down the tunnel. They heard if slide for quite a way before they could no longer hear it.

"What did you do that for?" asked Skip.

"I set off the GPS recover app I have on my phone. Even without Wi-Fi I should be able to track it with my laptop once we get back to the meeting area."

"That's brilliant," cried Melissa.

John shrugged. "Time to head back. There's nothing we can do here now. Harry has helped us, but he'll understand that we can't take him with us without putting ourselves in more danger."

* * *

Melissa's comment weighed on Sir Arthur. He knew she was right. He also knew that he had to do something to make it better. As soon as the others had left, and Bob was distracted, he grabbed Melissa's phone, turned on the app, and headed to the kitchen.

It was getting darker outside even though sunset was still some time away, and what little light there was did not reach the kitchen. He found a light switch and turned it on, but that only lit up one small section of the room. He could have crossed to the other side, where he saw a row of switches, but decided to forego them. The kitchen lights would not help in the wine cellar. Regretting not giving into popular demand and buying a smart phone he started looking in the drawers for a flashlight. He was afraid to use the light on Melissa's phone as he did not want to waste what power was left, saving it for the app that was protecting him. Finally in a lower cupboard he found a small kerosene lantern and some matches. Shaking it for fuel he discovered it was over half full. He adjusted the wick and lit it. Fortunately, it had been well maintained and lit with ease.

He made his way to the wine cellar door. Even alone he was able to push the refrigerator away from the door enough to be able to open it that is. He had no idea if them pushing it there in the first place had made any difference. He put his ear to the door but could not hear anything. *You fool,* he thought. *The door is like a refrigerator door. Even if she was right on the other side, I would not hear anything.*

Since he was wearing a dress shirt with pocket, he placed the phone in the pocket, gripped the lit lamp in his right hand and grabbed the door handle with his left. Turning the handle, he quickly pulled the door open and shoved the lantern in front of him. Jane was not standing there waiting for him. He cautiously made his way down the stairs. The lights were on, but remembering what happened the last time he was there he was unwilling to let go of the lantern.

Once he reached the bottom, he slowly made his way down the center corridor, stopping at each wine alcove and looked in, hoping to see Jane. He was halfway down when he heard the noise of a wine bottle dropping.

"I hope that was a cheap bottle you knocked over, Jane." He was angling for some response so he could pinpoint where she was. Still nothing.

He was almost three quarters of the way to the end of the cellar when he heard a groan. Then he saw Jane's foot sticking out from the second to last set of wine racks. Looking around to make sure there was nothing nearby ready to jump out at him, he went over to Jane. Her leg started moving. He finally reached the point where he was able to see her entire body. She was sprawled out on the floor, a broken bottle of wine beside her. She had blood on her hands, blouse, and shorts, as well as her legs. He kneeled beside her and touched her face. She opened her eyes and stared at him. Her eyes were no longer red.

She appeared dazed and did not seem to recognize him for a moment. He checked her over for any signs of major injuries. Other than some cuts on her hands and legs she looked fine. Her vision cleared and she gasped as she saw Sir Arthur.

"What happened. And where did you get a lantern from."

"What is the last thing you remember?"

"We were having a glass of wine, and then the lights went out. I kind of fell over and I guess I must have banged my head and passed out."

"We don't have enough time for me to tell you everything. Can you sit up?"

She was able to get to a sitting position, but was too dizzy to stand right away.

"We have to get out of here, but first you need to get your strength back. Whatever you do, don't try to open yourself up."

"What, now you are a believer?"

"After what I have seen today, absolutely."

"So why should I not open myself up. Maybe it will help."

"Because until a few minutes ago you were Josef Mengele."

She stared at him in disbelief.

"You have been down here for a couple of hours. A lot has happened, mostly bad, some good. See this?"

He pulled Melissa's phone out of his pocket, holding it tightly.

"The tech gurus have an app on it that emits an EMF field that seems to counter that of the spirits. I think it was what drove Mengele's spirit from your body. The group has also found the diary of Peter Vanderbilt and it explains what is going on here. They are searching for his resting place which is somewhere on these grounds. We need to destroy his body to stop what is happening. That's the brief news. But I don't think it is safe to stay here. We need to join the others. Do you think you can stand now?"

He helped Jane to her feet, although she was still shaky and she leaned on him as they headed back towards the staircase. Suddenly a wine bottle flew at them, hitting Sir Arthur in the back. He turned around to see a shadowy shape near the back wall. From there another wine bottle flew at them, this time just missing Jane. Sir

Arthur realized they would never make it to the stairs. He pulled the phone out of his pocket and shoved it into Jane's hand.

"Go. Whatever you do, don't let go of this phone. It is the only thing preventing him from taking possession of you again."

"What about you?"

"I have an appointment with the doctor. Now go."

He let go of her and gave her a little push. She managed to keep her balance by grabbing one of the wine shelves with her free hand. Her legs were a little steadier and she was able to keep moving forward.

"Hey doctor. I hear that you like little boys. How about a big boy like me. Think you can handle me?"

Jane heard Sir Arthur mocking Josef Mengele as he made his way towards the back of the room. More wine bottles flew, but none at her. As her strength returned, she was able to quicken her pace, soon reaching the staircase. She looked back. Sir Arthur was almost at the back wall now, but was on his knees. He was bleeding from his scalp, which must have been hit by one of the wine bottles. The dark shadow was hovering over him. He looked towards Jane and mouthed "*Run!*"

In a last act, as the shadow almost encompassed him, Sir Arthur threw the lantern. It flew through the shadow, smashed against the far wall and lit one of the wine shelves on fire. The shadow roared. That was all the incentive Jane needed. She found a last burst of energy, ran up the stairs and through the door, and pushed it closed behind her.

The last thing she heard was Sir Arthur's screams.

* * *

Jane stumbled out of the kitchen and into the hallway leading to the entrance area. She heard footsteps coming, but her strength had left her and she couldn't run, no matter what the danger. She saw shadows coming and was about to scream when she recognized the figures of Blaze, Ron, and Jackson. Jackson had a large cross in his hand, and Blaze was holding a small bottle.

Jackson was the first to see her.

"It's Josef Mengele!" he shouted. "We need to run back to the entrance. Our emitter is no longer working."

"No," replied Blaze. "It is Jane again. I can't sense anything influencing her."

Jackson calmed down. But it was Ron who went to Jane and held her arm.

"How did you escape his influence" asked Blaze.

Jane showed them the phone in her hand.

"Sir Arthur brought it to me. But I think he is dead now. He told me to run. The last thing I heard was him screaming." She put her head on Ron's chest and cried. He held her for a moment. Then pushed her back a little and looked into her eyes.

"There will be time for crying later. Now we must join the others and plan how we are going to destroy the monster that made all this happen."

Jane was able to stop her tears and nodded. She held onto Ron's arm though. As the four of them were making their way back they heard more steps coming. Running down the staircase were John, Melissa, and Skip. They met up at the foot of the staircase.

"Success?" asked Jackson of the other group.

"Yes and no."

"Us too," replied Ron. "Let's join Bob and share experiences."

It was only then that they saw Jane with the other group. Before they could ask how she got there Blaze signaled for them to meet up with Bob. They could share everything there. Yet as they filed into the entrance hall Bob rushed up to them as he was bursting to tell them the good news, maybe the first real good news they had received since entering this godforsaken mansion.

"Tippy and Michelle are okay," he cried. "He got to her in time and got her out of that room." In a few words he described the walkie-talkie conversation and explained about their idea for finding the crystals. "But I don't know how they're going to do it," he said "They're still trapped in the garage because of some cougars."

"Cougars?" asked John, looking as confused as he sounded.

"Lets sit and discuss this in the entrance and as close to the ghost machine as possible," said John. "We can fill everyone in."

CHAPTER ELEVEN

THE PLAN

The eight of them sat on the floor, passing around a couple of water bottles they had pulled out of one of their coolers. Another cooler held beer, still cold, although most of the ice had melted, but they all decided to forego alcohol, wanting to keep their heads as clear as possible. They had handed the cameras to Bob on their arrival and he had downloaded the videos.

First, they started filling in Jane on all that had passed while she was busy being possessed. They finished by telling her about the letter on James Neighbors' body.

"But why are the animals acting so strange?" she asked.

"It looks like Peter can control the animals, too," said Bob

"No, he can't control the animals," explained Blaze. "He controls the spirits that possess the animals."

"That explains why the deer that had treed Tippy left when he built his emitter," said Bob.

"It also explains why Josef fucking Mengele left me when Sir Arthur came down to the cellar," added Jane.

"Speaking of which, do you remember any of the time you were possessed?" asked Blaze.

"Nothing. As I told Sir Arthur when he rescued me, the last thing I remembered was sitting on the floor having a glass of wine when the lights went out. I think I fell over or something, maybe banged my head. Next thing I know Sir Arthur is touching my face and I'm lying on the floor a number of feet from where we had been sitting, with blood on my hands and legs."

"He had more guts than I gave him credit for," said Ron.

"There's a lot about him that no one knew," said Jane. "He told me about himself while we were drinking the wine. In a way he was like Blaze. Hiding himself behind a false persona." She paused for a moment. "Anyway, please continue filling me in. Sir Arthur told me you'd found Peter Vanderbilt's diary and he also said something about a search."

John quickly described Michelle finding the bodies in that small room and the letter on James Neighbors' body. "This diary gave us a lot of information," he said, going on to provide her with a rundown of what it contained.

After that, he brought the other group up to speed on the horrors they'd found in the third-floor room, finding the passageway and deploying his phone, and finally ending with the fate of poor Harry." John handed the diary to Jane. She glanced through it as the two search groups told their experiences. With the stories they told, the tension and fear in the room had notched up several degrees.

"I guess we all figured he was probably dead," said Jackson, speaking into the stunned silence. "But it's awful to hear the details—and we're so sorry for your loss."

Murmurs of shock and grief circulated among the group before Jackson continued. "Our experience in the chapel was also productive," he said, laying out the cross and oil they'd retrieved as he outlined what they had seen and heard.

"Well, I think this means we're making progress," John said. "And I think it's time for next steps." He got up and grabbed his laptop, retook his seat, and opened it up. He punched in a couple of commands. "Bingo! The GPS app is working." He watched the screen for a few moments in silence. "But this just doesn't make sense."

Turning the screen so the others could see, he pushed replay. They followed the track of the phone sliding down from the third floor. It continued down to the second floor, then to the first and came to a stop halfway between the basement and the first floor. They couldn't triangulate it exactly, but it appeared to be just outside the house.

"What about those crystals you mentioned, Bob. Do you really think you could use them to figure out a more exact location, if Tippy and Michelle could find them?" asked Jackson.

"That will depend on how many there are and if they can find enough of them. Also, I will need to have some kind of map of the property so we can place them."

This time it was Melissa who got up. She walked over to the table where they had left the house plans and picked up one of the pages from the roll.

"Peter said in his letter that the plans omitted parts, so I am not sure if those will help," said Ron.

"Not the house plans, but this might." She handed the page to John.

"Property survey plan! Brilliant Melissa."

John rolled it out in front of them, objects being pulled from pockets to place on the corners, keeping it unrolled.

"How many points would you need?" asked Ron.

"Probably four, depending on where they are, along with a base point."

"Blaze, would you know how many crystals Peter was likely to have placed to get the psychic energy to do what he wanted it to do?" asked John.

It was Jane who answered. "Ideally he would have used seven, to represent the seven senses."

"Okay, I have heard of a sixth sense, but seven?" the look of puzzlement unusual for the professor's face.

"The five that everyone knows of course are touch, sight, hearing, smell, and taste. The sixth sense, which few know about, let alone understand, is proprioception. It refers to how your brain understands where your body is in space. Proprioception includes the sense of movement and position of our limbs and muscles. For example, proprioception enables a person to touch their finger to the tip of their nose, even with their eyes closed. It enables a person to climb steps without looking at each one. People with poor proprioception may be clumsy and uncoordinated. What people commonly refer to as the sixth sense is really the seventh sense, and that is psychic ability."

Blaze nodded at Jane, although she was surprised at the depth of Jane's knowledge.

"So we need Tippy and Michelle to find at least four of these," said Jackson.

"And they need to be spaced apart. Ideally one on each side of the property," replied Bob.

"Kind of like the four points of a compass," added Skip.

"Once we have that we will use the point of John's GPS signal as the base. It should give us the exact location," finished Bob.

"Then we will just have to figure out how to get there," said Jackson.

"One thing at a time," replied Ron.

"Okay, we have a plan. Let's get going," said John.

"It's getting dark out. Maybe we should wait until morning. They may have a hard time seeing out there," piped up Melissa.

"We might not have until morning," pointed out Blaze. "We don't know how long this machine will keep working, nor if Peter can find a way around our emitters. Besides if they use a bright enough flashlight, it might be easier to find the crystals. They should glisten like diamonds when they shine the light on them."

"But do they have a flashlight with them?" asked John.

Bob was practically beaming.

"Better than that. They have an APL."

"What's that?" asked Jane.

Bob walked to the equipment table and picked up a piece of equipment. "All-purpose Light. Way brighter than any flashlight, and also works in UV so they can practically see in the dark."

Just then the walkie-talkie went off, causing all of them to jump.

"Hey Bob, any news for us?" Tippy's voice came through loud and clear.

"Partner you're going to give Blaze a run for her job. We were just talking about you."

"Good stuff I hope."

"Always. Were you able to equip yourselves?"

"Yep. Lots of stuff in a garage like this. Tire irons, cordless tools like a drill used for undoing bolts, which also makes a lot of noise to scare away the animals, and more. We even found a phone charger and have been charging Michelle's phone so it's almost at full charge. Funny thing though we found a bunch of batteries just lying around. Michelle says that they had gone missing from Bryans backpack. I was able to boost the charge to my home-made emitter. Only thing we are missing is a flashlight. Other than that, we're ready to go."

"Oh, but you do have one. There's an APL in Bryan's backpack."

"I forgot about that!" they heard Michelle exclaim in the background as Tippy was about to respond.

"So, what's the plan, partner?"

Bob quickly filled them in on what the group had been doing.

"So, if you can find at least four of the seven crystals at equidistant points, we should be able to locate Peter. At each point you must let us know exactly where you are in relation to the house."

"Got it. Michelle and I will head out now. Any idea on the placement of the crystals? Like will they be at ground level, or high up?"

Blaze responded this time. "I would say between eight and twenty feet off the ground depending on the slope."

Bob relayed that to Tippy.

"It should be dark enough now for the crystals to shine when we put a light to them. We'll use the UV setting first to check for heat signatures. See what creatures are waiting for us. Unless it's an emergency don't try and call us on the talkie. It might attract unwelcome company."

"Got it partner. Good luck. Out."

* * *

"What now?" asked Jane.

"Come with me over there," replied Blaze. "Let's see if I can help you to resist possession again." They moved away from the rest of the group, but still well within the range of the emitter. John had gotten up to turn on more lights, as dusk was taking hold.

"To know what you will need, I must know what type of training you have had until now."

"The parapsychologist I worked with started me off with basic steps. First, she had me practicing Psychometry. Simple objects at first. Things that she knew something about so she would know if I was just making stuff up, or actually getting a reading. A pair of glasses, a pen and so on. It took some time but soon I could get feelings on every object I touched. As I told you before my ability comes in colors. So, each time I saw a color I would tell her, and she would confirm if the color matched what she knew about the person. At first, I could only sense when people were really bad or really good. With practice though I was able to get a larger range, and in some cases could even touch a little on the emotions the person was feeling when they had last handled the object, although it had to be an intense emotion, like sadness or anger."

Blaze nodded in understanding. "Go on."

"From there she made it more difficult, emotionally, when she took me to antique stores. Some of the objects I touched there gave me really intense readings." Jane shuddered at the memory. "While doing this she also had me practice meditation and breathing. This helped me calm my mind and body. She set up a regular meditation schedule. I found that after meditating it made it easier to control myself when I read antique objects."

Jane took a sip of water from the bottle she'd pulled from a cooler provided for the crew. "Next came visualization techniques. Especially after meditating I could close my eyes and allow my senses to bring me images. When I felt drawn to a particular image, I would try to visualize it with as much detail as possible. I would describe this to her and this often was an object she had nearby, but which would not have been visible to me. The more I practiced the better I got."

"I'm sure you did," said Blaze, with an encouraging smile.

"Once I became proficient," Jane continued, "she had me do the same thing with people but looking for their auras. That's how I was finally able to refine my ability and see auras in almost everyone, no matter how strong or neutral. From there she helped me train my mind to ignore the auras when I didn't want to see them. I think, though, that it is something I really needed to practice more. Like when I was in the pool room earlier and that blackness overcame me. I'm afraid of what might have happened then if you hadn't come in."

"I think you know what would have happened," Blaze said, placing a comforting hand on Jane's shoulder, "because it *is* what had happened to you in the wine cellar. So, what else did she show you."

"The concept of the third eye. I would close my eyes and concentrate on the center of my forehead, visualizing a third eye there. I would think about opening and closing it. After a while she would think thoughts and I would use the third eye to try and catch the message she was sending me. It took time but eventually I was able to understand the message she was sending. Not like telepathy, but more like she was speaking to me in a foreign language, and I was able to decipher the language."

"Uh-huh …"

"She also had me keep a sleep journal by my bed. Every time I had a dream, I had to write it down immediately so I would not forget it. With that she had me focus on my dreams and I was able to control them, to some extent."

"Control them?"

"Yeah. I could follow along as the dream started, and then change the direction I was going in, or get myself out of a scary situation I found myself in. I remember one particular dream. I was in a dungeon and was about to be tortured by a witch. As she approached me, I kept telling myself, this is only a dream. I am not really here. Next thing I know I'm standing outside that same building, safe from the witch."

"This might help," said Blaze, her tone thoughtful. "You were actually dream walking. It's a difficult ability to learn but using the basics I think I can help you avoid being possessed again."

"Really?"

"Yes. I want you to go into your usual meditative state."

Jane closed her eyes. After a few seconds her breathing slowed and she felt herself slipping into her meditative zone. She could still hear Blaze's voice but from a distance.

"Now using the concept of the third eye, and focusing on what you did in your dreams I want you to push your senses outward. Do not go beyond the influence of the emitter. Tell me what you sense."

As if in a dream Jane was able to see what was around her, even with her eyes still closed. Her body did not move, but she felt herself standing up, and walking out of the room.

"Do not fear. I am right beside you. Stay close and it will be all right."

She could feel Blaze beside her as she "walked" Blaze's hand in hers, yet knew they were still sitting on the floor. They passed the emitter and went into the corridor. Going further they came to a point near the theatre.

"What do you sense now?"

"Blackness. The theatre is shrouded in a blackness I can't penetrate."

"Good. Now I want you to push against the blackness, like you would if you were trying to escape an evil place in your dream. Not too far and not too hard. A little at a time."

Jane followed her instructions.

"It is pushing back. Oh God, make it stop!"

"No Jane. It is you who can make it stop. Concentrate. Use that same sense to build a wall around yourself. Visualize a concrete wall that is impenetrable. Nothing can enter unless you want it too."

"I can't! It's getting closer!" she cried, her breath coming in short gasps.

"Yes, you can Jane." Blaze's voice was gentle but firm. "Think about all that is good. Think about good auras. Use those auras as part of your wall. A wall that no dark presence can enter."

Using every bit of her willpower Jane worked on visualizing a concrete wall full of white auras. The more she put her will in to it the stronger it got. Then she pushed her wall forward, against the darkness, and was able to push the darkness away. With a sense of relief, she watched the blackness falter and then dissipate.

She opened her eyes and saw Blaze beaming at her.

"Well done! You are stronger than you realized, aren't you."

Jane nodded.

"To be honest you are stronger than I thought you were. In time you can learn to harness that strength in ways you cannot imagine."

"I just hope we survive this house and get that chance."

At Jane's words, Blaze shivered as she had a case of precognition, something she had never had the ability to do before.

"Jane, when this is over, and I promise you it will end, you must seek out Allie Montore. She lives in Los Angeles and should be easy to find. She can help you with this. Just tell her I sent you."

Jane drew her brows together in confusion. "Why can't you teach me?"

Blaze looked her in the eyes.

"Because I will not survive this house."

* * *

Tippy pulled the APL out of Bryan's backpack. Testing it he saw that each setting was working as it should. He then pulled out the remaining contents and laid them out in front of them.

"So, we have an EV recorder—not sure how that will help—a hand-held video camera, a laser sensor pack, an EMF, and the APL. That's it for the equipment but he also put this lunch pack in."

Opening it up Tippy pulled out a couple of sandwiches and two cans of beer, although they were somewhat warm by then, along with two bottles of water. Opening one of the beers he handed it to Michelle and opened the other.

"Liquid courage," he said before draining the can. Michelle followed suit. They then ate the sandwiches and drank some water.

While eating Tippy examined the equipment. The laser grid was in working order, other than one of the laser posts missing batteries. Fortunately, Bryan had thought to add some plastic stakes that could be clipped on to the emitters. He had probably planned to set up a couple of them outside the garage. There were only five stakes, so they would have to hope to find some places to set them up without the stakes. There were also some long plastic ties they could use. He set up the system to be functional, turning on the junction box and putting it back in the backpack, then starting up the laser posts. These he also put in the backpack, but in a way that would allow for them to be easily removed.

"We'll set these up behind us as we go. It might give us a heads up that something is following us."

"Good thinking!"

He then handed the camera to Michelle.

"You want me to film our trip?"

"I will be carrying the APL. If you hear a noise nearby, you can use the video cam to shine a light on it."

He picked up the EMF, looked at it twice, then put it in the backpack without turning it on.

"I don't think this will work since our emitters will effectively block it from picking anything else up, but we'll bring it just in case we find another use for it."

The last piece of equipment was the EV recorder. Twice Tippy put it aside, but finally he turned it on and put it in one of his pockets.

"You never know. Maybe one of the spirits will want to give us a message."

Finally, they arranged the "weapons" they had selected from the garage. Each of them would carry a tire iron. Both had stuffed screw drivers in their pockets to use for stabbing. A tire drill went in the backpack, not so much to use as a weapon, but to make noise to scare off unpossessed animals. They also put a couple of extra tire irons in the backpack. With his free hand Tippy would carry the APL. Michelle would have a heavy wrench in her other hand, with the camera on a cord around her neck.

Tippy pulled the backpack over his shoulders, and they were heading towards the door when they heard the revving of a car.

"Have the emitters stopped working," asked Michelle, the panic evident in her trembling voice.

Tippy pulled his out of his pocket.

"Working fine. We must be past the range of the emitter for where the car ghost is."

"Phew!"

Weapons firmly gripped, Tippy opened the door and faced what was there. Nothing.

They cautiously exited the building.

It was significantly darker than when Tippy had entered. Although the sun had not completely set, it was barely visible on the horizon, and most of the property was now in deep shadow. Tippy engaged the APL in infrared mode and scanned around but found no immediate heat signatures.

"Kind of strange that there are no animals around now," said Tippy, keeping his voice just above a whisper. "You would think that Peter would have his 'army' out in force to stop us."

"Maybe they're planning an ambush somewhere. It is getting dark, and animals see better in the dark than we do," replied Michelle.

"True, but the advantage is that this level of light should make it easier to find the crystals. If I remember correctly from the notes Jackson had us read about the property, the garage is near the eastern edge, the property limits probably about another two hundred yards from here. I'm going to switch the APL to light mode and scan the trees from there. Every few feet I will switch it back to infrared mode to check for animals."

"Okay."

"I'll go about another hundred yards. I can't see him having placed the crystals too far from his home. At that point I'll turn left and we will circle the property in a counter clockwise direction. I think I can picture it enough to make sure we stay on the property. Once we turn though, I want you to take one of the laser posts out of the backpack and set it up."

"Got it," said Michelle, her voice sounding anything but confident.

They reached the point where Tippy planned on turning. Still nothing in the infrared, so he switched it to light mode and shone it into the trees. The light cast a brightness that lit everything he shone it at up to a good hundred yards. Nothing shone back.

He switched the APL back to infrared.

"Okay, set up one of the laser posts."

Michelle took one out and set it up. With nothing to tie it to she had to use one of the stakes.

"This is real guesswork, but from what I remember the entire property around is about a mile and a half. Walking at a normal pace I could do that in about twenty-five minutes. Since we have to stop every once in a while to check for animals and set up the posts, I figure about double that time, so just over three quarters of an hour," said Tippy.

He continued, half talking to himself as he calculated. "To figure out where to put the posts, a mile and a half is close to eight thousand feet and divide that by ten and we need to put one each eight hundred feet or so. Since the average human step is two and a half feet, that gives three hundred and twenty paces. So, we need to put a post each three hundred and twenty steps. Since we haven't got a GPS with us, we need to count it off as we go."

"Wow you are good with math!"

"Yeah, Bob says I'm a human calculator. Doing calculations like that has been easy for me since I was a kid. I also absorb useless pieces of information like the number of feet in a person's step—that seems to stick for some reason."

"Well about now I am glad it does. Lead on Mr. Calculator."

Tippy stifled a laugh. They had just positioned their second laser post—this one they could attach to a small tree, thereby saving a stake—when the APL glistened off something about eight feet up in a tree. Getting closer they could make out a crystal, inside a setting almost like a diamond ring would be, attached to a post bolted to the tree. The post was well camouflaged with foliage and would have been almost invisible without the APL. When he moved aside some of the foliage, he saw markings.

Tippy reached for the walkie-talkie. "Bob, we found one."

"Great buddy!" came the instant response. "Can you give me an idea where it is?"

"I can do better than that. This is what is marked on the pole holding the crystal."

Tippy read off a series of numbers spaced with degrees, feet, inches, and a direction.

"Map coordinates! I can use my laptop to place this at the exact place on the survey plan. He is making this easy for us."

"Don't want to get too excited yet Bob. We still have to find at least three more and at the right distances apart. And I'm willing to bet Michelle and I will have guests soon enough."

Then a beep.

"What's that," asked Bob, hearing the sound through the walkie-talkie before Tippy released the talk button.

"Our first laser post reported movement," Tippy replied, his voice tense. "We'd better get a move on. If the next crystal is too close, I'll pass it by and try to find one about two thousand feet away, more or less, if I calculated it right. Signing off for now."

Tippy turned down the volume and turned to Michelle who stood close by his side looking nervously about.

"We'll have company soon. Keep an eye out. Let's try and find the next crystal as quickly as possible."

Taking one last look behind them, and still seeing nothing, Tippy led the way. The sun had fully set, and the only natural light was provided by the rising half moon. He set the APL to infrared and scanned around. At the edge of where they had just been, he could see heat signatures. For now, whatever was following was keeping its distance, most likely because of the two emitters they had on. But how long that would last, they didn't know.

CHAPTER TWELVE

GOTCHA

"Not a word to anyone," said Blaze as she and Jane moved to rejoin the group. Jane started to protest but Blaze held her finger to her lips.

"It's okay, girl. I'm fine with it. We all have to go sometime, and I get to do it battling evil."

"Are you sure? Maybe it's just Peter planting ideas in your head?"

"I would know if it was that. No this was a genuine case of precognition. I don't see how my end will come, but I do know it will be in this house. Since I can't see how it happens there is no use trying to avoid it, as that might just put me in that place anyway. Worrying others also will not help. So, nothing to the others."

Blaze stared at Jane until she nodded yes.

"Don't worry, baby doll. This old bird will not go down without a fight."

"What were you two doing?" asked Jackson as the two psychics came and sat with the others.

"I was just showing Jane how to control her abilities. I don't think they will be able to possess her again."

Jackson looked doubtful but John looked optimistic.

"I'm glad there's someone here to teach her. We can't have her suddenly attacking us," Jackson said.

Blaze ignored the comment.

"Any news from Tippy?"

"Yes," replied Bob. "He found the first crystal. It was on a pole stuck in the ground but camouflaged by foliage, about eight feet off the ground, placed in a setting like a diamond ring. Oh, and on the post were written map coordinates. Peter is making it easy for us.

"I doubt Peter ever thought anyone would go looking for the crystals, since the only place he talks about them is in his diary," said Blaze. "Most likely he had the poles built and installed to his specifications, then added the crystals in himself. The coordinates were most likely there so he would know which crystal to place where."

"Huh?" was all that Melissa could say.

Jane jumped in.

"Crystals usually come in different shapes and sizes, especially natural ones that have not been chipped or manually shaped. He would want them as pure as possible. So, he would have the crystals measured and the poles made to the specification of each crystal. He would mark on the pole something that would tell him which crystal to put in. Since he would want to plan the spacing properly it would be less confusing to have the coordinates marked on the poles rather than some type of code."

"Makes sense," said John.

"How long will it take Tippy and Michelle to find enough of them?" asked Jane.

Bob had been writing some numbers down as they spoke.

"I'm not as good at this as Tippy but I calculated the area he has to cover and the time to search. I figure about forty-five minutes to an hour, if he doesn't come across any complications."

"Complications?" asked Melissa, and then it hit her what Bob meant. Seeing her expression Bob knew he did not need to respond. Instead, he referred back to the survey plan spread on the floor. "Now to figure out where on the plan to put the first crystal."

John retrieved his laptop once again. He put it down in the center of the survey and ran a program. Once the program was open, he turned his laptop so that the N on his screen aligned with the N on the map. He referred to his notes, adding in the numbers he had there. Then he typed in the coordinates that Tippy had given them. The screen showed where those coordinates would lie.

"Fun program I found a few months ago. It can tell where any coordinates would be in relation to your position. I just had to align it with the survey—and voila."

"Tippy said he was about a hundred yards or so away from the property line so that would put the crystal right there." Bob put an X on the survey.

"If all goes well, we should have Peter's location within the hour. Then we can start looking for him," said Jane.

"In this house I doubt all will go well," said Ron.

Then the lights went out.

* * *

"Are they still behind us?" asked Michelle, her voice trembling.

Tippy turned the APL back behind them.

"Still there, still keeping their distance."

Switching back to the regular light he shined it around at about an eight-foot height, expecting the next crystal to be at the same level.

Michelle grabbed his arm, then moved it upwards. About twenty feet up something gleamed.

"I'll have to be more careful. They are obviously not all at the same height."

They approached the crystal, trying to find how it was being held. That was when they noticed the electric pole. Near the top they saw the crystal, with the inset actually carved into the pole.

"How the hell are we going to get to it and check it's coordinates?" asked Tippy.

"Like this." Michelle handed Tippy her tire iron and wrench, pulled one of the screwdrivers out of the backpack and proceeded to shimmy the pole. Tippy watched her in amazement.

"Shine the light up here, directly on the crystal and not on my face please."

Tippy did as she asked.

"I can see part of the coordinates, but they are partially covered by the crystal inset. Let me see if I can remove it from the pole."

With one hand securely gripping the pole, and her shoes almost dug into the wood, she used the screwdriver to pry out the inset. After a moment it popped free and fell to the ground.

"I can see that the coordinates were marked here," Michelle called down, "but when he put the crystal in it damaged them too much. I can't read them."

"Okay, come on down. Let's hope we find another one soon. We are almost a quarter of the way around from where we started."

While Michelle shimmed back down, Tippy took out another laser post. By the time she reached the bottom he had managed to secure the laser post to the electric pole.

Michelle reached down and picked up the inset with the crystal still in it. "This looks kinda neat. It shimmers with only a bit of light touching it. It's faceted almost like a diamond. I think— Wait what's that?"

They heard leaves moving from where they had come. Tippy switched the APL to infrared. What he saw frightened him.

"Many shapes heading our way. Check your emitter."

Michelle pulled hers out of her pocket. Tippy noticed that although his was still working, one of the batteries was forming acid at the top, weakening the emitter.

"Why is my phone app glowing red?" asked Michelle.

"It means the app is losing power for some reason. Check your battery life."

Michelle moved the emitter app to background and checked her power.

"Down to twenty percent. When we left it was one hundred percent."

"My batteries are being drained of power as well. Looks like Peter is finding a way around out emitters."

Tippy pulled the walkie-talkie out of his pocket.

"Hey Bob, we've run into a situation."

"Us too," came the quick response. "The power in the house just went out."

"Well, the batteries in both my emitter and Michelle's phone are draining at a fast rate. We have to quicken our pace as we have heat signatures moving on us. How's the ghost machine holding up? The battery in it is much more powerful than what we have here, but who knows what Peter is capable of."

Silence for a minute and then Bob responded.

"Yeah, it is draining faster than usual. At this rate we have at most two hours before it's toast."

"Okay, Michelle and I are going to break some speed records. As fast as we can we'll call back with the coordinates. Hopefully that will give you enough time to find Peter and neutralize him."

"Good luck Tippy—and be careful."

"Will do. Back to you soon."

Putting the walkie-talkie back in his pocket, Tippy picked up the tire iron, and did one more scan with the infrared setting. Michelle had already picked up her improvised weapons.

"You'll have to keep an eye out behind us as best you can, while I look for more crystals. It's become a race. Are you ready?"

"Let's fucking do this."

With a last glance behind them, and the APL back to light and shining upwards, they ran as fast as the unseen ground would allow them.

* * *

Skip had managed to set up some lighting using portable battery light stands they had brought. With the sun having set, it only illuminated their immediate area.

Bob was checking the ghost machine.

"Anything you can do to extend it's working time?" asked Jackson.

"Although I have spare batteries, they are out in the truck. I've never needed to replace it before, so didn't think to bring one in. I've disconnected all other power drains on it, so the only thing it is using power for is the emitter. That might buy us an extra half hour."

"Any idea how he's draining the batteries?' asked John.

"It looks like he's somehow accelerating the level at which the power of the batteries work."

"So, if we disconnect anything battery operated, it won't drain them?"

"Yeah, but if we disconnect the machine, we have no protection."

"I was thinking of the portable emitters. We should take the batteries out of them until we have need of them. Also turn off the one phone that has a functional emitter app."

"Good thinking John. Melissa could you and Jane give me a hand?" asked Skip.

"What about the talkies?" asked Blaze.

"Leave only one on. We still need to listen for Tippy's calls."

While Bob worked on adjusting the ghost machine to use the minimum power, the others went around making sure all electronics requiring batteries were turned off, and to be extra safe, batteries removed.

Less than five minutes later the walkie-talkie crackled with noise.

"Bob, did you get that?" Tippy was breathing heavily.

"Barely. Repeat again."

Tippy gave them another set of coordinates.

"Got them. Turn your talkie off until you need to call again. Save the batteries as long as you can."

"Understood. Out."

Bob got down on the floor and marked the next set of coordinates on the survey.

"Skip how long do you think your lights will last?"

"Normally these babies could last for a couple of days. The way they are draining I would say four, maybe five hours tops."

"We'll be in the dark then," whimpered Melissa." Maybe we should only use some of the lights."

"We don't really have to worry about that," said Ron.

"Why not?" asked John.

"Because if we haven't located Peter by then, we will probably be dead," replied Blaze.

"Thanks for the dose of reality," muttered Skip.

"I need to take a pee," said Melissa.

"Did you have to bring that up," replied Jackson. "I've been holding it for a while but you mentioning it made it worse. It's actually starting to hurt."

"Where's the closest bathroom?" asked Bob.

"Next to the theatre," answered Ron.

"No one is going anywhere," said John. "Separating now would be the worse thing we could do."

"What if we went in threes," suggested Melissa. I could go with Jane and Blaze, then you guys could go."

"No!" exclaimed Jane. "I can feel the blackness. It is waiting just outside the emitter range."

"There are many presences there," continued Blaze. "Maybe with the portable emitters we would be safe, but I can't guarantee that."

Looking around for an idea John spotted his desk. Walking over to it, he cleared everything off it. Being a light frame portable job, he was easily able to stand it on its side, creating a screen.

"Maybe not the most hygienic of ideas, but it is well within the range of the emitter and the opposite side of the room from the theatre area. There's a waste basket there that we can all use."

"Okay then, ladies first," said Melissa making her way over to the makeshift bathroom.

She had just finished her turn, and Jane was heading there, when the walkie-talkie blurted static, followed by Tippy's voice. He was sounding more out of breath than before.

"Got your next set of coordinates." He reeled them off as Bob marked them down.

"Our visitors are closing in on us. I was able to change the batteries on my emitter, but it won't last much longer. Michelle's phone just ran out of power. The next crystal we find will have to do even if it is not quite equidistant."

"We'll make it do somehow. Once you get it find a safe place," answered Bob.

"We'll try. Out for now."

Bob went back to the survey and marked down the new coordinates.

"Do you think we have enough with this?" asked Jackson.

Using one of the metal backs of the chair like a ruler, Bob took a pencil and drew a line between the two opposite coordinates. Then lining up from the third coordinates with an imaginary fourth point, and aiming it for the base where John's cell phone had ended up, he tried to pick an exact spot.

"Not quite exact enough. We need that fourth coordinate to be sure."

John pulled out one of the plans of the house and laid it beside the survey, positioning it as best he could in relation to where the house was shown on the survey plan.

"We can narrow it down to this area though. What is that room?"

"Damn! That's the pool room," replied Ron.

"Even if we get those last coordinates, it won't help us. We can't blast through concrete. Even if we had a jackhammer, it would take days," said Skip.

"We must be missing something," countered John. "Two points. First, how would Peter have gotten out of there to get Betty, and second my phone shows it is between the basement and the first floor. If it was in the pool room, it would be sticking up somewhere in that room. Part of the floor would have to be higher, and we have seen it is not."

"Maybe those last coordinates will reveal what we're missing," said Blaze.

Everyone gathered around the survey, hoping that someone would spot something different. Minutes passed then the walkie-talkie hissed static again.

"Repeat Tippy. We can't make that out."

Again, the talkie made static noises, but no voice came through. Nothing they did could make his voice come in, even switching walkie-talkies. Then a series of static noises followed by silences between. After that nothing.

* * *

"There's another one there," hissed Michelle. Her voice revealing her panic.

"Not quite equidistant, but it will have to do. Those animals are closing in and my emitter is almost finished."

This crystal was attached to a lamp post. What a lamp post was doing there they could not figure out since there did not seem to be any way to connect it to a power source.

"I can't read it. He put these coordinates higher up for some reason."

"Can you shimmy it like you did the electric pole?"

"This is metal. No grip."

Tippy got close to the pole and took the backpack off, putting everything on the ground.

"Okay, climb up my back. It should give you just enough height to read it."

Dropping all her equipment Michelle piggybacked onto Tippy and using the pole for leverage climbed on to his shoulders. Using one hand to grip the pole to give Michelle more security, Tippy tilted the light up, doing his best not to shine it in her face. Michelle read the coordinates back to Tippy and quickly climbed back down. Just as her feet hit the ground, she heard a huge growl. Turning she saw one of the cougars standing just a few yards away. She picked up the tire iron, ready to fight to the last.

Tippy looked at his emitter just as the last battery popped. He heard the breathing of the other cougar advancing from a different direction. Taking the APL he shined it right into its face, forcing it to back away, then did the same to the cougar closing in on Michelle.

"That will only buy us a few seconds. I need to reach Bob.

Pulling out the walkie-talkie he called out.

"Mostly static."

"Keep trying."

He briefly heard Bob's voice, but when he tried to talk himself, all he got was static.

"Damn what now?" Michelle's voice had an angry edge to it.

"I have one last idea, and it had better work."

Tippy pushed the talk button in a series of short and long sequences.

"What are you doing?"

"Morse code."

"You know morse code? Does Bob?"

"Nope. Tried to teach him once but it went over his head. He couldn't grasp it. I just hope there is someone there who does."

He repeated it a few more times, then the walkie-talkie went dead.

"Now what?"

"Now we find a place to hide."

Just then a fox ran at him and bit his leg. Another jumped on to

Michelle's back, trying to bite her neck. Using the tire iron Tippy slammed it into the fox on his leg driving it to the feet of one of the cougars, then bare handed the other fox off of Michelle's back. He could hear the hooves of the deer moving in. He turned the light towards where he heard them and saw the red shining eyes staring back at him. Just then the APL went dead, it's battery out of power. He threw the light at them, slung the backpack over his shoulder and then with one hand waiving the tire iron, and the other grabbing on to Michelle's arm he ran straight at the herd.

"What …" was all that Michelle had time to say before she was pulled along.

"We have only one chance. We need to make it to those trees. Swing your tire iron like I am. I don't want to hurt the deer, but I want even less for them to hurt us."

Charging forth, they ran to meet their fate.

* * *

"We're screwed," said Melissa, the tears flowing down her face.

They all stood around, staring at the walkie-talkie in Bob's hand. All except Ron. He grabbed the pencil Bob had left on the survey and started writing on the bottom of the house plan. Blaze started to ask what he was doing but Ron just held up his hand, not wanting to lose his concentration. When he was finished, he handed the paper to Bob.

"Your final coordinates. I hope they help."

"Morse code," laughed John.

"Tippy, you're brilliant little buddy. I hope you're safe out there," said Bob.

Crouching back down to the survey, Bob marked the point of

the last set of coordinates on to the paper. Using the metal piece, he made a line between the two opposite coordinates like they had done with the other two. From the point where they crossed he drew a line to where John's cell phone had sent its last signal. He then circled the area.

"That is where he must be."

Pulling out the house plans they compared the spot.

"Not possible. There is nothing there. It's between the pool room and the theatre, but the walls connect those two places together," said Jackson.

Ron pulled out another page from the plans. This one showed the basement. He laid it out beside the first-floor plans.

"Look there. According to the basement plans there should be something there, but the upstairs plans show the pool and theatre adjoining each other. That is where Peter is."

"But how to get to him?" asked Jane.

Bob and Skip looked at each other and smiled. "The wine cellar," they said in unison.

Ron looked once more at the plans and said, "Gotcha!"

Suddenly the ghost machine started sparking, then it went dead.

CHAPTER THIRTEEN

PETER'S ARMY

"Who goes and who stays?" asked Jackson. They had quickly turned on the portable emitters and they all stood close together.

"We all go," replied Blaze.

"What, safety in numbers?" asked Melissa. "Wouldn't it be better if we separated into two groups? One group as a back up in case the other group fails."

"Blaze is right," replied Ron. "We will only get one chance at this. Peter knows now that we are on to him. He's going to throw everything he has at us. Everyone, pick up something heavy to swing."

"Swing at what?" asked Skip. "You can't hit a spirit."

"At the wall, I presume," answered John. "We won't find an arrow pointing to a door with a sign saying this way to evil ghost. We're going to have to make a door."

"Also be ready to protect yourselves. When I was down there, when Sir Arthur fell, the ghost of Josef Mengele was throwing wine bottles at us." Jane had to fight back the tears. The thought of seeing the body of Sir Arthur was almost too much to bear.

Blaze went over and gave her a hug. "Don't worry, we will be there too. You will not face this alone."

Jane smiled at Blaze and whispered thanks.

"There's something I just don't understand," said Jackson. "I've studied the paranormal for years. In all that time I've never heard of ghosts actually being able to physically attack someone. Oh yeah, I've heard about poltergeists that can move and throw objects, but not physically contact people. Also, how can Peter be adapting to what we do? Ghosts should only be able to react based on what they did in life, not learn and plan. Especially to technology that wasn't even invented when they died. He can't be alive, can he?"

Everyone turned to Blaze as she might have the most knowledge about this. Even John, with all his years investigating the paranormal had no idea how this could happen.

She looked at everyone, especially concentrating on Jane, before she responded.

"First, no Peter is not alive, at least not in any sense that we could comprehend. In his diary he spoke about what he learned from the swami in India. Also, the ceremonies he performed. I do believe that Peter had some psychic abilities. My guess is that the ceremonies he performed enhanced his psychic abilities. With that he was able to call for the spirits that had been embedded in the materials he used to build this house.

"Furthermore, I don't believe these are truly the ghosts of the dead, at least not the really evil ones. I think they are the essences that were left behind and Peter was able to bring them out and manipulate them to make them into what he wanted.

"A last point. My years of training as a psychic have taught me that almost everyone has some ability in this, but unless you believed in it and trained to use it, this ability would never show itself. With each incident that people in this house went through, Peter was able to channel that psychic energy into himself. I think that is what has kept him capable of still being fully aware of what goes on. Physically he is dead. Psychically he isn't."

"But where does the shaman fit in all this?" asked Melissa. "You said before that you believe the shaman may be somehow controlling Peter. If that's the case, will we still be able to end this by destroying Peter?"

"I think I can answer that," said John. "My research showed that there were many rumors and stories of the evil that was carried out on this property. Long before Peter bought this land and built his house, there is a story of a cult of Devil worshippers who called forth the spirit of that shaman. In their ceremony they claimed that they had given the shaman the ability to control all the dead spirits of any that had ever set foot on this property without them even knowing it, and could send them off to do his commands. Of course, I blew it off as nonsense, but what if it wasn't?"

"Still, for him to control Peter like this, he would have had to be physically close to Peter's body at the time of Peter's death," said Blaze. "In his diary Peter said he had found some bones that he thought might be those of that shaman. Most likely he had them with him when he died. They should still be with his body. If we destroy those bones with Peter, it should break the hold of the Shaman."

"That makes sense, Blaze, but I have a question," said John. "If he can manipulate or use psychic abilities of those that enter here, and he now has two powerful psychics in this house, how do we know he isn't using your abilities to augment his own?"

Jane looked at Blaze. "That's why you wanted me to build a psychic shield!"

Blaze smiled. "Yes John, it would have been possible except I have trained for years and am not vulnerable in that way. What I taught Jane makes her equally protected. But it does give me an idea. Maybe Jane and I can use that to help defend the rest of you."

"How?" asked Jackson.

"I'm not sure yet. Give me some time to work on it."

"Time is not something we have the luxury of," Ron observed.

"Then I will have to think faster, won't I?"

"Meanwhile we need to get going on our plan, and prepare ourselves," said Jackson.

"Can those lights be removed from the stands and still work?" asked Ron.

In response Skip walked over to one of the stands and disconnected the light, which continued to shine.

"Had these custom made. Notice the handle. It fits into the stand but can be used to carry the light around. And the handle will protect your hand from the heat of the lamp. The only thing is that half the power source is in the stand. So once disconnected, they will only have about an hour of power left. Less with what Peter is doing."

"Right. We have three lights and three emitters." John handed the equipment around. "We should have three people in the rear, one holding a light another an emitter, and the same for two in the front. Two of the three in the middle will hold the same."

"Wait," said Blaze. "We need holy water."

"How do you propose to get some of that. You're a psychic not a witch or a priest. You can't just conjure some," said Jackson.

"Like this." She smiled as she opened one of the coolers, removed the last few bottles of water from it and placed the large cross they had taken from the chapel within it.

"I don't know the proper prayer for this though."

Melissa stepped forward.

"Okay, everyone come around the cooler and join hands."

Once everyone was prepared, she told them to follow along if they could. She then proceeded to quote psalm twenty-three.

The Lord is my shepherd; I shall not want.

He maketh me to lie down in green pastures: he leadeth me beside the still waters.

He restoreth my soul: he leadeth me in the paths of righteousness for his name's sake.

Yea, though I walk through the valley of the shadow of death, I will fear no evil: for thou art with me; thy rod and thy staff they comfort me.

Thou preparest a table before me in the presence of mine enemies: thou anointest my head with oil; my cup runneth over.

Surely goodness and mercy shall follow me all the days of my life: and I will dwell in the house of the Lord for ever.

As soon as they had finished, the water in the cooler started swirling around the cross. It did this for almost thirty seconds and then stopped.

"Okay, that is some powerful cross," said John. "Were you expecting something like that to happen?" he asked Melissa.

"Not at all. I just remembered that passage from Sunday school and thought it would be appropriate for our situation."

"We can't exactly cart the cooler around," pointed out Ron.

Skip looked around, saw some empty water bottles, and gathered them up. There were eight in total.

"Looks like one for each of us. Give me a hand please."

Bob lifted the cooler, and with Ron and Jackson helping him to balance it, and Skip holding the empty bottles, they managed to fill all the bottles without spilling any.

It was just enough to fill them.

Blaze picked up the cross and the bottle of oil, putting the oil in one of her pockets.

"We need a dependable lighter and the white candles we have."

Bob found the candles in one of the bags, along with a Bic lighter and some matches as a backup. He handed the candles to Melissa, who repeated the prayer over them that she used for the holy water, before handing them to Blaze.

"Too bad Tippy wasn't here. He has a Zippo lighter that never fails."

"We'll just have to hope that what we have works," replied John.

Looking further Jackson picked up a couple of metal backs from the broken chair. Bob went into his bag of tools and pulled out a long screwdriver and a hammer. Skip still had the metal bar they had taken up to the third floor earlier. Ron picked up one of the light stands, commenting that he hoped it would be strong enough. Carrying it with the light still on would have been awkward, but holding it as a spear he was able to balance it and leave a hand free.

"Not to worry. They may be made from aluminum, but they are quite strong," said Skip.

Hearing that Melissa and John took the other two light stands.

Once they had gathered their equipment, they set their order.

Ron and John would lead the way.

Jane, Blaze, and Melissa would be in the center. Jane held a light, Melissa an emitter, and Blaze carried the cross. Her elaborate gown had plenty of pockets so she also had the candles, lighter and holy oil.

Jackson, Skip, and Bob would bring up the rear.

Each had a bottle of holy water in a pocket.

Melissa was about to say something about sexism, but quickly changed her mind. This was one time she was happy to let the men feel protective.

"Blaze, do you feel anything?" asked John.

"Nothing different yet. The presences are still there, but so far the emitters have them keeping their distance. Their numbers are growing though. Peter is calling them from all over the house. Jane what do you sense?"

"Just blackness, but the blackness is getting deeper. I think you are right about Peter calling in his forces."

"Then let's go before they all get here."

Suddenly the front door flew open.

"He's giving us an opportunity to leave," exclaimed Melissa. "We should take it." She was about to head towards the door when Jackson grabbed her arm.

"Are you forgetting the possessed animals out there?"

"Peter is afraid, maybe for the first time since he started this horror. If we don't stop him here and now, it will never end. And leaving the house will just give him another opportunity to knock us off. I say we carry on with the plan," said Blaze.

She looked around and everyone nodded in agreement. They turned away from the door and proceeded forward. The door slammed behind them. It caused them to jump, but not to change their mind.

"One more thing," said Jackson. He picked up one of the video recording cameras. "We document everything."

It was a surreal experience for all of them. Leaving the entrance area and passing by the theatre, their lights casting shadows every which way, yet not a noise from anywhere. Each of them kept looking around, expecting something to jump out at them any moment. They walked by the dining room and Jane made a little peep.

"What is it?" asked John, his voice low.

"Just more blackness. It is getting thicker with each room we pass."

"Bob, Skip, Jackson, stay close to each other. Grip arms if you can. We don't want to lose anyone along the way."

The three men looked at each other and then linked arms.

Soon they reached the kitchen and came to the cellar door.

"Anything before us Blaze?" asked John.

"Something, but not close to the door. Further down. Something purely evil."

"Josef Mengele," said Jane.

"Whatever it is, it has gone beyond being just the ghost of an evil man. It has become powerful in itself," replied Blaze.

"You mean like Peter has made him his field commander?" suggested Jackson.

Blaze didn't reply, but her silence spoke volumes.

Ron pulled the door open, and John shone his light into the stairway. Nothing was close.

"We will head down two by two. Three won't fit side by side on these stairs. The last person must pull the door shut. Don't let go of his arm until the door is all the way closed."

"You got that right," said Bob.

"Melissa, you take a step back and walk beside one of the men back there. Jane and I will follow right behind Ron and John and see if we can reach our senses forward to see what is waiting for us."

Once they were all in the stairway, Bob pulled the door shut and took position beside Skip, with Jackson moving forward to be beside Melissa. Bob held one of the lights with Skip holding the emitter. Looking down at it he saw the light flashing red.

"This thing looks like it will run out of power soon. We had better get a move on."

Melissa looked at her emitter and saw the same thing.

Knowing time was running out Ron and John quickened their

pace, reaching the bottom of the steps in short order. Down the aisle they went past wine shelf after wine shelf, expecting at any moment to get hit by a bottle, surprised when nothing happened. Soon their light cast far enough ahead that they could see the body of Sir Arthur, still in the same position as Jane had seen him last, on his knees. He was covered in blood and from the marks they could see, it appeared to be all his own. Just before they reached him there was a loud hiss and a black form lifted from his body and flew over their heads, back to the staircase.

"What the fuck was that," cried Bob.

"That was Josef fucking Mengele," said Jane, emphasizing the middle word like she had a previous time.

They reached the form of Sir Arthur. As John circled around him to check for vitals he knew would not be there he saw the expression on Sir Arthur's face. An expression of pure horror. Suddenly Sir Arthur's arm raised into the air, pointing to an area beyond John, and then his form collapsed. Jane screamed, with Skip following suit.

"Damn, what the hell just happened?" asked Ron.

"It was Sir Arthur's last act of defiance. Look where he pointed," said Blaze.

At the end of the corridor, the last shelf of wine bottles had shattered and a fire had partially burned one wall, with the remains of a lantern at it's base. What caught their attention though, was the pattern the fire had left. It was a giant arrow, pointing at the wall near the end of the last wine shelf.

"So, I was wrong. There is an arrow pointing the way. We're just missing the sign that says evil ghost here," commented John.

Ron went to examine the wall where the arrow was.

"This wall is solid concrete, as are most of the rest of the cellar's outer walls."

Jackson passed him by and went to the remnants of the burnt shelf. Pulling what remained from the wall, he knocked.

"Still solid." He continued to the end of the shelf until a knock produced a slight echo. "This must be it," he said.

The words were barely out of his mouth when a wine bottle flung at the group narrowly missed Bob and hit the wall with a crash. They all tried to fit into the narrow alcove, but Bob and Skip, being the last two, were being mercilessly hit with wine bottles. They both crouched as low as they could, arms over their heads to offer what little protection they could.

At the front of the group Ron and John were using the metal bars to smash at the wall. Pieces of Gyproc were coming apart as a hole began to appear, but progress was slow. As they smashed the wall the frame of what used to be a doorway began to emerge.

"Hurry guys, Bob and Skip are taking a beating," said Jackson. Still mindful of what he was holding, Jackson pointed the camera at Bob and Skip.

Suddenly the bottles stopped. Risking a glance up Skip saw the shadows closing in. He looked down at the emitter he saw that its power was gone. "Oh, Oh. The emitters have failed. They may have stopped throwing bottles but now they are coming at us."

Blaze pushed her way through. Looking at the figures coming, she opened herself up to see what was there. Those closest to her saw her face go pale.

"What is it?" asked Jane who had made her way to Blaze's side.

"They're coming. Can you use what we practiced to hold them off?"

Jane was able to slip into her meditative state, building the wall of good auras and casting it forth. She felt resistance and kept pushing. For a moment she was able to push them back, but soon they advanced again.

"I can hold them a bit, but not for long. There are too many of them and they are too powerful."

"What do you sense Blaze?" asked John.

"Leading the way is Josef Mengele. With him are Joseph Stalin, and Adolf Eichmann. I guess Peter did not get anything belonging to Hitler. Behind them I sense Thomas de Torquemada, the first Grand Inquisitor of the Spanish Inquisition. With him are Vlad the Impaler and Pol Pot.

"Next comes serial killer row. There's Charles Manson, Jeffrey Dahmer and Ted Bundy. After them is Jim Jones and members of his cult. And yes, John, this time I am using my psychic powers and not my powers of deduction. I can feel their essences.

"Damn it sounds like Peter has brought his entire army," said Jackson. "Let me pass. I want to capture this on video."

Instead, Blaze grabbed the camera, did a quick angle shot past Jane and handed it back. "Now get the fuck out of here."

Stunned by her language, which was quite unusual for her, Jackson just stood there gawking. She turned away from him to face what was coming.

"We're through," said Ron.

"What do you see?" asked Bob.

"A short staircase and then a landing. What's there I don't know."

"No time to check it out. Everyone in now."

They all headed towards the hole in the wall, except Blaze. She grabbed Jane's arm.

"They will never make it on time unless we slow down Peter's Army. I might be able to do something, but I will need your help."

Jane looked at the oncoming hoard of shadows, and back at the comfort of the hole in the wall that the last of the group were passing through. She knew that Blaze was right.

"Of course I stand with you."

"That's great girl, but no matter what happens you must do as I say.

* * *

Michelle stumbled and fell. A fox landed on her back, but Tippy, seeing her predicament, stopped and kicked the fox, sending it back into the group of deer.

"Give me your hand."

She reached up and grasped his hand. Pulling hard he got her on to her feet.

"They've stopped. I think we are beyond Peter's range," said Michelle.

"Don't count on it." Tippy pointed back the way they had come. The deer gave ground and the two cougars passed amongst them.

Michelle's face showed resignation, but Tippy was not about to give up.

"I guess this is it for us," she said

"No way. I have a boyfriend back at the house, and he would never give up. Neither will I." He pulled the backpack off his shoulder and unzipped it, pulling out the drill and two of stakes for the laser posts.

"Whatever you're doing it had better be quick. No time for some fancy tech stuff."

"How about some non-fancy, non-tech stuff?"

Standing up Tippy displayed what he had improvised. Attached to the drill, in place of a bit, was a stake for a laser post strapped to the drill using the ties. He pointed it at the closest cougar and started the drill. The action of the drill caused the ties to wind up, then snap and that sent the post flying, hitting the cougar directly in the eye.

"Good shot!"

"But I think I just made him mad."

The cougar howled in pain and shook his head. However, he paid no attention to the two humans standing there. Instead, he focused on the other cougar, roared a challenge, and charged. He caught the other cat unaware, knocking it over and slashing its face. The other cougar got to its feet, looking dazed. Then it sensed the first cougar about to attack again and ran into the woods, its pursuer hot on its trail.

"Fucking brilliant!" Michelle cried, raising her fists in a victory pump.

"Well, I didn't exactly expect that to happen." Tippy sounded truly surprised. "But at least it worked. We still have the deer and the foxes to worry about, but the cougars were the more dangerous ones."

"The foxes might bite, but we shouldn't have much to worry about with the deer."

"You think? See these bites?" he demanded, holding out his arms and indicating the wounds on his legs.

"No way!"

"Yes way. So, I suggest we get moving."

"But where?"

Tippy looked around, getting his bearings. "If I remember correctly, when we arrived, I saw a small shack. Bob said something about it being used for maple syrup or something. It can't be too far away. It should provide us some protection."

"Our own little sugar shack," Michelle quipped, breaking the tension if only for a moment. "Lead the way."

The deer however, were not going to make it easy. With the cougars gone, they had closed ranks again and were moving in.

"Give me the drill," shouted Michelle.

Tippy handed it to her, a questioning look on his face.

Not responding, she faced the deer and started the drill. The closest two stopped, then started looking around, their confusion evident. They started to drift away, but after a few steps stopped again and turned back.

"I noticed this when you fired your new-fangled arrow at the cougar," Michelle said over her shoulder. "I think it somehow drives the ghosts possessing them away, though only for a short while."

"Long enough to get out of here. I just hope there's enough power left in it the way batteries keep draining. The good news is the moon is higher up. It's only half full, but it'll provide us with decent light now. Time to make a run for it," said Tippy. Slinging the backpack over his shoulder, he grabbed up the tire iron. "Okay, start up the drill and let's go."

With Michelle pushing the button intermittently to save power, they made their way through the herd of deer. They had just passed the last of them when the drill stopped.

"Time to start running!"

CHAPTER FOURTEEN

BLAZE'S BATTLE FORCE

Six of them continued on, not realizing that two had been left behind.

After passing through the hole in the wall, they followed the short flight of steps that led to the landing Ron had seen on his first glance through the opening. It was an area about ten feet by ten feet, with no other access that they could see.

"There's your phone, John," said Melissa, pointing to the only object in the room. John went and picked it up and then looked around, seeing the tube it had come down. The floor itself seemed to be just dirt and sand, with red blotches in places.

"Is that what I think it is?" asked Melissa pointing at the stains.

"Yes it is," replied John thinking of the torture room. "But where are his trophies?"

"Everyone, search each wall," called John. "Rap on them. There has to be another passage."

Knowing that time was running out everyone picked an area of wall to check.

Ten minutes later and still nothing. No hollow space, no area that looked like it could provide access to anything.

"Damn, how could we be so off in our calculations?" asked Bob.

"Maybe we just misunderstood what Peter was saying in his diary," said Skip.

"Or worse. What if Peter set that entire diary up to trick us into wasting our time," added Melissa.

"That makes no sense," replied Jackson. "That he could see a group like ours finding James Neighbors, finding the diary and someone actually guessing about using the crystals for triangulation and having someone drop a cell phone with GPS down the chute from the third floor, when cell phones of this type had not even been invented yet."

"We're missing something," said John. "We have to keep looking."

"We don't need to keep looking the way we have been. We need to start looking at the right place," said Ron, who was standing in the middle of the room. Everyone turned to look at him, and when he had their attention, he stamped his foot. The metallic ring was unmistakable.

"For his resting place to survive a fire that burns the entire house down, it needs to be underneath the house and protected."

Skip. Bob, Jackson, and John got down on their knees and started wiping the floor where Ron had been standing. After a few minutes they had uncovered a large metal plate.

"How in hell are we going to remove this?" asked Bob, straightening his back after working with the other three trying to shift it. That was when he noticed Ron was no longer with them. "And where the hell is Ron?"

Melissa quickly replied. "He muttered something about wandering psychics and went back to get Jane and Blaze. I think they were trying to set some type of psychic defense or something."

"No time to worry about them now," said Jackson. "We need to figure out how to get this open."

"Let me take a look," said Melissa, pushing him aside.

Skip was about to comment on that but John raised his hand forestalling him. "Unless you have any ideas, let her look. She may catch something we're missing."

After only a few seconds Melissa stood up and pulled a bottle out of her pocket. She took the cap off, got back down on her knees and starting pouring the water around the edge of the plate.

"What? You think water will melt this," scoffed Jackson. "He isn't the Wicked Witch of the West, and this isn't Oz.

"No, but he had to have a way to open this, and then seal it after he got Betty. Something that doesn't require major construction, maybe something he learned from the swami. And this isn't just water, it's holy water."

She completed the entire edge of the three-foot-by-three-foot piece of metal, then stood up. Nothing happened at first, and then the edges started bubbling.

"Quick now, get your tools and try to move it," said Melissa.

Using whatever they'd brought with them the four men got back down on one side and pushed their tools against the edge, lifting at the same time. They were all turning red in the face from the effort when pop went the plate, flipping over. From the hole that opened up came a puff of smoke, and a stink of sulfur.

John picked up one of the lights and shone it into the hole. They could see a set of stairs heading down.

"I guess we head into the pits of Hell after all," said Jackson.

"Sure smells like it," said Melissa.

"Why would it smell like that?" asked Bob.

"If my Jackson was here, he might be able to answer that," replied John. "He was a chemist and a geologist."

"In a way, he is here," said Skip.

John gave him a strange look.

"No, I don't mean spiritually. I mean his knowledge. He's been teaching me a lot about chemistry and geology the last year or so. He said it was just in case we encountered a cave or something when he wasn't around.

"He especially talked about sulfur and to be careful if we come across it. It's either a sign of gas buildup or is caused by bacteria giving us this characteristic rotten egg odor we smell. It's highly unlikely to be gas here so it must be bacteria caused by decomposition doing this."

"What if it is natural gas?" asked Jackson. "Couldn't lighting a match in there cause an explosion?"

"If it was natural gas, I guess it would. But Peter isn't likely to let that happen and destroy his resting place," replied John.

"You make it sound like he's some all-knowing deity or something," said Melissa. "He was only a man. A weird man who wanted to turn himself into a deity, but a man nonetheless."

"Says the person who thought he could see the future," joked Bob.

"A very smart man though," answered Jackson. "One that would have taken as much into account as possible, and protecting his resting place would have been paramount with him. I agree with John on that."

Taking one of the lights Skip moved to the top of the steps.

"Instead of gabbing about it, let's march into the depths of Hell."

"Shouldn't we wait for the others?" asked Melissa. "We might need Blaze or Jane's psychic abilities when we find this resting place."

John shook his head. "We need to get there first. They can join us when they're done doing what they are doing—no doubt laying some type of protection to give us time to do what we need to do."

"We can't wait," Jackson agreed. "We'll have to depend on Ron to get them and bring them here. He, of us all, has an idea of what we'll be facing and will do all he can to get us the help we need."

With Skip leading the way and Jackson filming over his shoulder, the five remaining in the party braved the steps to Hell.

* * *

"What do you want me to do?"

"I need your protection. I am going to perform a ceremony I learned a long time ago, and never thought I would ever want—or be able—to perform. But Peter's ceremonies have opened this up and made it possible. While I am doing this, I will be vulnerable, not only to Peter's army, but to Peter's influence and maybe the shaman too. You must use every bit of strength you have. I don't know how long it will take."

"Any ideas on how I can strengthen my shield?"

"Think about the others. About protecting them. About caring for them. Add that into your meditation. Hurry girl, we're running out of time."

The spirits were only steps away.

Jane stepped in front of Blaze, then slipped into her meditation, feeling the spirits pushing through her shields. She pictured the faces of her companions. The fierceness of Ron, who she'd come to realize she had feelings for. The studiousness of John. The glow of Melissa she remembered from when they first met. Bob's cheerful round face. Skip's eager look at anything technological. Jackson's excitement when they first arrived. And of course, the serene look that Blaze gave her when she was teaching her to build a shield. With that in mind she poured the feelings she had come to have for this group into her shield. The aura around them flared bright, and the blackness of the evil advancing towards them was pushed back.

Blaze emptied her pockets, putting the holy oil, candles, lighter and matches behind her, along with the cross she had been carrying.

"When I tell you to you must leave me and go join the others. Take the items I have put down with you. They will be needed."

"I will never leave you!"

"You must. What I am about to do will stir forces that I may not be able to control for long. If I lose control, it will destroy you. The others will be needing your help."

"What about you?"

"I will be fine. Trust me. Now do all you can to hold your shields!"

The distraction of her worry caused her shields to slip a little, and the evil blackness to advance. Putting her worry aside Jane again pictured her companions and used this to add strength to her shields. She thought of a solid barrier of light, holding back the blackness. Her shields strengthened and held, but she felt herself getting weaker with the effort. Behind her she sensed Blaze somehow manipulating the psychic forces around them, and then Blaze spoke.

"Victims arise. It is time to fight back. I offer my body and psyche as a vessel for you to work through. In exchange I ask for your help to defeat the darkness that comes and protect my friends. The darkness is made of those who have harmed you. Of those who have destroyed your lives, your families, and your eternal peace. I give you the chance to fight back. To tell them that you are no longer their victim. Cast the yoke of darkness from you forever."

"Deus, has animas cruciatas custodi et protege, ut contra malum pugnare valeamus. Offero me tibi et faciam omnia, quae possum, ut eorum bonitas a tenebris non vincatur.

Da nobis fortitudinem tuam, ut omnes hostes superare possimus, et pacem dare tuis fidelibus semel et semper servis tuis."

Although Jane did not recognize the words, she realized that Blaze had been speaking Latin. Then her friend's voice changed. "Okay baby doll, your part is finished here. Go and protect the others."

Jane felt that the pressure on her shields had lessened. She turned and looked at Blaze. What she saw shocked her. Yes it was Blaze, but she also saw so many others. Men, women, children. Most looked like they had been tortured, some had bodies that were burned black. How could so many people fit in that small area. And yet at the same time there was only Blaze. She shook her head trying to clear her vision, thinking that she was hallucinating.

"No, you are not imagining things," said Blaze. "I have called on the forces that were harmed by the evil that is now in this house and given them a chance to fight back. When Peter brought the spirits of those evil beings here, they brought the spirits of their victims. It is time for the victims to fight back. Now go and join the others. Help them find Peter's resting place and put an end to this. Once that is accomplished these spirits will know peace for the first time."

Jane looked at Blaze and again at the forces that were standing behind her. She looked once more at Peter's army, that for some reason were not advancing, even though her shield had drawn back. Blaze moved forward and Jane slid past her.

She still could not stop watching her friend. Jane kept her eyes on Blaze the entire time as she backed towards the hole. She watched as Blaze stepped away from the alcove and into the corridor, advancing on Peter's army, her forces changing as Jane watched. From the pitiful beings she first saw, they now looked whole, restored, full of energy, and anger. The two forces met. As they collided Jane felt something behind her.

Before she could even scream, she was grabbed and pulled away.

* * *

They ran as fast as they could, or more like as fast as the terrain would allow them. A number of times one of them would stumble, the other would stop to help.

This time it was Tippy who fell. As Michelle stopped to grab his arm he told her to go on without him.

"What do you mean!? You remember you have someone at the house who will be severely disappointed if he learned you were dead because you gave up."

"He will never know."

"Of course he will, because I will tell him every detail."

"You're one mean bitch."

"You bet I am. Now get on your feet."

She pulled him up and they started trotting again.

"How do you keep going like this?" asked Tippy between breaths.

"Marathon training. Ran the Boston and Montreal marathons last year.

"I see a shape ahead. It must be the shack."

"It had better not be those bloody cougars."

"Always the optimist, eh."

"Usually it's Bob who's the pessimist and I'm the optimist, but not today."

A quick glance behind showed that the deer had fallen back a little.

"Looks like being possessed slows them down," remarked Tippy.

"I wouldn't count on that lasting. Pick up your feet."

"Now who's being the pessimist?"

With a last burst of energy Tippy gave it his all and was happy to see the shape forming in the moonlight be that of a structure. They reached the front and saw the outline of the door. Tippy grabbed the handle, turned, and pushed, ecstatic that the door was not locked, and opened easily. They slipped inside, Tippy slamming the door behind him.

"We need something to block this. Can you find anything?"

"We have no lights and it's pitch black in here. How am I supposed to find anything."

"Here." Tippy had grabbed her hand and shoved something in it.

"Your Zippo! Thank God you have it still."

Michelle flicked the flint wheel and a nice sized flame instantly erupted. With the help of the flame, she spotted a solid metal rake with a thick wooden handle.

"How about this?"

She put it into Tippy's hand. He quickly turned it upside down and jammed it into the door handle, digging the other end into the lose dirt that made the floor of the shack, then took the lighter back from Michelle.

"It should hold them. Let's see if we can make more light."

Using the Zippo Tippy was able to see enough of the cabin to get an idea of what was there. Near the door was what looked like a work bench and lying on it were a couple of outdoor torches.

"Our luck is changing," he said as he picked up one of the torches and applied his Zippo to it. The torch caught right away, casting enough light for them to see the remainder of their sanctuary.

"Damn that burns." Tippy sucked his fingers that had been holding the lighter for too long. "Maybe it's a hint that I should quit smoking."

"If you had quit yesterday, we wouldn't have the Zippo today."

"Point taken. Let's see what else we can use to brace the door. Also check for any windows in case we have to make a quick exit out of here."

The cabin was not large, maybe twelve by fifteen feet.

"I guess Bob was wrong about this being a sugar shack. It looks like they mostly kept gardening tools here."

"This isn't the shack that Bob told me about. I don't remember seeing this place when we arrived. It's too small to be the sugar shack. Which means we are not where I thought we were."

"What difference does it make. At least we are safe for the time being."

"I guess you are right. It's just that the sugar shack looked a lot more solid than this tool shed. I hope it holds."

"What's that noise?"

Tippy stopped walking around the shed and listened. Now he heard it too.

"Sounds like chewing," he answered.

"I don't like that possibility," responded Michelle, her voice quavering. "Maybe you were too quick to say that our luck was changing."

Looking around they spotted a hole in one corner. A hole that was getting larger by the minute. Then they spotted the red eyes staring at them. Whatever creature had those eyes scampered through the hole, followed by another and then another. Soon there were dozens in with them.

"Oh, rats!" yelled Tippy, before the first one ran up his leg, taking a chunk out of his thigh. Then he heard screaming, and it wasn't just his.

* * *

The flight of stairs was longer than they had expected, going down at least twenty feet. At the base of the steps was a small circular area barely ten feet across. From there the only egress was beside the steps leading into a cave. Following along they realized that it led back towards where the pool would have been if they were still in the house itself. It followed along for another ten feet and ended at a stone door. Beside the door were two coffins. Etched into one was Adolf Hitler and in the other was Eva Braun.

"So, he did have something from Hitler," said Jackson. "I guess he was able to find the corpses after all, despite the Soviets claiming they had cremated them."

"If he has the body, how come we have not been confronted by his ghost?" asked Skip.

"Maybe his ghost is waiting for us just inside this door. Peter's final guardians," replied Bob.

"Or maybe Eva somehow contained Hitler," added in Melissa.

John started laughing, the others staring at him, wondering if he had gone mad.

"Don't you see? No matter how much money you have, it doesn't mean you can't be fooled. Someone sold these two coffins, which probably have bodies in them by the smell, to Peter claiming they were the bodies of Hitler and Braun. Maybe the features of the two inside were similar, or there was some type of fraudulent paper trail, but Peter was duped."

John then turned back to the door, their object of immediate concern.

The door itself had markings on it, some words they could not make out and some images that were quite visible. Snakes predominated, but they also saw carvings of rats. As well there were a number of pyramids etched into the stone.

"I see how he felt the destruction of the house would hide his sanctuary," said John.

"How so?" asked Melissa.

It was Skip who answered. "If the house collapsed, say after a fire, everything would be buried up to this door. Even if a contractor dug out most of the house all they would come to would be the stone of the cave. Peter must have discovered the cave before building the house and set his sanctuary here."

"That place would appear to be exactly where the crystals would have pointed. From his diary he said that he had constructed the house to focus the spiritual energy here." John moved the light around and then continued. "See the markings on the walls of the cave. Hard to see unless you are close, but there appears to be writing on the walls. Maybe part of the ceremony he performed would cycle that spiritual energy through the cave to this point."

Jackson made sure to get the coffins and the markings on the cave wall on video.

"The question now though is how do we get through that door," said Bob.

"The answer to that is behind you," came a voice from the other end of the cave, causing Melissa to scream.

* * *

"Relax, I've got you," said Ron. Jane continued to fight against him.

"You can't help her now. This is her battle. You would only distract her and get her killed."

Realizing that Ron was right, Jane stopped fighting him. The two watched as the forces collided. Then they lost sight of everything as blackness settled over the wine cellar. They could hear screams and what sounded like battle cries.

"We have to leave. Now!"

Pushing off of Ron, Jane bent down to pick up what Blaze had left there.

"Blaze said we will need this stuff," she said as she picked up the bottle of holy oil, candles, matches and lighter. Ron reached around her and grabbed the cross, slipped the handle of the light he had taken from the group through his shirt, then took hold of Jane's hand and led her through the hole.

They took one last look back, hoping to get a final sight of Blaze's battle force, but the darkness there showed nothing.

They followed the flight of stairs up to the small landing area.

"Wow, how did they get that open?!" exclaimed Jane.

Ron bent down to lift the cover and found the weight was too much for one person.

"Teamwork for sure. This thing is heavy."

Looking down the hole they saw the staircase leading into darkness and smelled the sulphur.

"Something is missing here," said Jane.

"What's that?"

"The sign that says *Abandon all hope, ye who enter here*," replied Jane.

That elicited a small smile from Ron.

"Yeah, this does look like something Dante would write about."

They continued in the steps their companions had taken moments before.

Reaching the bottom of the stairs they heard the voices of their companions coming from a cave beside the stairway. They could see the light being cast by their lamps.

They heard Bob ask how to get through the door, and Ron answered.

CHAPTER FIFTEEN

CONFRONTATION – BETTY'S REVENGE

"You scared the shit out of me," hissed Melissa. "What the fuck were you thinking."

"Only that you will need these things to finish off Peter."

"What have we here?" asked Jane looking at the two coffins.

"Peter thought they were the bodies of Hitler and his wife, but apparently they aren't," answered Jackson.

"Where is Blaze?" asked Bob.

"She raised her own army and is in battle with Peter's army as we speak," replied Ron.

They stared at him in shock, all except Jane and John.

"She happens to be the most powerful psychic I have ever met, and yes I have met a few," said John. "So, no I am not surprised."

"But she said she has no idea how long she can hold off Peter's forces, so we had better get a move on," urged Jane.

"We have a problem," said Skip. "This is a solid stone door with no sign of how to open it. Shit the only thing that tells us it is even a door is the carvings on it and the edges it has."

"Let me take a look," said Jane. But as she passed the coffins she let out a cry.

"What is it?" cried out Melissa.

Ron went over to Jane and held her until she stopped shaking.

Once she had calmed somewhat she looked at the coffins and then responded.

"Those coffins contain evil. No not Hitler or Eva. Something more North American. I can feel it is something from this continent. Killers of some type. A man and a woman. I just can't place them yet."

"Can they hurt us?" asked Bob.

"I don't know. Their bodies are there and the essence of the evil they have committed, but something is missing. I sense that they have killed many times though."

"Before or after they arrived here?" asked Jackson.

"A bit of both I think."

"Let's worry about that later. Right now we need to find a way to get this door open," John said facing away from the others and studying the etchings.

Jane moved closer to the door, Ron holding her arm to keep her steady.

"These patterns kind of look familiar." Jane brushed some dirt off of one of the snake carvings.

"Yeah, like Harry Potter. Does anyone here speak parseltongue?"

"That's parselmouth, and no this is not a witch movie, you dumb cop," snapped Jackson.

Ron turned to look at Jackson. Seeing trouble coming Bob intervened.

"Come on Jackson. We're all uptight, but no reason to get bitchy."

Jackson looked sheepishly at Ron.

"God I'm sorry. This place is getting to me."

Ron continued to walk towards Jackson. Thinking things were about to get violent John stood up, but Ron walked right past Jackson, to where he had put down the cross when he took Jane's arm.

"So many times this cross has been mentioned that it may be even more important than we thought."

He picked it up and brought it back to Jane, standing by the door.

"What are you thinking?" asked Skip.

"I have an idea what he's getting at," replied John. "In his note James Neighbors talked about the cross being something that Peter misunderstood. About it not being evil."

"Also, in the chapel the ghost of William Taylor said that what we needed to stop Peter was in that room, and Blaze went right to the cross. She was insistent that we take it."

"But it served its purpose when we made the holy water," said Melissa.

"What if that wasn't its only function," replied Jane. "Look at these etchings on the door. The way the grooves form right where the large snake's eyes are. Like maybe something is missing from them."

Looking at the cross Jane put her fingers around one of the glass bubbles, the one containing the silver, and twisted it. Like a light bulb it unscrewed. She took this and put it into the right eye socket of the large snake and screwed it in. It was a perfect fit. She repeated the procedure with the bubble containing the earth putting it into the left eye socket. Finally she took out the last bubble and saw a groove in the tongue of the snake where she screwed it into place.

She stood back and waited. Nothing happened.

"It was worth a try," said Melissa. "After all they fit so well."

"Maybe if you switched them around," commented Skip.

"No. The grooves are all slightly different. They wouldn't fit any other way."

Ron took the cross from Jane's hands. He noticed a smaller square notch at the end of the snake's tongue. He put the base of the cross into the notch. It fit perfectly. Acting on a hunch he started pushing the cross towards the opposite end of the door. The door shifted, sliding into a recess, leaving an opening before them.

"Why would Peter have left that cross in plain view if it was the key to his sanctuary?" asked Jackson.

"He didn't," replied Jane. "While he was making his plans, psychic forces were working to stop him. Peter made the design of the door according to some ceremony taught to him by that swami. The swami in turn probably found these ceremonies somewhere else. It seems that when something evil is created, so is something good to counteract it. Yin and Yang. The psychic forces just made sure that the cross was in this house when it was needed."

"Well, that makes about as much sense as anything else here," said Skip.

"The lair of the dragon awaits," announced Jackson. "Who wants to lead the way?"

"You're holding the camera, why don't you go first?" snapped Melissa.

"No." said Jane. "I will go first. I sense evil ahead and I am the only one left here with the psychic abilities to fight it."

"Not alone you don't," said Ron, taking his place beside her.

Before they entered Jane handed the holy oil to John and the candles and matches to Skip.

"I may have to hold him at bay while you take care of the body," was all she said.

With the others following, and Jackson filming, they entered Peter's lair.

*   *   *

Blaze had been training and practicing her psychic abilities for over thirty years, yet in all that time she never imagined herself in a confrontation like this.

The ceremony she had performed had been taught to her when she was in her late teens. At that time she had thought she was a witch, and that the abilities she had were magic. Being the late nineties, research resources were thin, but she had finally found a coven of witches that she thought was legitimate.

She wasted almost a year of attending circles, reading spell books, visiting stores that catered to witches by selling supplies to be used in spell casting, and more. The day that she showed one of the witches in her circle her abilities, was the day she was thrown out of the circle. It turned out that they were actually afraid of anyone who had real power.

Fortunately, she met someone at one of the witch stores who understood her. Allie Montore explained that almost all supposed witches you can find easily are just wannabes, that the few witches who have abilities keep them hidden. Then she added the explanation that mostly those who have abilities are really psychics, and that is what Blaze was.

Allie took Blaze under her wing. She helped Blaze to learn and understand her abilities and her limits. Ironically this person also practiced a form of witchcraft she called Blending. When Blaze asked why that name, she was told it was because it blended psychic abilities with the commitment of witchcraft. It was from this that Blaze learned the ceremony she had just performed.

Blaze had been spending the week with Allie, and had already turned in after a long day of learning and practice, when she heard noises that woke her. Getting up she had left the guest room she had been using and descended the flight of stairs to the basement where the noise was coming from. When she got to the bottom of the steps, she was unsure of what she was seeing and hearing. Sitting in the center of the room, inside a chalk circle was her mentor chanting something in a language Blaze did not understand. She could hear a whistling in the distance that matched the cadence of Allie's chant. Then she saw figures of people floating above Allie's head. That was when Allie noticed Blaze. She smiled, looked up at the figures above her and waived. With that they disappeared.

Blaze replayed the conversation in her head.

"You were able to see my friends," stated Allie.

"Who were they?" asked Blaze.

"Dead friends long gone. Come sit and I will teach you this ceremony. But you must only use it in the case of a need most urgent."

"Why? It seemed all right."

"These are friends I had known for years, and they were all psychics. Furthermore, I was able to control the time and place. Without that you might call spirits that would mean you harm, or would want to remain with you to experience life again, taking over your body."

She had sat within that circle with Allie the remainder of the night, as Allie called back her friends. She could feel what Allie did and how she did it. She also knew that it was a ceremony she herself would never perform unless she absolutely had to. Using her abilities, she could see that Allie controlled the spirits, but as well, the spirits controlled her to an extent. Without the full trust of the forces she was dealing with, Allie could have had her spirit taken and lost.

She felt it now. The spirits she had called forth with the ceremony wanting to take control of her. She knew it was not their intention to harm her, but they wanted to feel normal again, to touch, to smell, to taste, even if for a moment.

Beyond that she could feel the malevolent forces of Peter, and beyond him the shaman. Peter and the shaman were not close right now, but she could sense them in the background. They were ordering their forces forward. Reluctantly the evil spirits they had trapped advanced, but they felt fear for the first time ever. Arrayed against them were those they had tortured, but now those forces were whole, strong, and united.

Sensing that the key to the forces against them was Blaze, they focused their attack on her. She felt pain like she never had before and would have collapsed, but the spirits she had called forth supported her, washed through her, removed the pain, and then attacked the forces of Peter.

She felt the tide of battle shifting in her favor. But only for a moment. Suddenly more blackness entered, coming from outdoors. The spirits that Peter had sent to possess the animals that had attacked Tippy and Michelle were being called by Peter to defend him. For a moment she was certain she faced Peter and the shaman and then they disappeared. She realized that the team must have breached Peter's inner sanctum and he was rushing to defend it. She hoped Jane would be strong enough to hold them off long enough for the others to destroy Peter's remains.

She could not give it any more thought as the assault on her mounted and it was all she could do to hold them back. Then she felt biting on her legs and arms. The spirits that had inhabited the animals overwhelmed her. The last thought she had was the hope that Jane could get them through to Peter.

* * *

In desperation Tippy threw the torch into a pile of stacked wood. It took a moment for it to flare up, but the wood chips finally caught fire and the pile of wood soon became a blaze. The rats nearest the wood pile started to burn, and as the pain reached them, they panicked and tried to escape, pushing back on those still entering the shack and spreading the fire.

Tippy grabbed the rat still clinging to his leg and pulled it off, taking a chunk of flesh with it. He yelled in pain and threw the rat into the blaze, then kicked away the two rats at his feet. This created enough of a gap for him to grab a nearby spade and started swinging.

The fire intensified, brightening the entire shed. He saw Michelle lying on the ground, covered in rats. Rushing over to her he swung the spade, getting some of the rats off of her. Using the point of the spade he stabbed those rats that did not let go. Still there were some that would not leave. Looking around he saw the unlit torch on the bench. He ran over and grabbed it, using the fire from the wood pile to light it. He started lighting the fur of the rats still clinging to Michelle. He was finally able to get the last one off of her.

Most of the rats that were still in the shed were dead or dying. The remainder had fled the fire, the fear of which had chased away the possessors. Tippy put the torch aside and got down beside Michelle, checking for vitals. She briefly opened her eyes, but then they glazed over and she passed out.

Tippy did a quick scan and saw that she was covered in blood and bites in multiple places. Her face in particular was so badly bitten that he could see her cheek bone through her skin. Yet he knew there was no time to check her out further. The fire burned intensely, with two walls completely ablaze, and half the roof. The smoke was making him hack and breathing was difficult. In moments the doorway would be engulfed in fire. He had to get them out now.

He knew he did not have the strength to lift her so getting behind Michelle's head he reached under her armpits and pulled her towards the door. He kicked aside the rake. Embers were falling all around them, burning his arms and neck. Bracing Michelle as best he could he reached the door handle, turned it, and pulled the door open. The smoke was now so thick he couldn't see anything. It billowed out the open door, obscuring everything.

Grasping Michelle, he pulled her out the door and away from the burning shed. Finally, almost overcome with smoke, he collapsed to the ground, drawing in huge breaths of fresh air. His vision was blurry, the tears running down his cheeks. His eyes finally cleared enough to see Michelle. Seeing the blood on her face he ripped off a piece of his shirt and wiped it away from her eyes, not wanting to touch the damage on her cheeks.

Michelle opened her eyes and looked at Tippy.

"It hurts," was all that she got out.

"I know. Try and hang on. I need to get us somewhere safe and then get help."

"Are they gone?"

"Yeah, I think most of the rats were in the shack and it's completely ablaze. No worry there for now, and we're far enough from it that neither the fire, nor the smoke should bother us."

"What about the other animals?"

Tippy had been so worried about getting out of the burning shed, he had forgotten about the deer, the foxes, and the cougars. It had grown very quiet and then Michelle's eyes opened wide, staring at something behind him.

He turned to look and saw them. Just feet away were at least a dozen deer, along with a score of foxes and some more rats.

They were closing in on them. Tippy looked at Michelle.

"I'm sorry."

"You have nothing to be sorry about. You did all you could, and we gave the people in the house a chance."

Tippy bent over Michelle and held on to her. He knew it would not be enough to protect her, but at least they would not die alone. He closed his eyes, waiting for the attack.

How long he stayed like that he did not know, but he could not understand why the attack did not come. Fearfully he opened his eyes and looked up. The animals were no longer there.

* * *

They entered Peter's sanctuary and were stunned by what they found. It was more like a pharaoh's tomb. The room itself was spacious, about twenty feet by twenty. The walls were mostly mirrors, with hieroglyphs etched into many of them. Scattered around the room were various objects, many of them looking ancient Egyptian in origin, although some appeared Mayan, Native American, Hindu, and other cultures. On many of these objects were various pieces of human anatomy—fingers, skin, and bones—Peter's "trophies."

What occupied the largest area was what must be Peter's resting place. Against the far wall lay a sarcophagus on top of a flat-topped pyramid. The pyramid itself was not tall, maybe seven feet, and resembled more the Mayan pyramids than the Egyptian ones. It was stepped in a way that would allow anyone to climb and then look upon the sarcophagus, which had a glass lid in place of wood or stone. The base appeared to be made of stone almost entirely covered with both hieroglyphics and Mayan glyphs.

Next to the pyramid was a smaller, less elaborate sarcophagus. It also had a glass lid, and carved into the lower part was the name Betty. There were a few hieroglyphics and Mayan glyphs on it as well, though not to the extent of Peter's.

The ceiling, which was about fifteen feet above, also had carvings on it. But instead of hieroglyphs, it had constellations, the moon, and a giant sun, emitting beams. Somehow the ceiling was also emitting light, enough so that their lamps were redundant.

"How the hell did he do that?" asked Jackson in awe, filming every bit of the room.

"Forget about that," replied John. "There is his resting place. Let's destroy his body before his army gets here."

With Jane leading the way they started across the room. They had only taken a few steps when a blackness formed in front of them, blocking their way.

"What the hell?" muttered Melissa.

"Do you really think I would allow you to harm my body before my spirit has finished transitioning?" asked a voice from the blackness.

The black coalesced into figures. Up front were a man and a woman, both holding guns of some sort. Behind them was a larger figure, that they could recognize as Peter from the photos they had seen of him. Then off to his right was another figure they could not make out.

"I recognize those two," whispered Skip. "They're Bonnie and Clyde."

"It must be their coffins up front," replied Ron. "That's the evil that Jane felt."

"They're holding guns," said Melissa, her voice shaking. "You don't suppose they fire real bullets, do you?"

"Not real in the sense of physical lead, but more along the lines of spiritual. I am willing to bet that they will kill us if they shoot us," answered John.

"For sure," replied Peter. "You were smart enough to reach my inner sanctum, but not smart enough to realize I would have protective spirits with me."

Jane stared Peter in the eyes.

"We have not made it this far to be thwarted by ghosts. Blaze has stopped your army from harming us, and I will not allow you to kill those of us who have made it here."

"Kill you? I think not. At least not right away. That bitch in the other sarcophagus has bored me to no end. I want more company. You two women will give me hours of pleasure. The men will make admirable additions to my torture chamber. There are still a few tools I have yet to try out. Of course, if you women give me any trouble there is one tool there that will be especially fun to make use of. It is called a breast ripper."

Ron nodded at John and then moved up once again to stand beside Jane.

"Why would a spirit, that has no body, want a woman to have pleasure with? Your manhood is not exactly active you know. I doubt it was ever really of any use anyway, otherwise you would have had children. Are you a eunuch?"

Peter's form got blacker, losing some of its cohesion.

"You dare mock me!" his voice boomed.

Melissa reached forward to grab Ron's arm, hissing, "What the hell are you doing?"

Jackson pulled her back.

"Shut up," he whispered.

Meanwhile, with Peter's attention on Ron, John inched his way to the left, looking to get around the spirits facing them. Skip did the same thing, moving to the right.

Peter noticed them and was about to issue orders to his "guardians" when Ron spoke again, this time playing on Peter's ego.

"Well, you must have had some plan for what to do, having brought a woman into your sanctuary with you. So far you've shown a brilliance and knowledge well in advance of your times. I would assume you had thought that part out."

Peter's attention shifting back to Ron. "The ceremonies I followed give me physical feelings even in spirit form. However, for some reason, the ceremony did not translate well to Betty. I have had to rape her spirit as she takes no pleasure in what I do."

Ron laughed.

"You think that's funny? Or is rape your thing, little man?"

Ron smirked. "With all your preparations you forgot to take one thing into account."

"Oh, and what is that?"

"Human nature. I guess it never dawned on you to find out more about the person you chose. You see Betty is gay."

That caught Peter by surprise—and John and Skip made their move. Running and jumping John brought all the force he could bear, swinging the metal bar onto the glass of the sarcophagus, expecting it to shatter so that Skip could toss the holy oil onto Peter's actual body. His surprise was complete when the bar bounced off, causing no damage, except to his hands, which stung from the contact.

It was Peter's turn to laugh.

"You thought I would not have adequate protection for my resting place. That is acrylic not glass and the glyphs give it an added strength."

Two large hands coalesced from Peter's form, grabbing both of them and flinging the two men back against the wall near the door they had entered, cracking the mirrors and knocking them out.

The form of the shaman leaned over Peter and touched his head. Peter looked at him and nodded.

"I guess there will be no playtime then. Time for all of you to die. My army has overcome your spirit guardian and they will join us soon."

He gave a sign to Bonnie and Clyde who raised their weapons and fired at the group, point blank.

Expecting this, Jane waived her hands, creating a psychic shield. Whatever ammunition they used bounced off Jane's shield and smashed against the mirrored walls causing more damage. Then Jane brought her hands together and the shield formed around Bonnie and Clyde, pushing them back. The two former gangsters started pushing back. Jane was able to hold them but it was a stalemate.

Once again the shaman touched Peter and once again he nodded.

"Your psychic can't help you now. If she tries to help you, my gangsters will kill her. You five have no power to stop me. Now I will make you suffer before you die."

He advanced on them, growing larger as he came. Bob stepped forward and threw a punch that just passed through Peter. Laughing Peter back-handed Bob sending him flying against the wall, more mirrors cracking.

That was when Melissa noticed that with each crack of the mirrors, the acrylic lid to Peter's sarcophagus also cracked.

"The mirrors. We need to smash them."

Jackson saw what she meant and picked up the bar that had landed near them when John was thrown. He turned and smashed the closest mirror.

Peter's hands grew in size, reached out and grabbed both Jackson and Melissa by the neck. Ron tried to intervene but found he was unable to move. Glancing down he saw that there was another spirit holding him. Looking up at him was a woman's face. He realized it could only be Betty.

"I will take care of Peter. You must finish the job."

She released Ron, and with a screech jumped on Peter's form. Her attack caught him completely by surprise. Releasing the two he held he turned his attention to Betty.

They say hell hath no fury like a woman scorned. The same could be said about a woman who has been spiritually raped for over twenty-five years. She tore into Peter with all her fury, unleashing the hate and anger that had built up over that time.

Ron wasted no time. He picked up whatever loose objects he could find. Statues, urns, whatever was handy. Then he started throwing them against the mirrored walls.

Jackson and Melissa, recovering quickly, got to their feet, and prepared to do the same.

"No," said Ron. "Take the oil, candles, and lighter from John and Skip and do what we came to do."

John and Skip were lying nearby, their forms still. Jackson knelt next to Skip, feeling for a pulse.

"No time Jackson. We do it now or we all die," shouted Melissa.

Realizing she was right he reached into Skip's pocket and found the jar of holy oil. Melissa had already gotten the candles and lighter from John's still form. Grabbing the metal bar, Jackson and Melissa ran to the sarcophagus. The shaman moved to block them.

They came to a stop, not knowing what to do.

Jane yelled at them.

"He can't touch you. Just go through him."

Trusting Jane was right they ran on and passed through the form of the shaman.

"Most of the mirrors are broken. Do it now," yelled Ron.

Once again, the metal bar was swung at the lid of the sarcophagus, this time with much different results. It shattered completely.

"NOOOOO," screamed Peter, trying to throw Betty off of him and rush to defend his final resting spot. But Betty would have none of it and held him with all the spirit strength she had.

"You have fucked me against my will for over twenty-five years. Now it is my time to fuck you," she yelled.

Clearing as much of the acrylic as he could Jackson unstopped the jar and poured the holy oil over Peter's body. Melissa lit the candles and was about to toss them onto the body when she spotted the diary. She reached in to grab it.

"What in hell are you doing?" Jackson yelled.

"The secret to immortality is in that book. We can't just let it burn."

"You want to be immortal like that?" Jackson pointed to Peter who was raging away at Betty but could not get free.

Melissa took one look at Peter, made her decision, and tossed the lit candles onto the body, one at his head, one on his chest, and one on his groin for good measure.

"What's that lying beside the sarcophagus," asked Ron.

"Looks like a bone of some sort."

"Toss it in too," yelled Jane. "Make sure you have all of him."

Melissa bent and picked it up, tossing it into the growing fire. This time it was the shaman who appeared to scream in agony, but nothing came out.

"That must have been the bone of the shaman that Peter found," said John, sitting up and rubbing his head. Beside him Skip let out a groan.

Once more Peter screamed, finally able to toss Betty off him. He tried to reach for his sarcophagus, but he could no longer hold his form. As Peter's body burned, the shaman faded away, as did the spirits of Bonnie and Clyde, releasing Jane from her battle.

Soon Peter himself began to fade. He gave one last cry and was gone. Betty's revenge was complete. She also started to fade but made one last request.

"Please open my coffin and pour some holy water on my body. It will release my spirit."

Unlike Peter's sarcophagus, Betty's was easy to open. Taking the bottle from his pocket Ron poured it over her form, which began to smoke. Betty took one last look at the group and mouthed thank you, before she faded away.

Suddenly the sarcophagus of Peter flared, the flames rising to the roof. The roof immediately caught fire. They realized the ceiling must be made of wood.

"We need to get out of here," yelled Melissa.

Ron went to help John and Skip to their feet, while Jackson went to Bob, shaking his still the form til Bob finally opened his eyes.

"Come on buddy, we need to get out of here."

"What did I miss?"

"A lot, but if we don't get out of here now you will be missing your life as well."

He had just gotten Bob to his feet when the stone door slid shut.

Laughter permeated the chamber, then the presence of Peter was gone for good.

Jackson raged in frustration. "We're trapped here now. He got his last laugh it seems."

"Peter got his final revenge," added Bob, coughing as the smoke got thicker. Soon they would all be overcome.

"Not if I can help it," said Jane, her voice tight, but fierce. "Bring me all your holy water."

They had already used two bottles and Blaze still had one with her. That left five, which Jane collected and emptied over the door. "Okay everyone, push against the door with all your strength."

Jackson, John, Ron, Bob, Skip, and Melissa leaned into the door, using their legs, and what leverage they could without getting in each other's way, putting everything they had into it. Jane then reached out with her senses, pushing psychically. At first nothing happened. But they kept at it as their faces turned red from the strain. Suddenly ... *Bang!* ... the stone door fell over like it had just been leaning there, and not sealed.

"How—?" asked Melissa.

"I don't care how. Let's just get the hell out of here," shouted John.

Jackson bent and picked up the camera he had put down to have more leverage. After all they had gone through, he was not going to lose the proof. When they entered Peter's sanctum it was running at red so he was afraid there would be no power left by now. But the camera had jumped back to thirty percent power. Peter's ability to drain the batteries had passed with him. He decided to leave the camera on.

Half crouched to avoid as much smoke as possible they followed the cave back to the staircase and climbed as fast as they could. The smoke followed them. They soon realized that the entire house was now on fire.

"How could that happen?" coughed out Bob.

"The entire house has absorbed his presence. In essence he has become the house. When we set his body on fire we set the house on fire," answered Jane between gasps.

"I'm fine with that," replied John. "As long as we get out of here before it burns to the ground."

They reached the small chamber where they had found John's phone. The smoke was not as thick here, but the heat was intensifying. They crawled through the hole they made in the wall and into the cellar.

"Where's Blaze?" asked Jane. "We need to find her."

"No time to look," answered John. "Let's hope she made it out."

They raced through the wine cellar—bottles bursting as the fire reached the wooden shelves. They had made it to the stairs when a darkness coalesced at the top, blocking their way.

"If Peter's dead, what's that?" cried Melissa.

"Peter may be dead, but the spirits he captured still have a little of their presence left," answered Jane. "Let me through."

Jane made her way up the stairs, coming within a few feet of the blackness.

"Blaze if you can hear me, we need your help."

The door behind the blackness brightened around its edges, then burst open sending a powerful light into the blackness, ending its power. They heard Blaze say, "Go now. Hurry. I can only hold them for so long. Once the house has burned to the ground their power will end."

Without hesitation Jane led the way. Through the kitchen, then the hall, they ran. As they got to the entranceway, where their equipment still lay, John grabbed his laptop and Bob the memory sticks from the filming they had done, then they ran out the now open door. As they passed through Skip called, "What about the bodies of our fallen companions."

"Unless you want to join them, we have no choice but to leave them," answered Jackson.

"Jane, will their spirits be trapped here if we do that?" asked John.

"I really don't know. That's a question that only Blaze might have been able to answer."

"Where is Blaze?" asked Bob. "She must have made it to here if she was able to help us n the cellar."

"Blaze is dead," replied Jane. "I knew that as soon as we reached the cellar stairs. That is why I called for her help."

As the uni-pave stones of the driveway and the water fountain at the front burst into flames, they continued running, not stopping until they had cleared that part of the driveway.

"I've never seen stones and water fountains on fire like that before," said Bob, panting out the words as he doubled over trying to catch his breath.

"I have," said Skip, looking back at the driveway. "But that was when I was fleeing from forest fires in California."

Then they saw flames coming from a different direction. The separate garage was now also on fire.

"Tippy!" yelled Bob racing towards it. Jackson grabbed his arm, pulling him to a stop.

"If he is in there, then there's nothing you can do."

"Let go of me," he yelled at Jackson. "He means everything to me. If he dies I would prefer not to live."

"I would prefer you did live," said a voice coming from a clearing between some trees. Nearby a shed was also on fire, but that fire was dying down.

"Tippy!" yelled Bob in glee. He ran over to hug his partner, but Tippy held up his hand.

"Later," he said. "Right now, I hurt all over. And we need to get help for Michelle."

That was when they noticed Michelle lying beside him, bleeding from many wounds.

"Oh my God, what happened to you guys?" cried Melissa, joining Bob and Tippy.

"Rats, deer, foxes and cougars to start with," answered Tippy. He looked over to so the rest of the group making their toward them. "Where's Blaze? And Sir Arthur? And everyone else?".

"We're all that made it," replied Jackson.

"Damn! What about Peter and his ghostly army?"

"We destroyed Peter's body and when we did, he, the shaman that controlled him, and his spirit army vanished."

"Shaman? Wow looks like I missed a lot. Then again, we had our own battles to fight. But right now, we need to get help."

"Does anyone have a cell phone that still works?" asked Ron.

John pulled his out of his pocket. Even with all it had gone through it still functioned and had ten percent power remaining.

"Who should I call?"

"Give it to me," said Ron.

Realizing the ex-cop would have the necessary contacts he handed it over.

"Who are you going to call?" asked Jane.

"The chief deputy. He worked with me during the last two incidents here. He can arrange everything as I tell him to."

Jackson gave him a look as if to ask what he meant by that

comment, but Ron ignored him and dialed the number, which was answered after only one ring.

"Deputy Gardner."

"Hey Todd, it's Ron."

"Ron, glad to hear your voice. You still out at that crazy house. I couldn't believe it when you told me you were going back there. What can I do for you?"

"There's been another incident here. Send medical assistance—and the coroner."

"Oh God, no! How many this time?"

"Six dead and a number injured, some seriously."

"Hold on while I make the calls." The phone went silent for less than a minute, then Todd was back. "Damn will that house ever stop taking victims?"

"It will now," Ron said, his voice firm. He paused a moment then added, "And Tood, send the fire department too. But tell them to take their time. I want this house to be ashes by the time they get here."

"Got it. I'll call it in, and then I am coming out there."

"Thanks, pal."

Jane was kneeling beside Michelle, giving Tippy a hand as she was the only one there with some medical training. The remainder of the group was standing nearby when they heard strange noises coming from the house and turned to look.

They all seemed to yell at once. "WHAT THE HELL!"

CHAPTER SIXTEEN

DENOUEMENT — THEY LAID THEM IN A ROW

They could see a rush of spirit forms leaving the house. Hundreds of them—marching as if in a funeral procession—carrying five objects. A group of spirits broke off and headed towards the garage. Minutes later they exited, also carrying something.

That's when it hit them. The spirit forms were carrying bodies.

They walked through the flames of the burning stone driveway until they reached the grass area and set their burdens down. The spirits from the garage joined them and set down the body they bore. They laid them in a row.

Jane got up and walked towards the bodies. Ron, John, and Jackson joined her.

As they got closer, they saw that the bodies had been laid in the order of their deaths. Bryan first, the camera he had set up in the garage beside him, followed by Jackson Brown, Harry Worth, Matt Capiro, Sir Arthur, and lastly Blaze.

One of the spirit forms broke away from the group. They could see that it was Betty.

"We did not want to leave your friends behind. You have done so much by releasing us. It was the least that we could do to thank you. For now we are free, even the spirits that had been held by the serial killers and despots. The spirits of your friends are also free."

As the spirits faded away, the last to remain was Betty. "Ron, please tell Anita that I am so sorry not to have been able to live our lives together as we planned. I never stopped thinking of her, even while Peter ravaged me. It is the only thing that allowed me the strength at the end to fight him."

"I will tell her," Ron promised. "You should know, Betty, that she always believed in you. That you had been killed and were not a killer. She set up a memorial for you, and most of the townspeople have visited it. Only the FBI thought you were involved."

Betty smiled and then faded away.

Jane ran over to Blaze's body almost falling beside it.

"Oh Blaze, you taught me so much. How am I going to get by without you."

"I will always be there when you need me."

Looking up through her tears, Jane saw the form of Blaze standing over her body.

"Remember baby-doll, to go and see Allie Montore. She will teach you to use your abilities in a way that is safe. You are a more powerful psychic than I am. You just need to be taught so you can reach your potential. There are more people like Peter Vanderbilt out there, and more evil that needs to be fought. She can help you with that. I feel you will be called on again to use your abilities."

With a final smile Blaze faded away.

"Baby-doll, huh," said Ron, now standing beside Jane.

"That's what she called me. I don't know why, but I will always treasure it."

Ron held out his hand to help Jane up. She took his hand and he pulled her towards him, giving her a hug. She looked into his eyes and kissed him.

For Ron it just felt right. Almost like it was meant to happen.

They heard the sirens in the distance.

"Come, let's join the others. We'll have a tale to tell the authorities when they get here. Not that they'll believe us."

"There are always Jackson's cameras. Bob got the remainder of the data before we left the house. That should prove we're telling the truth."

"We'll see about that."

They heard a large crash. Everyone turned to look at the house as it collapsed in on itself. It was followed moments later by another crash as the garage did the same thing.

The first of the siren-wailing cars reached the driveway. It was a sheriff's car driven by Ron's friend. Todd got out and walked up to the group. He picked out Ron and went to shake his hand.

"Thank you for finally ending this.

"Once you get the fire inspectors to sort through the rubble you should be able to find the bodies of most of the missing people in the garage. Since where they were stored was surrounded by concrete, you should be able to recover and identify them. The only body missing is that of Betty."

"Not anymore," said Jane walking up to them and pointing to the bodies of their companions lying on the ground. An additional body had appeared when no one was looking. It was partly decomposed, but enough was left that it would be identifiable.

"I guess the FBI are going to be running damage control, then," said Ron. "A lot of families will be suing them for defamation after what they said about the missing people."

"You know the FBI. They'll find a way to cover up their

incompetence," replied Todd.

"Maybe they will investigate who Peter paid off and he will become their sacrificial lamb," said Ron.

Moments later a couple of ambulances pulled up. A doctor jumped out of one, took out his bag, and ran to where Michelle was lying on the grass. He waived over at the ambulance to immediately bring a stretcher.

Todd had made sure there was a full force at hand.

Others, paramedics, moved to examine Tippy, as well as the others who had lesser injuries.

Jackson walked up to Ron and held out his hand.

"I want to thank you for all that you've done and apologize for all the nonsense I said in the house."

Ron pushed his hand aside and instead, to Jackson's surprise, gave him a hug.

"We survived because we all worked together. And I owe you and your crew an apology for calling you all fakes and your equipment garbage. Shows how little a dumb cop can know."

Jackson smiled in return.

"So, what now for you and your crew? Back to your *Ghost Eliminators* show?"

"Yes and no. It will be different going forward. But I plan a special episode to start the new season. It will be dedicated to those who lost their lives here. I would really like it if you could be part of the show."

"As long as I agree to the presentation, I will join you for that one episode. After that I'll have had enough of ghosts to last me a lifetime."

"I don't blame you. Maybe that season premier will also be the series ender. I never realized how much Blaze actually protected us. I would not want to go to a real haunted house now without a legitimate psychic."

Jane walked up and put her arm into Ron's.

"Give me a chance to learn a bit more, and maybe I will become your psychic," she said.

"Really?!" exclaimed Ron and Jackson at the same time.

"It's something that Blaze said to me before she left. About there being more evil in the world then we thought. But like Blaze, I will also hide my abilities behind a sham, if that's acceptable."

Jackson held out his hand for Jane to shake.

"Agreed!" he said "You know there's something I still don't understand. How come, when we were in Peter's sanctuary, we couldn't break the acrylic sarcophagus lid until after the mirrors were smashed?"

"I think that was another error that Peter made. I noticed that some of the glyphs marked on the mirrors were the same as some that were on the sarcophagus. He probably used them as a connection to focus the psychic energy towards him. It also may have been what helped make his protection stronger. When we smashed the mirrors, we broke that connection. In doing so the acrylic cover lost that extra protection and went back to its normal form. Even acrylic, especially what was built back in the nineties, would not stand the type of smashing it was given. That lid was not really that thick."

"I hope that every trace of those glyphs and any notes of the ceremony he used have been destroyed. We don't need another Peter Vanderbilt spirit hanging around," said Ron.

"Oh, there will always be another person somewhere trying to cheat death and doing anything to achieve it," replied Jane. "And by the way Jackson, there's one more condition that will have to be fulfilled if you want me on your show."

"Anything," he answered.

"It is not something that you can say yes or no to."

She turned to Ron.

"I would want you by my side as my protector. That is if you don't have other commitments."

"Where you go, I will follow," Ron replied.

"Then pack for California. I have a meeting with my new teacher to arrange."

CHAPTER SEVENTEEN

EPILOGUE – THE GHOST ELIMINATORS

"I want to welcome you to another season of *Ghost Eliminators*. However, it is with a heavy heart that I do so. When we ended last season, I told you that we had been invited to eliminate the ghosts of one of the most haunted places in the world and promised you that it would be our most exciting episode ever. This will be a three-part episode as there is just too much to show in only one hour. These will also be the only episodes of this season. Due to our loses we will be recruiting new members and will need time to make sure everyone is adequately trained.

"In the end it was the most dangerous place we had ever been. We had to fight entities that tore us apart both physically and mentally. Although when all was said and done, we had succeeded, it was at a very high cost. We will be showing you scenes that will scare you, and make you ill at the same time, and for that reason this will be our first episode that comes with a ratings warning. For those with weak hearts we recommend that you do not watch this show. If you have children, please do not let them watch this without your guidance. The professionalism of our team is why almost every scene you will see was captured as it happened. As our regular viewers know, when on an investigation our team has a policy that cameras go with them everywhere. In this case though some of the scenes captured are quite graphic. We have edited out some of the bloodier scenes, yet enough remain to justify this warning.

"I said it is with a heavy heart that I bring you this episode. The house we were at was commonly known as Blood Mansion, and many of you will have heard of the deaths that have happened in that house over the last almost three decades. Before the ghosts were eliminated it claimed more. Fifteen of us entered the house on that fateful day. Two investigative teams, our own Ghost Eliminators, and the university team headed by John Samuels along with retired police officer Ron Harris. Only nine walked out. John Samuels has graciously allowed us to include the scenes that his team were in. When we first arrived, he was adamant about not including any scenes showing his personnel. However, with what has passed he wants the world to know about this, and his fallen companions to be remembered.

"Please join me in a minute of silence to honor our fallen comrades:

"Bryan Chan of the Ghost Eliminators. He was the first of our group to fall, taken in an ancillary building, but even in death doing what he could to help a fellow team member.

"Jackson Brown of the University Investigative Team. After seeing the footage of what happened to him you might never enter a theatre again.

"Harry Worth of the University Investigative Team. His interest in astronomy caused him to suffer the most painful death of all.

"Matthew Capiro, director of the Ghost Eliminators. He used his knowledge, and gave his life, so that we could have the means to stop the evil in this house.

"The honorable Sir Arthur James. World class narrator who sacrificed himself, and died a painful death, to save another's life.

"Blaze Destiny. She stood her ground and guarded a passage, preventing the evil from getting us before we could destroy it.

"As well we must remember all the victims this house has claimed. There are too many to list here, but if you go to our website there is a dedication page to all who have died because of the evil of this place."

Jackson lowered his head. For a full minute there was silence. Then he continued.

"The house itself no longer exists. With the elimination of the evil that had built it, the house collapsed and burned to the ground. The authorities were able to recover the bodies of those who had gone missing, that the FBI had accused of being murderers. That is another issue that will be decided by the authorities.

"Now I want to introduce you to the survivors of Blood Mansion. I have to start with the only person who has seen the aftermath of every incident that has taken place in this house. You will learn more about him, and the others, as the episodes unwind."

Jackson, with his usual dramatic flare, pointed towards a group sitting in chairs off to the side. "Ron Harris please stand."

Ron stood, having been told by Jackson how this episode would play out, and agreeing to the script beforehand.

"His courage gave us the strength to do what was necessary. There is not another man in this world that I would rather have beside me when danger comes."

Ron was surprised by this ad lib that Jackson had not mentioned, but was able to hide it. He nodded to the camera and sat back down.

"John Samuels, university professor and paranormal investigator extraordinaire. I learned a lot from him during this expedition."

John stood, gave a wave, and sat back down.

"Jane Wilbury, apprentice psychic to our own Blaze Destiny. In our next season she has gracefully accepted to step into Blaze's shoes, although no one could ever take her place."

Jane stood at her introduction and blew a kiss to the camera. This was to become part of her persona going forward.

"Skip O'Reilly, renowned technician, who worked with our own Tippy and Bob to make our equipment the best in the industry. Without his aid we would have failed."

Skip stood and gave a quick nod.

"Now from our own crew, I am pleased to welcome back our two fantastic technicians:

"Tippy O'Hare." Tippy stood and doffed his cap.

"And Bob Selson." Bob stood and gave a big smile.

"A special announcement here. Bob and Tippy will be getting married later this year."

The remainder of the crew stood and clapped.

"Now returning as our lead investigator is Michelle Aysha. She lost her love on this last expedition, but has told me she will do all she can to honor his memory in our next season's episodes."

Michelle stood waved and then bowed. Something that would become her staple.

"The last of our survivors could not be here."

Jackson pointed to a screen showing a large picture.

"This last adventure was too much for her, so she has retired from ghost hunting, but we will miss Melissa Sanford."

"Now sit back and be amazed, shocked, and yes, frightened, by what you are about to see."

Jackson pointed to a screen and the camera zoomed in.

Ron turned to John.

"Do you think people will actually believe what they're going to see, or will they think it was all faked?"

"The true believers of the show will accept it as gospel. Those who think it's always been fake will continue to do so no matter what. However, there is that middle ground, some of whom will be swayed by what they see. Do you have any news from your friend Todd on where the authorities stand in this?"

"Not really. They've cleared all those previously accused of any wrongdoing, but beyond that nothing."

"So where are you off to now?"

"Back to California. Jane will continue her mentorship under Allie Montore. What about you? Back to the university?"

"That remains to be seen. I've been called before the committee. Apparently there is talk about revoking my tenure. When I told them that I had given Jackson Benders permission to use the footage showing our crew they demanded that I withdraw it immediately. I explained to them that doing that would diminish the memories of Jackson Brown and Harry Worth, two members of this university faculty. They threatened me if I refused. I guess this is their way of carrying out their treat.

"That's bullshit!" exclaimed Ron.

"That's the academic world. Appearance is everything. My friend is assistant dean and will fight for me, but at this point I don't care. I plan on starting my own paranormal investigative firm and have been offered a talk show by a major network. Jackson Benders also offered me a job, but I prefer the freedom of making my own decisions."

"You know if you need anything just contact us. Jane and I will be more than pleased to help, even be interviewed on your talk show," Ron said with a big grin.

Knowing how little Ron liked on camera work, John was honored by this offer.

"By the way. You'll be receiving your invitation to our wedding soon. I hope you can make it."

"I wouldn't miss it for the world!"

ACKNOWLEDGMENTS

I would like to thank two paranormal researchers who were kind enough to provide information on how they go about their investigations. Their information was quite helpful, but please note that any inaccuracies or artistic license taken are purely the fault of the writer.

James Underdown

Chair, Founder, Center for Inquiry Investigations Group

James Underdown has been the executive director of the Center for Inquiry West (Los Angeles) since 1999. He has written for both *Skeptical Inquirer* and *Free Inquiry* magazines.

He is also the founder and chairman of the Center for Inquiry Investigations Group in Los Angeles, CA, the U.S.'s premiere paranormal investigation team.

Hayley Stevens

U.K.-based paranormal investigator, and the author of the blog Hayley is a Ghost

Hayley Stevens takes a scientific approach to her work. In an interview she told *Newsweek*: "When people think they've had a strange, spooky experience I will research and investigate it to see if I can work out a cause for what they saw, and heard. ... However, unlike the ghost hunters you see in the media, I don't look for evidence of the paranormal but instead try to find rational explanations."

I extend a special thankyou to Laurie Carter, editor extraordinaire, for helping make this book the best it could possibly be. She pushed, she prodded, she suggested and she was right.

ABOUT THE AUTHOR

Robert Howell has gained a diverse range of skills and experiences. While studying business administration in college, he also took courses in literature, poetry, cartography, and supernatural studies. After completing college, he joined the military to satisfy his urge to travel and fulfilled that goal with travels across Canada and various parts of Europe. Following his military service, he spent forty years in real estate, starting as an agent and later working in acquisitions for an investment company, focusing on locations such as Florida and Texas.

Yet despite Howell's successful career in real estate, his true passion was writing. To develop his skills, he took a writing course through the Long Ridge Writers Group, affiliated with the University of Connecticut. Since completing his studies, he has written articles, web and newsletter content, short stories and found a love for writing novels.

Howell's young adult urban fantasy trilogy, The Charm Saga, is a mystical chronicle creatively woven with a strong plot, diverse characters, and a captivating storyline. The three titles are *Third Times the Charm*, *The Fourth Charm* and *The Charms Together*.

Blood Mansion is Howell's first venture into Gothic Horror. Expect more from him in this genre.

BLOOD CASTLE

They had thought that nothing could compare to the evil they encountered at Blood Mansion. They were wrong!

Although not all had survived Blood Mansion, Jackson Benders would continue to lead his team in the pursuit of Haunted places to investigate and purge of their evil.

However, it's the call from a former member of the team that sets The Ghost Eliminators on a hunt even beyond the horrors of Blood Mansion. A phone in the woods sends them on a course with an evil inhabiting an ancient yet modern castle set in a countryside bordering two nations.

To his surprise, other friends await there, as well as foes unlike any they have faced before and a death count that rivals any of their previous encounters.

How many will survive Blood Castle?